A DANGEROUS LORD

Forced to live with her enemy! Hollie Finch is horrified when the forbidding Earl of Everingham, Charles Stirling, places her under house arrest in his manor. Well, he may suspect her of sedition, but to her it's just freedom of the press—and she's determined to carry on her work right under his arrogant nose! Yet that turns out to be unexpectedly difficult, with his all-too-disturbing presence disrupting her days . . . and memories of his passion-dark eyes troubling her nights.

AN IMPOSSIBLE LOVE

Lord Everingham merely planned to keep a close eye on the lovely rabble-rouser—and he's appalled when her intoxicating scent and lithe curves make him burn to have her in his bed. Even worse, her generous heart and joyous laughter start him thinking about keeping her with him forever. But the powerful earl has a secret that could destroy him, so he dares not let Hollie into his life. Can the pride and deception separating them ever be overcome . . . by the miracle of love?

Other Avon Romantic Treasures by
Linda Needham

THE MAIDEN BRIDE
THE WEDDING NIGHT

If You've Enjoyed This Book,
Be Sure to Read These Other
AVON ROMANTIC TREASURES

THE BAD MAN'S BRIDE: MARRYING MISS BRIGHT
by Susan Kay Law
A BREATH OF SCANDAL *by Connie Mason*
THE MARRIAGE LESSON *by Victoria Alexander*
ONCE TEMPTED *by Elizabeth Boyle*
ONE MAN'S LOVE: BOOK ONE OF
THE HIGHLAND LORDS *by Karen Ranney*

Coming Soon

A NOTORIOUS LOVE *by Sabrina Jeffries*

LINDA NEEDHAM

MY WICKED EARL

An Avon Romantic Treasure

AVON BOOKS
An Imprint of HarperCollinsPublishers

This is a work of fiction. Names, characters, places, and incidents are products of the author's imagination or are used fictitiously and are not to be construed as real. Any resemblance to actual events, locales, organizations, or persons, living or dead, is entirely coincidental.

AVON BOOKS
An Imprint of HarperCollins*Publishers*
10 East 53rd Street
New York, New York 10022-5299

Copyright © 2001 by Linda Needham
ISBN: 0-380-81523-0
www.avonromance.com

First Avon Books paperback printing: August 2001

Avon Trademark Reg. U.S. Pat. Off. and in Other Countries, Marca Registrada, Hecho en U.S.A.
HarperCollins ® is a trademark of HarperCollins Publishers Inc.

Printed in the U.S.A.

10 9 8 7 6 5 4 3 2 1

Chapter 1

Everingham Hall
Hertfordshire, England
Late September, 1819

"Your prisoner's arrived, my lord. Summerwell's just pulled him round back of the courtyard."

Charles Stirling, 7th Earl of Everingham, paused as he entered his front door. His heart actually paused as well, and now it thrummed in his ears.

Success! So near, it was difficult to credit; even more difficult to believe that it meant so much to him.

"You're absolutely certain, Mumberton: Summerwell's got that bastard Captain Spindleshanks in the wagon with him?"

His starch-collared butler nodded, though there was a cautious cast to his old gray eyes. "That's what he said, my lord."

"Good, Mumberton." Extraordinarily good.

Charles wanted nothing more than to bellow in triumph, to drink a fiery toast to the bloody end of Captain Spindleshanks's seditious nonsense and his reign of terror, but he merely handed off his hat and gloves to Mumberton, then strode past him into the dim foyer. "Fetch Bavidge for me. I want to see him."

"Yes, my lord."

"Oh, and what of . . . uh, the other?" He had no words yet for the new resident at Everingham Hall, stumbled over the very idea. "The . . ."

"Your son, sir?"

My son. Where's the bloody proof of that, I wonder?

"The boy" was the best he could manage. He shrugged off the unfamiliar and irritating twinge of guilt and heaped his scarf and his cloak across the man's outstretched arms.

"He's abed, my lord. Finally." Mumberton's graying frown drooped, as though the process had required a team of roustabouts and a load of grappling equipment. "Though, sir, if I might be allowed to say so, I'm not suited in the least to the position of nanny."

Nor am I suited to fatherhood. And certainly not when it came to the capricious antics of a six-year-old. After three days, the title of father still pinched like an unjust accusation; it would always fit badly, if he allowed it to fit at all.

"I'll take care of the matter, Mumberton." One way or the other.

Charles shoved the problem from his mind entirely, tried to ignore the bedeviling image of the wide-eyed, thin-limbed boy who'd been left on his doorstep by that damned attorney.

"Tell Bavidge to meet me in my office in three minutes. And send Summerwell to me with the prisoner. Immediately."

"I'll do my best, my lord." Mumberton started away with his teetering load.

"Your best, Mumberton?" Charles caught the man's arm and turned him, plagued suddenly by a dark suspicion that all was not as well as it seemed. "Is Captain Spindleshanks in my courtyard, or is he not?"

"In your courtyard, yes. That's where your prisoner is, sir."

A sideways answer, if ever there was one. "He's still securely shackled and about to be delivered to me?"

"All appeared to be in order, my lord, last I looked." Mumberton's eye twitched as he backed up a dubious step, and then another.

God only knew what the hell had happened during the arrest. Spindleshanks was a large man, according to the local legends, agile as a cat, shoulders of an ox—mythical to the tip of his pointed tail. Blood might have been spilled; Charles could only guess whose and how much.

He'd know soon enough, and that felt damned good. "Then fetch Bavidge now. We've got work to do."

"Right away, sir." Mumberton scudded off down the hallway toward the cloakroom.

Charles freed a gloating smile once the man was gone. Captain Bloody Spindleshanks, at long bloody last. What a great pleasure it would be to finally meet the cowardly bastard face to face.

He'd memorized every word of every seditious broadside and placard that Spindleshanks had strewn about the countryside in the last two months.

The Old Corruption returns. Lord Everingham, the Government's Foul-hearted Commissioner of Lies and Mercenary Morals, along with his Nest of Vipers, can't be trusted to investigate the Bloody Massacre at Peterloo.

And on and on went Spindleshanks's familiar harangue. As clever as it was incendiary, but entirely and maliciously untrue.

Charles's charter from the Home Office was to inquire into the facts in evidence, to study the depositions and magisterial reports, and then to submit an impartial finding about the tragedy. Another three weeks, and he would be done with the matter, and peace would once again reign in his life.

He'd be damned if he'd allow the bastard to call his honor or his integrity into question. But far worse, the people could too easily be shaken to the point of rebellion with madmen like Spindleshanks riding through the night, spreading sedition, believing they could indiscriminately incite unrest and then outrun the law.

Charles was incorruptible, was his own man in all things. Captain Spindleshanks would pay dearly, and for a very long time.

Charles shrugged out of his coat, relieved to be home after that endless dinner with Liverpool and Sidmouth in London and the two-hour journey back. He strode into the orderly quiet of his office, where he had just enough time to rouse the oil lamp at his desk and light the chandelier above the circular table before Bavidge made his coat-tail-streaming, bleary-eyed entrance.

"Yes, yes, my lord. What can I do for you?" Bavidge hastily righted his cravat, drew his long fingers through his sandy-gray hair, and then stood at attention as though still in the army and prepared to do battle.

Charles retrieved the arrest warrant from his desk drawer and dropped it onto the tabletop, savoring the moment before he said, "We've caught him, Bavidge."

Bavidge blinked at him. "Who is that, my lord?"

Great God. "Spindleshanks, Bavidge. Get me the reports on the case. Every scrap of evidence."

"Yes, my lord." Bavidge went to the file shelves in the next room and returned hefting two large boxes, thick book files, the accumulation of the investigation into Spindleshanks's activities. "How did you find him, my lord?"

Spies. Charles didn't approve of them, the shadowy men who thrived on suspicions and terror and were wrong more than half the time. But his deputy commissioner had pleaded for quicker action on the matter, and it seemed the expedient thing to do. Anything to snatch Spindleshanks off the street and out of the way of his inquiry. And now, all had turned out well.

At least so far.

"I learned of his whereabouts this afternoon through a reliable source. From there it was a simple matter of sending Summerwell and Haskett to pick him up."

"Excellent news, my lord."

Yet Charles couldn't shake the memory of Mumberton's edginess.

Bavidge unlatched the lid of one of the boxes and lifted out a motley stack of papers. They shifted as he set them down on the polished mahogany, and then slid across the tabletop as though on a mission to escape.

Charles caught the stack before it went sailing off the edge. "Re-sort the lot of it, Bavidge. The St. Peter's Fields Commission, Spindleshanks, reports, news items. When Spindleshanks stands there on my carpet, protesting his innocence, I'll have plenty of evidence to show the bastard to the contrary. Let him know that the Crown's case against him is unshakable. He'll confess and—" Charles stopped as he recognized Lord Rennick's crest of ewe and fleece emblazoned at the top of an unfamiliar letter. "What the devil is this?"

Bavidge peered over his arm, lifted his spectacles. "It came this noon, my lord. After you'd gone off to Whitehall."

Charles hated being ambushed, hated that panicked foundering while he scrabbled for facts and strategies. He shook off his anger and jabbed the page into Bavidge's chest, then turned away to the spirits table and poured himself a brandy. "Read it then, quickly."

" 'Rennick Hall, 26th September—' "

"The details only, Bavidge. The bastard will be here any minute." Charles paced to the window and the many-paned blackness lurking beyond.

" 'I write, my lords, to inform you of still another secret union meeting that occurred at my Leeds Woolen Mill three nights past. Organized by Spindleshanks, attended by him, but he got away.' "

"Obviously." But a temporary reprieve. God, he was going to enjoy this.

"Seems your captain ran the length of the mill roof in his escape, leaped onto the carding shed, over a fence, then disappeared through the lanes and into the night. Oh, and this also came with Lord Rennick's report." Bavidge held up another broadside. "Another personal attack on you, sir."

Charles turned away from the bold black lettering, the shouting of more abuse. "Read it."

" 'Surrender the truth, Lord Everingham, if you dare,' " Bavidge read, " 'else we'll take it from you by cudgel and you shall rue the name of Spindleshanks as you do Peterloo.' "

At the moment he rued only his position on the bloody commission of inquiry.

And the boy. He rued that, too—the rakehell part of his past and the reasons for it.

"What else?"

Bavidge opened his mouth, but a pale knock sounded on the door and the right side panel opened a crack.

"My lord?" Mumberton peered inside, mustache first and then his nose, as though to guard himself against a thrown projectile.

"Bring him, Mumberton."

"Actually, my lord, it's, uhm . . ." Mumberton opened the door just far enough to let himself inside.

"My prisoner. Yes, bring him in, Mumberton," Charles said.

"Yes, my lord. Thank you, my lord. That is exactly what I mean to speak with you about just now. A detail." Mumberton pinched a gap between his thumb and his index finger. "A small detail."

"The only detail I care about is Captain Spindleshanks." Charles tried to ignore the rankling apprehension in his gut. "Do they have him or not? Bloody hell, Mumberton, if they've bungled this, I'll—"

"Oh, no, my lord, it's not that." Mumberton fluttered his hands in front of his chest. "It's just that—"

"Stop your blasted fidgeting, Mumberton, and bring him to me!"

The man flinched. "At once, my lord. But I think I ought to explain that there's been a slight . . . uhm . . ."

"A slight *what*, damn it all?"

"A slight misimpression about—"

"Bloody *hell*, I'll do it myself." As Charles started for the door, he heard the approaching sounds of voices, and the rattle and drag of chains against the marble corridor floor.

He nearly laughed in relief; satisfaction surged through him and settled in his chest.

Captain Spindleshanks, chained and stumbling under the burden of his guilt. Summerwell and Haskett were arguing like boys, yet there was something else . . .

Another voice dodging lightly among the others, a springtime scent, a melody out of place—one that left him suddenly expectant and exposed.

And then the pair of doors swung open fully.

Charles expected to see a cocky Summerwell

standing there with Captain Spindleshanks cowering beside him, manacled and abased.

But only Haskett filled the opening, as big as a barn, his eyes oddly soulful.

"Your prisoner, sir."

Charles savored the relief, the pure triumph. Despite all the stammering and stalling, Spindleshanks was here after all, though unexpectedly shy and cowering behind Haskett. He had expected a river of picturesque curses to flow from the man, just as they had from his broadsides.

A coward after all.

"Show him in, Haskett. I've a few choice words I'd like to say to the bastard before he's taken to the jail."

Mumberton gasped and turned crimson. "Please, sir! Your language."

"My what?" Charles would have laughed if his butler's remark hadn't been so absurd.

"Please, sir, you shouldn't—" Mumberton's brows were arched high, his color high, as Summerwell shoved his way out from behind Haskett.

"You see, it's like this, my l—"

"You've lost the bloody son of a whore, haven't you, Summerwell?"

"Sir, I repeat, you mustn't speak like—"

"Damn it, Mumberton, I'll speak as I bloody well like. The prisoner, Summerwell!"

Summerwell gulped, staggered backward into Haskett. "Yessir."

A singular voice came from nowhere and sent Charles's heart spinning and stopped his breathing.

"You've just made the greatest mistake of your life, Lord Everingham, and mark me well, you shall pay dearly for it."

It was the same buttery-soft voice he'd heard a moment earlier in the corridor, sunlight mixed in with Haskett's stammering and Summerwell's grumbling, lifting above theirs like an air. Even now it wreathed his senses.

Not a man's voice. A melody, coming from somewhere behind the nervous louts who'd been in his employ for decades. Men that he trusted.

Then, as though tumbling gray clouds had parted just in time to beam a ray of sunlight down upon a particularly spectacular miracle, a magnificent young woman wedged herself through the small breach between Haskett and Summerwell and came to stand before them.

Shackled in iron, hands and ankles.

Barefoot. Clad only in her nightgown.

And her eyes lit with balefire.

Chapter 2

Holy Christ.

He'd expected a hulking country dolt or a lordly buffoon, a broad-shouldered man, at least as tall as himself. One who stank of shoddy ale and rabid arrogance. He'd expected blustering and blasphemies and blasts of dark threats leveled against him.

But not this, not a superbly fashioned young woman with eyes of clear, crystalline green that set his pulse racing.

Not this study in brazen grace and white-hot defiance standing in his office, glaring at him in her heavy iron manacles and plain cotton flannel.

Not clouds of hair that grabbed the gold out of the lamplight, that tumbled off her shoulders and down the lightly broidered front of her nightgown.

Her nightgown, for Christ's sake!

He swung the full force of his astonishment and anger on Summerwell. "What the bloody hell do you mean by this?"

Charles pointed at the woman, trying not to stare openly at the willowy roundness of her hips, at the curve of her slim waist or the rise and fall of her unencumbered breasts.

"I mean nothing at all, sir." Summerwell shrank back against the door and squeaked out, "Just, well, he's your . . . well, that is to say, she's your prisoner, my lord. Isn't she?"

"I'm no one's prisoner, Lord Everingham, least of all yours." The dazzling woman raised her wrists and clanked the thick iron bands manacling them like a histrionic ghost in a Christmas pantomime. "You'll unlock these immediately, sir, and let me go!"

He'd like to do just that—to start the damned evening over again. But he couldn't move, was utterly powerless to think beyond the absurdity of the scene, beyond watching the compelling young woman whose chains rattled accusingly as she took a single step toward him across the polished floor.

"I don't know who you believe I am, sir, what crime you think I've committed, or where you come by the arrogant notion that you can send your barbarians to break into someone's home while they are sleeping and arrest them without cause, but I demand that you unshackle me and return me to my family immediately! Else I'll see the lot of you in jail for kidnapping or worse."

Worse? He couldn't imagine worse than this, this cogent, clear-eyed threat to his strategies and his reputation, with her perfectly, gracefully arched brows and soft, thickly sooted lashes.

Charles took an unsteady breath, then stepped back from the woman to empty his head of her befuddling scent. Why had Summerwell brought him this pagan offering instead of Captain Spindleshanks? This goddess gowned for his bed, scented for his deepest pleasure with flowers and pale moonlight.

Bloody hell! "Who the devil are you, madam?"

Her eyes flashed brightly green, setting off little warning flares inside his chest.

"My name is Holliway Finch, Hollie, as I told these louts of yours when they arrested me—in your name, sir—as though I were a common criminal."

She was as uncommon as any woman he'd ever met, the portrait of self-possessed indignity. A magistrate's indulged daughter or a mayor's or, God forbid, a lord's. He couldn't muster a single excuse that wouldn't later be used in a trial against him.

Abduction, plain and simple—by men in his employ.

A maiden ruined, her reputation sullied.

And his own reputation pulverized by the press, unrecoverable this time, given his misspent youth. Spindleshanks would certainly make hay when he learned of it.

Bloody, bleeding hell! He swung back on his bailiff. "What the devil were you thinking, Summerwell? Or were you thinking at all?"

Summerwell shot a glance at the woman in stark horror. "Only to serve the arrest warrant, sir, as you ordered."

"I ordered you to arrest Captain Spindleshanks," Charles said slowly, precisely. "You remember: the radical reformer who's been a blot on the landscape and a plague to me for the last two months. A man, Summerwell. Not a woman."

Certainly not this one. She was neither swooning with shame nor weeping in terror. She was following his every word, every move, with her discerning eyes, her shoulders squared and proud despite the staggering weight of the shackles on her wrists.

"Well, sir, me and Haskett went directly to the village of Weldon Chase, to the Tuppenny Press. A printing shop it was, just like you said. We found no one else there but the young lady. She was upstairs and so—"

"Bloody hell, Summerwell, if you had found a goat instead, would you have arrested it and brought it too?"

"Of course not, my lord. But—" Summerwell

edged back behind Haskett, who then seemed to shrink behind the woman, who arched her pale, graceful brow and one nicely rounded hip, and cast a searing glare at the pair of them.

Charles wanted to throttle them both with his bare hands.

"Enough. Spindleshanks is probably in Cornwall by now, thanks to your bungling."

"The fault is yours alone, my lord," Miss Finch said in a sultry voice that he knew he would remember to the end of his days.

He had a sudden, unnerving feeling that she was a fanciful vapor, moondust and a bit of madness come to torment him. A wayward fairie princess, caught by the castle guards as she escaped down the tower stairs, off to the ball to meet her eager lover.

Unsettled by the notion and by a small but unrelenting awareness that things still weren't as they seemed, Charles leveled a finger down at her. "You'll be quiet, madam."

"I won't be quiet at all, my lord Everingham. Not now, and certainly not when you return me to my home and family."

His thoughts scattered like useless bits of glass whenever he chanced a look at her, at the bedclothes wildness of her gold-strewn hair. He felt a burning need to rake his fingers through it, to taste the dusky rose of her mouth and toy with the ribbons that secured the front of her nightgown.

Hell and damnation! A months-long investigation, his reputation at stake, and all he had to show for it was a wide-eyed, iron-shackled, nearly naked young woman, who would surely report the incident to the Home Office. And then to every newspaper in the country.

This was going to take more than the smoothing of a few ruffled feathers.

And yet there was something niggling at him, something that didn't quite fit. Some path of logic he'd missed and ought to be carefully tracking.

He hated puzzles. And this woman was a puzzle, the worst kind of ambush: incongruous and damnably distracting in her nightgown and her bare feet, in the shackles which he couldn't quite bring himself to unlock. Because a kind of unexpected danger seemed to lurk in the woman's freedom, because she was glaring at his every move when she ought to be weeping, because she was intelligent, rebellious.

If it looks like a radical . . .

But Miss Finch looked nothing at all like a radical. Radicals were large-bellied men, full-bearded, abrasive and pipe-smoking, and arrogant far beyond their station. They were ink-stained publishers and belligerent weavers who reeked of unwashed wool and camphor.

Miss Finch was scented with sunshine. She stood unflinchingly in her cutting silence, a soft crimson tinting her cheeks, her chin perpetually tilted at him.

Besides which, Captain Spindleshanks was tall and broad; he rode like the wind, scampered across midnight rooftops—and he was a man.

Bloody hell, he'd be a year cleaning up this particular mess. Explaining to Mr. Finch, or Mayor Finch, or Colonel Finch that he hadn't meant to abduct his daughter, his sister, his wife, that he hadn't sundered her innocence—

"Bloody hell, Summerwell, did you even read the arrest warrant before you executed it?"

"I did do, my lord."

"Read it again."

Charles watched Miss Finch as the man fumbled with the paper in his pocket, unfolding it as he cleared his throat, and then read, " 'Wanted for the—' "

"I know the crime, Summerwell. The description. Read the description of Captain Spindleshanks."

"It says here that he's 'about thirty-five years of age, stands six feet or more, has long, dark hair and a beard to match, tends to broadness at the shoulders, and wears a cloak and an ancient tricorn. . . . ' " Summerwell's voice trailed off as he looked up again at the unlikely Miss Finch and then back at Charles.

"Six feet or more, Summerwell. Broad-shouldered. A beard. Black hair." Summerwell cringed at the litany of his errors. "Seems the Home Office reward is safe enough from you and Haskett tonight."

"A reward?" The question came from Miss Finch, the throaty lilt of surprise laced with something else. Pride, was it? Adventure?

That was preposterous, of course, but Charles watched her carefully as he answered, still plagued by an indistinct itch he couldn't name. "The Home Office has posted a generous reward for the arrest and conviction of Captain Spindle-shanks."

She made a small, unconcerned hum in her throat and raised an unconcerned brow. "How much?"

"A hundred pounds."

"Imagine that." Then Miss Finch smiled, almost imperceptibly.

Oh, Papa, I have a price on my head!

Chapter 3

Hollie Finch knew that she ought to be utterly terrified by the huge, shadowy man who loomed above her in his crisply elegant linen shirt and finely tailored waistcoat, who smelled of brandy and lime and leather. She knew that she should feel wholly chastened for her carelessness now that she was shackled to her eyebrows and standing in front of the great and legendary earl who was on the brink of bringing her down along with her dreams. But it was all she could do to keep from shouting with joy.

A hundred pounds!

A reckless, undeniable pride caused the fluttering in her stomach and the thumping in her chest. Not Everingham's fearsome glower, not the compellingly spicy scent of him as he circled behind her or the fear in his servant's faces or the chill that scuttled along the floor and brushed at her bare ankles.

It was a sweeping, towering joy, the sort she hadn't felt in months. Not since before her father died and the world had gone so far awry.

Oh, but this shameful pride would get her into even more trouble than she was in already. The tide was miraculously at bay; the earl thought she was an innocent bystander in his political affairs. With any luck, she'd be long gone before he discovered that Summerwell and Haskett hadn't made a mistake at all.

That she was Captain Spindleshanks, in the flesh.

In the bare flesh, or nearly so. Dear God, her father would have had her hide if he'd known what she'd been up to. If he hadn't been killed that day on St. Peter's Fields. She missed his scolding of her passion.

Patience, girl.

Oh, but Papa, they murdered you. Like they murdered all the other people who got in their way that day.

Heartlessly. Brutally.

And now the lot of them were going to get away with their abominable crime—the magistrates and the yeomanry, Everingham and his commissioners—while innocents were imprisoned and hanged and transported from their families to the ends of the earth.

Murder sanctioned by Parliament. Flagrant injustice. It must be exposed and put right before Everingham's commission issued its pack of lies in the guise of truth.

But she could only continue her campaign if she escaped. Her only hope was to stanch her hasty temper and encourage Everingham's belief that he'd made a huge error in arresting her, that she was indeed an innocent young maiden caught in his evil tentacles.

Though he wasn't at all the sort of man to make errors or leave them unexplored. And his brow had deepened precipitously in the last few moments, his eyes darkened to a chilly suspicion, sinking her courage.

She stood her ground, though she wanted to run, weighted to the smooth oaken planks by terror and the cool iron shackles around her ankles.

"Describe this print shop to me, Summerwell," Everingham said, his gaze so breathlessly dangerous that it was impossible to look away. He touched every stitch of her flannel nightgown with his gaze, blazing his intimate way through the inadequate fabric right to her skin, stealing her breath, pausing to stare at her mouth, as though tasting her there, and then back again into her eyes. "The Tuppenny Press."

Summerwell had slipped deeper into the shadowy room, just beyond Everingham's reach. "Well, my lord, there was . . . uh, printing, of course. And paper. Yes, yes, loads of printed paper everywhere."

Of course there was; printing was her business. She'd been pushing perilously forward in her campaign to expose Everingham's corrupt commission before he issued his findings. She'd been careless recently, had probably left a leagues-wide trail of sedition all across the Midlands.

Leave it to Everingham to follow that trail directly to the Tuppenny Press—exactly where her life would end unless she could call upon a spectacular miracle and escape him. The door was open wide behind her, freedom just a step backward between the butler and Haskett, then out into the dim hallway.

But not with Everingham watching so closely, and certainly not when she was encumbered by a clanking chain. Dear God.

"Exactly what sort of printing, Summerwell? Tracts, handbills?"

"Oh, yes, sir. And newspapers and pamphlets and broadsides. Evidence, my lord! Just like this one here that you gave me with the warrant."

"Show me, Summerwell."

Summerwell dug down into his jacket pocket and then unfolded a sheet of paper. "Here, my lord."

Hollie easily recognized the incendiary woodcut that she'd bought from a Manchester engraver: a bloodthirsty yeoman slashing off the head of a young weaver.

Oh, this was a deadly game with but one outcome. She'd accepted the risk from the beginning, when she'd made her first midnight ride, when she started printing her sedition. And when Everingham's men had awakened her into this nightmare, she'd known she was in great trouble, even in their confusion at finding a woman instead of the man they had been expecting.

"Read it, Summerwell."

The man's hands shook as he began: " 'The full and truthful inquiry into the massacre of the unarmed weavers of Manchester, their wives and innocent children, by the yeomanry cavalry, under the direction of . . . of the evil magistrates . . . ' "

Summerwell trailed off feebly and raised wary, pleading eyes to Everingham.

A terrible fury creased Everingham's brow, becoming a palpable threat when he shifted his gaze to Hollie. "Go on."

Summerwell flinched but continued, " 'A truth that has been squelched and corrupted by the infernal designs of the . . . uh, the . . . wicked"—Summerwell gulped before he raced through to the end—"Lord Everingham.' "

A cold clot of stillness hung in the room, Everingham's suspicion keeping Hollie frozen in place with visions of a damp and dreary jail cell, of the gallows, oblivion.

The silence was broken at last by the squeak of

Summerwell's quiet defense. "Sounded like Spindleshanks to me, sir."

Everingham took the broadside from Summerwell and dropped it onto the table. "Indeed."

"Yes, indeed, sir." Summerwell brightened, approached the table, and lifted a stack of handbills. "We found a lot more 'n that: page after page of this sedition stuff."

Haskett nodded eagerly at his master. "Hanging on lines downstairs they were, sir, stretched every which way between the rafters. An' dripping with words from every page. Looked like a bleedin' laundry room on a Monday afternoon."

"We were so sure that we'd found Spindleshanks's shop, we packed up a few boxes and brought 'em back with us."

Hollie's heart collapsed and fell into her stomach. So that was the chicanery they'd been up to when they went back inside after they'd shackled her to the wagon seat. Rifling her bedroom, digging around for evidence.

Everingham's eyes flickered for the briefest moment, a lick of searing flame against her cheek, then he turned his blazing attention from her and moved closer to the paper-cluttered table, the lamp casting deep shadows across his face as he spread his broad hand across one of the stacks of paper.

"Where are these boxes of evidence now, Summerwell?"

Summerwell's chest rose. "Still waitin' out in the wagon, my lord."

This seemed to please Everingham; it tightened a muscle in his jaw that served as a smile.

"Take a close look here, Summerwell: do you recall seeing any of this in the shop?" Everingham gestured at the sea of sedition: her printing shop flayed open, ready to be dissected, every handbill and placard familiar to her and ultimately indicting.

Hollie wanted to rage at Everingham, for the drowning hollowness in her chest, for the echoing memories, for stealing her voice, her words.

"Oh, yes, my lord," Summerwell said, picking up a handbill. "We found plenty of these, announcing a meeting of handloom weavers in Leeds."

At Rennick's mill, only three nights ago. She'd barely escaped with her skin, had nearly lost her cloak and that blasted tricorn and its wig. And now here she was, trapped and about to be exposed, chilled to the bone but fiercely clinging to a familiar point of heat in her heart, a spot of courage and outrage.

Because Everingham had left her alone at the doorway. She took a quarter-step backward, just to see how far she could move away.

Clank went the blasted chain.

Everingham's dark eyes found hers sharply from across the room and narrowed as he studied her more deeply. He slid his smoky gaze along her cheekbone and across her mouth, then back to her eyes, questing where he didn't belong, with a scorching interest that sifted through her flannel and had nothing to do with sedition or treason or shackles.

"What else, Summerwell?" he finally asked, holding her gaze fast with his own.

"I do remember this piece, sir, though I don't think we brought it along. 'The Lancaster Hymn,' it says. 'Smuggled out of Lancaster Prison by Captain Spindleshanks to lift the spirits of the victims and innocents of the wicked massacre in St. Peter's Fields.' " Summerwell jabbed his finger at a large-font block of print, and Everingham turned his attention back to his bailiff.

Just in time, because, dear God, when she'd taken her slow step back, her heel had lifted out of the shackle. The iron band was too large for her foot when she pointed her toes. Freedom! So unexpected and precious it took her breath away.

While Everingham studied her broadsides at his graceful, lordly ease, while Summerwell read aloud from them, and the three other men focused all their attention on the heaping mound of sedition, Hollie carefully, silently worked on ridding herself of the remaining shackle, angling her toes just right.

Clank, chink.

She held her breath as they all looked her way again, Everingham's piercing, devil's gaze more suspicious now than ever, as though he could lift the hem of her nightgown with the power of his thoughts, as though he knew she'd freed herself of one of his iron bands. And that it pleased him.

A wave of fear came roaring through her that she would fail her father if she were thrown into prison now. She was damned either way: running from the law would mean that she could never return to her print shop, could never again publish the *Tuppenny Press* on her father's beloved Stanhope. But if living underground for the rest of her life was the only way to expose the truth of the massacre that took her father's life, then so be it.

She deliberately sighed impatiently and shifted her weight to her other hip with another clanking rattle. "You're trying my patience, Lord Everingham!" she said for good measure.

She felt wickedly prideful, because it was only a matter of time before Everingham would realize that he'd actually had Captain Spindleshanks in his office all along.

And that I got away, my lord.

The man studied her with his impossibly dark gaze, a muscle tightening beneath his clean-shaved jaw, before he finally frowned and returned to his deviltry.

"My lord, there were a couple hundred issues of a newspaper—the *Tuppenny Press*, like the name of the print shop—all bound up neatly, looking like they were ready to be carted off to London."

Everingham studied the newspaper with care, and Hollie prayed.

Please don't look up! Not yet.

She held her breath as she finally stepped completely out of the last shackle and stood blessedly free. Her pulse thrummed a deafening rhythm against her ears as she clasped her manacled hands together to keep the short chain between them from rattling.

Just a half-dozen stealthy, sliding steps backward, and she'd be in the darkened hallway. And then out the door and away into the woods.

But the beast looked up and into her eyes, as though he could hear her thoughts and see right down into her heart.

"Leave us, gentlemen," he said suddenly, gesturing for the others to scatter.

"But, my lord—"

"Now, Summerwell. Deliver the boxes of evidence to my library. That will be all, Bavidge."

They were alone a moment later, the door closed, the room darker and absolutely silent save for the thundering of her heart. The shadowed corners pressed in as he strode toward her, his mood changed entirely. He'd been a blur of powerful bureaucracy just a few moments ago. Now he was a stalking beast. A beast who wore his fine linen shirt with a dark and dangerous grace, an elegant silk neck cloth and the scents of bay, all the tones and textures of rank and privilege.

He stopped in front of her, an overwhelming

threat as he touched his searing fingertip to her breastbone, an intensely intimate pressure that set her heart spinning and sent her stumbling backward a step. She followed his slow, sinuously possessive gaze down the front of her nightgown, then to the damning tangle of chain and iron bands that now lay piled on the polished floor.

"Clever, Miss Finch." Everingham swiftly stooped and then dangled her ankle shackles from his finger, with a devilish, falsely admiring lift to his brow. "You were about to run from me. Perhaps I misjudged you."

His voice was dark and thoroughly personal, curling around the tips of her hair and against her ears, pulsing through her fingertips, threatening dire consequences if she didn't quickly master her paralyzing fear and prove that she was innocent of his suspicions.

Hollie scooted past him and put a chair between them so that she could think better. "It's very late, my lord."

"Indeed." A solitary, darkly silken word, a test, a challenge. He let it hang between them as his gaze swept across her face in a methodical fashion, ending at her eyes.

"I'm tired—"

"So am I."

"And I'm not your Captain Spindleshanks fellow."

He raised a brow slightly, insufferably amused

and more than dangerously suspicious. "Obviously," he said too mildly.

Obviously! Then he still didn't suspect the truth. There was hope after all, if she played this right.

"Then, you finally recognize your error—the first step to righting a terrible wrong. Which means that you'll also understand that I want to go home to my bed, where I belong." She stuck out her hands, bound by the two D-shaped steel bands and the short length of chain between them. "Unlock me. If you please."

But he made no move at all. "I don't please at all, madam. As I don't please to have anyone running from me."

"I didn't."

"You didn't get the chance."

"You seemed to be finished with me, my lord, so I—"

"I'm not finished with you, Miss Finch." The flick of his dark eyes set her heart loose of its orderly rhythms, made it skid around in her chest. "Not nearly finished."

Chapter 4

Hollie swallowed hard, terrified that Everingham suddenly knew everything about her, that his favorite game was cat and mouse and she was now his plaything, to be tormented to her last breath.

She'd seen his powerfully rugged profile hundreds of times: that strong blade of a nose, the hard-edged jaw, the precision of his brow as he pinned a man with his glare. Sketches of his features had been printed often enough in *The Times*; in her father's own newspaper, as well. Caricatures of the man, to be sure, etched into tin, inked, and then pressed by her own hand into the heavily taxed newsprint—but those caricatures hadn't prepared her for the power of the man in the lifting shadows, and at this dizzyingly close range.

Nor had the years of secretly, shamelessly watching him from the press gallery in Parliament, listening to his imperious speeches and meticulously committing them to her notebook for her father's newspaper, wondering all the while how he could be so compellingly thickheaded. But far more disturbing, wondering how the man could sometimes be so wise.

"We can be done with this quickly, Miss Finch."

"Good, my lord, because I—"

"Where is he?"

"He?" Blast the man and his unbalancing questions, for the dizziness he caused as he closed in on her and the darkness in his eyes that left her senses reeling, left her searching for light, for the normal sense of things. "Where is who, my lord?"

"Your husband, madam," he whispered, now just inches from her temple, his eyes starless midnight. "Where is he?"

"My *husband?*" Hollie nearly choked on the word, on the absurdity. On her relief at the earl's poor sense of direction—away from her and onto some more capable man who existed only in Everingham's misogynistic suspicions. But he'd managed to back her slowly against the round table heaped with all the evidence of her crime, the heat of him blending with her own, his scent becoming part of hers. "I don't know what you mean, sir," she said breathlessly. "I'm not married."

That seemed to please him in some way, though he made a dark, disbelieving sound in his throat and lowered one of his tall, broad shoulders, bringing him closer to her ear. "Your father, then, Miss Finch. Tell me where he is, and I'll go easily on him."

"What do you mean, my father?"

"Sheltering a criminal is a crime in itself, Miss Finch, punishable by long years in prison. Protecting him will only gain you more trouble."

The blackguard! She hadn't been able to protect her father when he was alive, could only watch him fall under the yeoman's blade and then hold him as he died.

It was too late to protect him; honoring him was all that was left to her life.

Tears stung her eyes, stuffed her chest and her throat, but she swallowed back the salty heat. She be damned if she'd cry in front of the earl, who was carefully watching her and waiting as a lion awaits his supper.

"My father is dead, my lord. Buried in the family crypt." *And the fault belongs to you and men like you.* Her father's death and so many others.

But saying that would give Everingham too much knowledge against her. He would surely understand her cause and her conspiracies, might sense the danger to him, the stakes in this dance of theirs.

Everingham stepped away slowly, the lamplight striping his black hair with glints of bright-ness, his eyes narrowed and studying her. "When did your father die?"

The truth would lead to Peterloo and to her rabble-rousing, and then to her. "Several months back."

"When exactly?"

"After Christmas." Yes, that lie would do— unless he decided to poke around the parish records.

"I'm sorry for your loss, Miss Finch. But I need to know the whereabouts of the man who calls himself Captain Spindleshanks."

"I can't help you." *Won't. Ever.*

"He's a danger to the peace of the country, an even greater danger to the people around him. You know the man. You must."

"I haven't the slightest idea which *man* you're talking about, let alone where you might find him." It was a simple falsehood, yet it rang in her heart like a pledge to her father. "Is he such a dangerous creature, my lord, to put the fear of God into a whole Parliament?"

Oh, what a blistering dunderhead she was, baiting the earl of Everingham! She prayed that he hadn't noticed, that he'd been too busy loos-ening his neck cloth and his shirt collar, exposing the bronze imprint of the sun on his throat and the promise of hard muscles beneath the fine fabric.

But the gaze he lifted to her had a feral gleam,

as though he suddenly recognized the enemy and knew his plan would succeed.

"Tell me, Miss Finch, why did Summerwell find you sleeping above a print shop?"

Damn his blindsiding questions! She'd seen him bring down mighty lords and their unshakable opinions with his unexpected strategies. "He found me there, my lord, because that's where I live."

He studied her as he tossed the neck cloth across the back of a chair. "And *why* do you live above a print shop?"

"Why?" Dear God, the answer would give everything to him. There was a ragged-toothed trap behind each of his questions, and she couldn't judge where to step next.

"Because the shop is mine." It sounded like a question even to her own ears.

"Yours?" The beast laughed without a stitch of humor, plainly unbelieving that a woman could bear such a responsibility. "The truth, Miss Finch. Why were you sleeping in the print shop? At whose bidding?"

"At my own bidding, my lord, because the Tuppenny Press belongs to me, and I live there." She inhaled the dangerous spice of him, and her courage came back again at full force, allowing her to glare up at him and all that tethered fury. "And now will you remove your medieval chains from my wrists and send me home? I have work to do that cannot wait."

He raised her chin with his knuckle almost gently, as though he would kiss her when he finished. As though she wished for him to, yearned for it.

"I applaud your loyalty, madam, but it's past time you stop your lying and tell me who you're protecting. Who is Captain Spindleshanks, Miss Finch?"

"I don't know."

"Is he worth that much to you, madam? A quick trial and a brutal prison term for aiding a criminal?" His heat billowed against her nightgown, seeped in through the seams where the breezes that roamed his cavernous house caught and swirled. She'd been standing blithely inside the circle of him to keep warm. Her skin had been pinched and dimpled from the cold, and now it seemed to crave him and his heat all the more when he walked a few steps away from her, though his gaze never wavered.

"I don't know what you're talking about, my lord. The shop is mine. I've never heard of Colonel Whatever-His-Name-Is."

"Is he your printer, Miss Finch?"

"My what?" That breeze slipped across the floor from the buffeting shadows, danced at her ankles again, and all the while Everingham stared at her.

"The man who operates the equipment. Does he work at night when you're asleep or away?"

"*He* is *me*, sir. Hollie Finch." She might well be signing her own death warrant by the admission.

"I am not only the publisher, but the printer, the compositor, and the charwoman, and everything else since my father died."

"Are you?" His quietly rumbling doubt settled low in her belly, a disconcerting intimacy that softened her knees to putty and sped up her heart. "Then what is it that you print in your . . . little shop?"

Sedition, my wicked Lord Everingham.

"Why?" she asked, angry to her bones at his prejudice. Let the lout disbelieve her, dismiss her entirely. That's where she would hide from his inquisition: deeply inside the truth. "What has my work to do with setting me free of these blasted shackles?"

"Answer my question."

"I am innocent of anything you believe this Captain Spindleshanks has done."

"Good, Miss Finch, then you'll answer me truthfully." He crossed his arms and leaned easily against the paper-cluttered table, a beast guarding his treasure trove of evidence. "What is the nature of your printing business?"

"I print the sort of things that any printer does, various jobs for various customers."

"Jobs such as?"

"Sale notices for local merchants. Playbills for the touring shows when they come."

"And . . . ?"

"Announcements."

"Of . . . ?"

Secret trade union meetings. "Births, deaths, market fairs, traveling minstrels."

"What else?"

"Billheads and booklets and posters." Hollie hadn't blushed in years, had never suffered such a rush of breathless, unfocused heat. His studied silence disturbed her more than his insufferable questions. As though he were looking through her, leaving traces of himself, warm streaks of mystery and wanting. "Recipes and wallpaper patterns, a book of remedies, primers."

"What else?"

Seditious handbills, likening you and your commission to a foul nest of vipers.

"Almanacs, of course, my lord. They are very popular."

"With whom?"

"With ordinary people. Those of us who must live by the tide tables and planting days, and those who are interested in the chronology of the archbishops of Canterbury and how many square feet in a hectare."

Hollie wanted to stop herself, but Everingham was the enemy, and she had a huge burning in her chest that needed airing. And his brow was cocked at a jaunty, arrogant angle.

"And your newspaper as well?"

"Yes. My printing press is busy constantly. Anything my customers want, because it's my livelihood. Though I can't imagine that you would understand the need to work for a living."

"What I don't understand, Miss Finch, is this: if you are truly the proprietor of the Tuppenny Press, a shop that obviously prints Captain Spindleshanks's sedition by the bushel full, then how is it that you've never met the man?"

"I—" Oh, blast! She'd plowed headlong into his trap.

He leaned closer. "You what, Miss Finch?"

"Well, that is to say—" The tip of Everingham's finger was fitted perfectly against her lips like a hot kiss, taking her breath as he pressed her back against the desk again.

"Enough, madam." His words brushed at her temple, made her want to turn her mouth to catch them, to feel them against her cheek. "You've done a fine job protecting your captain; no man could ask for a more loyal champion. But it's time you end this dangerous charade."

"My lord, I—"

He shook his head, as he slid his fingers along her jaw and then through her hair until she was tilting her head back, exposing her throat, and the telling flush that was rising out of her bodice.

"You may not know Captain Spindleshanks beyond the profitable custom he brings in secret to your shop. He may pay you well for your silence. You may not even approve of his illegal activities. But it's your press that prints his seditious tracts and your silence that is keeping the secret of his identity intact."

She was skating on such thin and crackling ice.

And yet an idea was forming there, just beyond her reach. "But, sir, I don't—"

He wound a lock of her hair around his massive hand. "Would your captain be as loyal to you, Miss Finch? This paragon of the people, this flawed hero of yours?"

She swallowed roughly and braved the man's gaze, terrified by the foolish risk she was considering. "Loyalty, my lord, is a delicate thing."

"Profoundly so, Miss Finch. The basis of trust. I'd consider my loyalty wisely, if I were you. Don't be foolhardy enough to waste it on the unworthy. I'll assure your captain that you were shackled against your will. That you struggled bravely to the bitter end, protecting his name and his cause. But that at the last, you realized that the right thing, the sane thing to do, was to reveal his whereabouts. Tell me his name, and you go free."

His name. Her name. A phantom.

"Now, Miss Finch." He braced his hands on the edge of the desk behind her and met her thighs with his own, all hard muscles and heat, his minty breath playing at the curls along her hairline, lifting them lightly in a growl. "You'll tell me his name, else I'll have you clapped in prison with the fleas and the rats."

It was now or never.

"Oh!" Hollie whimpered for dramatic effect, drew back in abject horror, and cried out, "No! No, my lord! Not the rats, pleeeease!"

Looking surprised, Everingham let her up slightly, but his eyes were still narrowed and doubting, still testing. "That's what prisons are all about, Miss Finch. Dripping walls and dark pits. Hunger and privation. And rats."

"No!" Hollie hissed and clasped her shackled hands to her chest, hoping she wasn't pouring it on a bit too thickly. "Not the rats, sir! Tell me you wouldn't throw me into prison, my lord, just for being too loyal."

Everingham blinked down at her, his brows winging suddenly toward his dark hair, a quirk to his fine mouth.

"Make no mistake, Miss Finch: I'll see you locked inside the dankest and darkest prison possible, if it means finding Captain Spindleshanks."

Hollie hauled her chained hands up to cover her eyes and gave a good, long wail. "I don't know what to think anymore, sir, or what to do."

"Just tell me the truth," he said between his teeth.

"Oh, please, sir, don't force me to do this! Not to . . . to . . . *him.*" Hollie peeked at Everingham through her fingers as she sobbed.

He was rubbing the knuckles of his fist along the hard-edged ridge of his jaw, as though he didn't trust his sudden good fortune.

"Whom do you mean, Miss Finch?"

"I—I mean—"

A brother? No, she'd never betray a brother. Who else would he believe she'd protect with her life? Someone she loved, adored. Someone she'd walk through fire to save.

Of course!

Her heart in her throat, Hollie dragged her hands away from her eyes, unexpected tears burning at the back of her nose, as though such a beloved man truly existed and that she was in terror of his life. "Promise me that you won't hurt him if you find him, my lord."

"*Who*, Miss Finch? Tell me now, else you'll find your delicate little ankles manacled once again and yourself on the way to Coldbath Prison!"

"*Please*, my lord, I'd never forgive myself if he was injured."

"Tell me, Miss Finch."

Tears that Hollie hadn't wept since her father died now came in huge, drowning gulps.

"My name is actually Hollie Finch ... MacGillnock, my lord."

"What the devil do you mean, Miss Finch?"

"The man you've been looking for, is . . ."

"Is who? *Tell* me, dammit all."

Hollie took one last, long breath of fortitude and prayed for the best.

"He . . . he's my husband."

Chapter 5

~~~~~

*H*usband.

Charles felt his heart thud and then stop. He took a sharp breath to start it again, but there was still a cold lump in his gut.

Married. The woman was married. She should have said earlier that he'd stolen her from her husband's side.

But the man hadn't been there; she'd been alone in her bed when Summerwell found her. Her coward of a husband had doubtless fled down the back stairs, leaving his innocent wife to face the consequences of his folly.

Bloody blazes!

"Spindleshanks is your husband, madam?"

"Alas, my lord, he is!" She was weeping into

44

those rusty iron chains at her delicate wrists, and they suddenly seemed horrific.

Christ, how he hated this. A woman weeping in his office. *This* woman.

"What is your husband's name?"

"MacGillnock, of course."

"His Christian name, madam?"

"It's, it's—" The bastard's name became a flood of weeping and clanking as she snuffled and wiped her nose. "It's Adammmmmmmm."

The coward. "Adam MacGillnock," he said, hating the stabbing taste of it on his tongue.

"Yes." She gathered herself up on pitifully wobbling legs, her face beautiful even streaming with tears, her shoulders sagging now, her fingers laced together among the folds of her nightgown and the lank chain. "I've told you all I know. Now you must let me leave, my lord. I'm so very tired. To the inside of my heart I am."

"Not quite yet, Miss . . . madam—" He couldn't bring himself to say *Mrs. MacGillnock*; the name didn't suit her in the least. Miss Finch did. She was far better than MacGillnock; so magnificent in her defense of her rotter of a husband, in her foolhardy attempt at perjury to save his lousy skin.

"But you promised, my lord! I've just betrayed the man I love and for what purpose? Do you mean to keep me here at your mercy?"

The man she loved—it set his teeth on edge to

hear it. That she would waste her life and her love on a man like that. Not that he cared a whit about the woman's private life; he merely detested injustice, and that was the case here.

"You'll be free to go as soon as you tell me where he is."

"Gone." She sniffled and shook her head, making all that cascading gold shimmer down her back.

"Gone where?"

That brought a little whimpering sound. "I don't know. He didn't say."

Bloody hell, he'd never had a bit of luck with weeping women. He usually sped off in the opposite direction, but this one made him want to dry her tears, to soothe her fear. To apologize, for God's sake!

"When did you see him last?" he snapped, because like an utter dolt he was reaching into his breeches pocket for a handkerchief, offering it to her.

She caught her lower lip with her perfect white teeth, snuffled again, and started to reach for the linen, but the chains dragged her hands down. Bloody hell.

"It was three loooong nights ago. Very late. I don't know where he'd been."

The meeting at Rennick's mill. "What did MacGillnock look like when he arrived home? What was he wearing?"

"His shirt." Another sob shook her shoulders.

"Trousers and a leather waistcoat, like always. He was tired and hungry."

He lifted her chin and dabbed at the dampness in her eyes. "What did he do then?"

"We'd been two whole weeks without seeing each other. So I fed him supper, and then he took me upstairs, and we—Oh." It was a tiny but telling sound and made his teeth hurt. She blushed absolutely everywhere he could see, leaving him to imagine all the sultry places that were hidden just beyond his jurisdiction.

"Well, he was gone when I woke up the next morning."

The thought of Hollie Finch warmed to her ears and naked and tangled up in cool linen sheets unbalanced his thinking and brought a roaring heat to his groin. Though he hadn't a single claim to her.

"You haven't seen him since then?"

She shook her head. "He tells me very little about what he does and where he goes. He says that I'm safer if I don't know." She blinked her huge eyes at him, the innocent green of springtime, fringed by spiky, gold-tipped lashes. "*Am* I safer, my lord?"

"Great God, madam, look at yourself. You're standing in a magistrate's office, manacled and in your nightgown, defending an indefensible husband, and you can ask such a question?"

She stiffened and frowned at him, in full possession of her earlier outrage, her voice husky and low. "Do you intend to torture me just to discover that I know nothing?"

His head had begun to ache, right at the base. This was still careening out of his control.

"How long have you been married, madam?"

Her face crumpled suddenly, and she swabbed her sloppy eyes with her sleeve, nearly clouting herself with the shackle.

"Two months, my lord."

Two bloody months. Bloody hell, now he was nursemaid to the muddled heart of a newlywed bride deserted by her unworthy swine of a husband. More weeping and wailing, a gushing spigot of emotion. As though she were—

Holy hell! A wildfire swept and through his chest, a jealous outrage that filled him with horror.

"Are you with child, madam?"

She dropped her hands and stared at him, wild-eyed. "Me?" It was a yelp, obviously an idea that the woman hadn't yet entertained.

Great Christ, he hoped to hell she knew where babies came from. The guilty thought pulled his attention to the young boy asleep upstairs, and to the unprovable claim on his name.

He couldn't remember a night that had disintegrated so swiftly and surely. Triumph turned to absurdity. He'd captured not Spindleshanks at all but the man's magnificently unruly wife, who'd only stirred up more questions with every new answer.

And there were boxes and barrels of questions waiting for him to unravel in his library. He'd be days sorting through it.

Days and nights with Miss Hollie Finch MacGillnock.

Bloody hell! "Come," he said, starting for the door.

"No." She plunked her lovely backside down on top of his desk, stuck her shackled hands primly into her lap, and thrust out her defiant chin. "I'm not saying another word to you or taking another step until you've released me as you promised you would."

"I can't do that quite yet."

"Then I'm staying right here."

"Like it or not, madam, since you refuse to tell me the whereabouts of your husband, you and I have an appointment in the library."

"I told you I don't know where he is."

He stalked back to her. "Then you haven't thought hard enough, Miss Finch."

He had intended only to lift her onto his shoulder and carry her off to find the key to the manacles, but her waist was small and curved exactly for his hands, and her breasts were shockingly warm beneath the flannel as they tucked themselves neatly inside the arc of his thumbs. So perfectly weighted, so buoyant, that his heart took off like a New Year's rocket.

"How dare you, sir!"

How, indeed?

"I'm a married woman!"

"You've made that eminently clear." He bent his knees and hauled her lightness up over his shoulder, trying not to think about the shapely, flannel-covered derriere that loomed at his cheek.

"I'm going to scream."

"Please do." Then he wouldn't be thinking quite so precisely about her wriggling, or how he could manage to spend another moment conducting an interview with her dressed for bed, while he imagined her in his own, writhing beneath his hands, begging for his touch.

Bloody hell! He gritted his teeth and then shouted, "Mumberton!" as he reached the hallway with his comely baggage and her threats.

"My husband will come after you for manhandling me, Everingham."

"That's a chance I'll have to take." It also sparked an astounding idea—an unsavory strategy that just might bring Spindleshanks finally to justice.

Though it might also bring about his own madness if he didn't take care with its execution.

"He's big, you know," she said against the back of his neck, a steamy little burst of anger that leaped down his back and lodged itself in his groin, becoming a bolt of pure, hot, uncivilized lust for her.

"So I've heard. Mumberton!" Charles was halfway down the stairway to the servants' hall when the man appeared on the landing below. He stopped cold, his eyes saucer-wide.

"Blazes, my lord! What have you got there?" Mumberton blinked quickly and then straightened his thin shoulders. "You can't really mean to do this!"

"Do what, damn it?"

"Do . . ." Mumberton indicated Miss Finch's wriggling derriere and Charles's hand spread so possessively across it to keep her still and in place. "Miss Finch."

The woman propped her pointy elbows on the ridge of his shoulder and whipped around to Mumberton. "That's *Mrs. MacGillnock,* if you please, Mumberton. And if his lordship tries anything at all, believe me, he'll regret it—exactly where men most regret their injuries."

Charles was quite sure of her aim. Though, God in heaven, she was willowy and fine-limbed. He could tell that easily through the flannel, warm flesh and scented invitations. But she belonged to another man—a cowardly bastard who sent out his wife to fight his battles. Still, she was a duly wedded and bedded bride. And he'd long ago made it a rule to stay clear of married women and their unpredictable husbands.

"My lord, do you hear that? She's a married—"

"Yes, Mumberton, but she's still shackled. I want the key."

Charles had always kept his private affairs away from the eyes of his household staff, but in

recent years he'd lost interest in those shallow
dalliances, and had begun to yearn for something more. A wife. A child.

Are you my papa, sir?

"Put me down this instant!" The woman ped-
aled her feet and he staggered sideways, then
caught his balance with his hip against the newel.

"Hold still, madam. The key, Mumberton, before she wakes up the entire county." Charles
held out his free hand, but Mumberton was still
staring raptly up at Miss Finch's backside with a
perfectly blended expression of scandalized horror and deeply male appreciation that Charles
resented.

"Keys, my lord? Oh, yes!"

"Now, Mumberton!"

Mumberton scowled, muttered beneath his
mustache as he dipped into his coat pocket and
drew out the key, then sniffed his dissatisfaction.
"Here, my lord."

Charles grabbed the key and set the woman
on her feet, but held fast to the appealing curves
at her waist to keep her from taking off down the
hall and into the night. "And make up the West
Room."

"The lady's staying here tonight?"

"No, I'm absolutely not staying here, Mumberton." Miss Finch fixed her fury on Charles
and pointed a finger at him in a clatter of iron.
"You said we had an appointment in the library."

"It's two o'clock in the morning, madam. We'll

sort this out tomorrow in the clear light of day."
When his head was less cluttered and the woman
was wearing a decent gown and garments that
would keep her from bobbing and swaying.

"Oh, no, you don't, Everingham! You
promised to let me go home if I confessed. I've
done just that and I'm not staying here another
moment!" The lunatic woman gave a sharp yank
to the side that would have sent her tumbling
down the stairs if Charles hadn't grabbed the
chain between her wrists.

"That's enough, madam." He stooped and
hoisted her over his shoulder again before she
could protest. "The West Room, Mumberton.
And hurry."

Charles tightened his grip on her backside,
which only intensified his irrational need for
her, and took the stairs two at a time, not certain what he would do with her once he got up
there.

"I might have known all those rumors of your
sins and your debauchery were true, Everingham!"

"Debauchery?" Charles would have laughed,
because he was long done with that facet of his
life, but the boy's face came back again: his supposed son's, the product of his past—knee-high
to him, with huge, dark eyes, chin upturned and
quivering.

Hollie hadn't actually ever heard anything
vile about Everingham's morals. On the contrary,

society ladies seemed to clamor for the privilege of his attention—at least according to the items she'd devoured about him in the gossip columns. Once or twice she'd even allowed herself to imagine herself on the man's arm at a ball, smiling up at him, dancing inside the circle of those strong arms.

"Hold still, madam."

And now she was his prisoner, draped over his shoulder like a sack of barley and on her way to the West Room. Which was no doubt some specially designed garret jail, a tiny, stifling tower belfry with no windows and bats instead of rats.

She shivered and stopped struggling to be free, because fighting against him only made him tighten his grip around her hips, which wasn't exactly an unpleasant sensation. His hands were brutishly large, his fingers brazenly familiar where they strayed in his single-minded mission. But most shockingly inexcusable of all, they were gentle and so very hot.

She was, after all, supposed to be a married woman. And with any luck, the ruse would gain her freedom tomorrow morning.

"I can walk myself, my lord."

"Yes, but you won't in the direction I prefer."

With his hands planted where they oughtn't be, the beast carried her down the upstairs hall, across the landing of the grand marble staircase that rose from the cavernously echoing foyer below, and finally paused at the last door in the hall. In one smooth swirl, he lifted her off his shoulder and set her on her feet on the woollen runner.

"In here, madam." He opened the door, fitted his broad hand to the small of her back, and ushered her inside, as possessively familiar as ever.

She went reluctantly to her cell, expecting the worst. But the room was palatial and inviting, deeply saturated with forest hues, rich wines, and autumn maples.

Flames burned in the hearth—Mumberton had been very quick in his preparations—producing a smooth blanket of dark orange that touched the drapes and the polished mahogany and the fine carpet that she curled her toes into as she stood amidst all this shimmering splendor.

And at its center was a tester bed so tall that a two-step stair was tucked against it, so broad and piled with pillows, so utterly inviting, that she wanted to climb up and lose herself beneath the sleek, silver-gold silk counterpane, lofted by the finest down.

The whole room smelled of bay and rare raw spices and . . .

And—bloody blazes—it smelled of—

Him!

She whirled on the man and his oppressive height, stuck her finger into the middle of his chest, and instantly regretted it because of the pulsing heat she found there. "This is your chamber."

"It is."

"I'm not sharing your bed."

"No, madam, you're not. To my eternal sorrow."

"What?" Her ears were burning crimson, muddling his words.

"If you recall, we have just left Mumberton, madam. Your bed isn't ready yet."

"It was when I got into it five hours ago. I should be fast asleep there now, Everingham."

"You have your husband to thank for that."

"My—" My what? she'd almost said. She gathered back her senses and left the heat of him for the hearth, and found it lacking. "If I ever see my husband again, I'll tell him how you abducted me. *If* he'll accept me back to the marital bed after my reputation's been so casually tainted by you."

"Believe me, madam, I have no intention of inviting you to my bed."

His outright dismissal shouldn't have stung, shouldn't have made her blush or worry that she was lacking; she should have been grateful.

"Good, my lord, because I certainly wouldn't accept the offer, being as happily married as I am. I'll scream the house down if you try."

"I assure you, madam, that I don't take women against their will."

"As if I'm going to trust you." But in the back of her traitorous mind, Hollie knew without a doubt that the beast wouldn't need to force any woman into his bed. They probably went there gladly, great hordes of them, standing in line to . . . well, to do whatever it was exactly that men and women did in bed together. She knew only which part went where and why and that by all accounts it was best done without clothing.

And just now she was having no trouble at all imagining Everingham's hands sliding across her bare skin. Starting with her ankles, rucking up her hem, ever upward—to the back of her knee, her thigh—

"Give me your hand, madam."

"What?" Her heart took off with her pulse.

"Your hands." The firelight played across the planes of his face, down the broadness of his chest and the flatness of his stomach, caught the firm, bronze shadings of his hand outstretched to her.

Wondrous hands.

"Why?" she asked, her throat dry.

"Do you mean to sleep in these, madam?"

"Sleep? Oh." A sultry band of fire burned around her wrist when he took her hand in his, and a zip of pure lightning raced up her arm, out of place and staggering.

Then she realized her shackles were gone, just like that. Her heart hammered in gratitude that she damned well shouldn't be feeling.

"I'd say thank you, my lord, but we both know I wouldn't mean it at all." Shouldn't, because he was the enemy.

That made him frown as he bent over her wrist. "What the devil is this?"

He ran his very capable fingers along the underside of her wrist and up her forearm, lighting more of his exquisite little fires as he went. Pleasure and promise, an astonishing trail of blue sparks and dizzying lightning that would make any blushing young bride forget that she was married, happily or otherwise.

She found breath enough to say, "The price of your justice, my lord."

"Bloody hell," he growled, then turned to the fire and examined her wrists in more detail, cursing under his breath. Then he glared down at her, more angry than she'd ever seen him. "You've brought this on yourself, madam."

"*I* have, my lord?" She yanked her hand out of his, though his warmth still wrapped her fingers like a glove. "You're blaming me for your high-handed mistake? You had no right to break into my home and bring me here and certainly no right to hold me."

"I have the right of law, madam, as magistrate of the county. And as far as legalities are concerned, since habeas corpus has been suspended—"

"Conveniently suspended—"

"I have not only the right to arrest you for no reason at all in these times of trouble, but I can also hold you for protecting an enemy of the king's peace. In fact, I have the obligation to do so until—"

"Until Lord Liverpool has crushed every breath of liberty out of innocent people who—"

"Until I damn well see fit to *give* you liberty, madam, when I'm satisfied."

Hollie caught her unrepentant tongue between her teeth. A short hour ago, she'd been nearly doomed to a trial and prison for sedition; then Everingham had handed her this miracle of a husband.

If she could keep her opinions to herself long enough to allay Everingham's suspicion, then she could fly back to her shop and pack it and cart it away to a place where she could continue her campaign in safety.

A half-day's head start was all she would need.

Oh, Papa, look what I've gotten myself into! A price on her head. A phantom husband. And now an earl breathing down her neck.

Which wasn't actually the case; he was standing at the foot of his magnificent bed in his linen shirt and waistcoat, bronzed and breathlessly handsome.

She closed her eyes to keep her focus. "I'm sorry, my lord. It's been a long day."

"Interminable, madam. And just so that you realize the extent of the jeopardy of your situation, you're being held here as a hostile witness who is withholding vital evidence in a serious investigation of sedition and high treason."

High treason too? A shiver tumbled down her spine. "I don't know what more I can tell you."

Except to claim the right of a criminal not to be forced to bear witness against herself.

The man lifted a small blanket off the end of the bed and thrust it at her. "I think you'd best wear this, madam. It's cold. And you're much too—"

"Too what?"

His eyes glittered as he stood there, frowning darkly as he studied her face. "Compromising," he said finally, the word tangled in a growl.

Not at all certain what he meant by that, Hollie took the cover and wrapped her shoulders, wondering why her heart was beating in wobbling circles.

Everingham strode away from her, clasping his hands behind him, the legalist once again. "So, madam, you say you've been married to this Adam MacGillnock for two months?"

She was pretty sure she'd told him two months. Because that was just after Peterloo, when everything in her life had gone so impossibly wrong. But Everingham had been firing his damnable questions at her so precisely, she'd had trouble keeping track of her answers at the time.

"As I told you, Adam and I—" Great heavens, was that the name she'd given him? Yes, Adam. "We were married almost exactly two months ago."

His gaze darkened considerably. "How long did you know MacGillnock before that?"

"A week." Let him think her recklessly, passionately, in love with her radical husband. That she'd do anything for him, an innocent, dutifully gullible bride. She turned a treacly sweet smile on him and wondered why he was asking.

"A week?" He raked his hand through his hair, then blew out a breath as though he'd been holding it for days. "Tell me, madam: before this marriage to MacGillnock, did the printing shop belong to you?"

"Why?"

"Is that when Mr. MacGillnock began printing his sedition on your press?"

The man was at his parliamentary best: the grand inquisitor. "What do you mean?"

"Where did you meet him?"

Dear God, where? Her answers would have to hold up to all of his questions. "In . . . my shop."

"And did he only begin courting you after he'd seen your printing press?"

Why, the arrogant bastard! "How dare you! If you mean to imply that my dear Adam married me solely for my printing press, then you're greatly mistaken. We love each other. Madly. Joyously. We always will."

"How wonderful for you both," he drawled, his dark smile anything but congratulations to the happy couple. "Where did he come from, madam?"

Oh, hell.

"From your village? Weldon Chase, is it?"

"No. He's from . . ." A place far, far away; the farther the better. "He's . . . Scottish, of course. MacGillnock."

"He's what?"

"From an old clan of wool weavers. A burr you can cut with a knife. But your spies must already have told you that."

"Madam, I'm—" Everingham suddenly went utterly still. His brows knit as he fixed his focus on something behind her. "What are you doing here?"

Hollie turned around to see what had so thoroughly caught his attention, and her heart melted on the spot.

A little boy stood in the center of the room, his face ghostly pale in the dimness, his eyes huge, his dark hair sleep-mussed, the hem of his nightshirt dragging on the carpet. He peered at Hollie, then at Everingham, and back to Hollie again with a worried little smile.

"Are you my mama?" It was the dearest, sweetest voice she'd ever heard.

"Me?" She was afraid to blink, certain the child was nothing more than a spirit, while the earl stood glaring at the apparition.

"Are you, ma'am?"

Hollie didn't know what to say to this gallant little boy who didn't know who his own mother was. She cast a glance at Everingham, who only bellowed out, "Mumberton!"

Then he strode coldly past the boy, past the

softly liquid gaze that followed him to the doorway and then found Hollie's again.

"Mumberton, come here!"

The boy shivered, and Hollie ran to him,
lifted him into her arms. He fitted perfectly inside her blanket and snuggled his cheek against
hers as though he were trying her out for size
and texture.

"Did you have a nightmare?" she asked, looking into all that worry. "Did we wake you?"

But the boy put two of his fingers into his
mouth and turned his head to the doorway, to
the man who shared his coloring and his strong
profile—though she couldn't recall hearing that
Everingham had any children.

"Is he your son, my lord?"

Everingham whirled on her, startled, his jaw
clenched as though he would say a hundred
things but he'd thought better of it.

"Mumberton!" he bellowed again, making the
child cling even tighter to Hollie's neck, making
her wrap him tighter in the blanket.

She heard Mumberton's running and skidding
footfalls before he appeared in the doorway.
"Oh, I'm sorry, my lord. I didn't know he was
out. Busy, you know, finishing Mrs. MacGillnock's chamber. I'll put him back." Then he said
to the boy in the stony silence, "You should be in
your bed, young man. Not running around the
halls. Come along."

Mumberton took the boy's hand, and Hollie

let him down softly, kneeling as she held his thin shoulders for a moment. "Sweet dreams to you."

"And you," he whispered.

And then he was gone with Mumberton, disappearing as quickly as he'd come.

Charles's heart had stood still during the exchange between the boy and the woman, the pair of them looking so very domestic in his bedchamber.

This other man's wife and the child he didn't know, hadn't claimed.

"Is he your son, my lord?"

To tell the woman or not? It wasn't a secret. At least, it wouldn't be one for much longer, thanks to the *ton* and its grapevine of gossips. Not that the opinion of that over-ornamented rabble mattered to him in the least. But telling Miss Finch seemed too much a confession of the reckless rakehell he used to be.

Yet it was better that she heard the truth from him. She already thought the worst of his character: breaking and entering, abduction, blackmail, coercion—what's a question of paternity after that?

"His mother's attorney says the boy is my son."

She nodded slightly. "Oh."

Oh. The quick catch of her lower lip with her teeth, and an unexpected concern that puckered her brow and made her shift a glance at the doorway and then back to him. For some reason that he couldn't fathom, he wanted her to absolve him—or at least to understand the untenability of his position.

"Does he live here with you?"

Now that was the question, not yet answerable. "Probably so."

"You're not sure?"

"Though it's none of your business, madam, I'd never heard of his existence before he arrived on my doorstep three days ago."

She drew her brows together. "Along with his mother, I suppose?"

"His mother is dead."

"I'm sorry for that."

"A woman whose name I frankly didn't recall, obviously from several years past." A shooting party at Bagthorpe's Manor, if he remembered rightly. The young woman was a chambermaid who had offered herself to him, and he'd taken exactly what she'd given, because that had been his way at the time.

Miss Finch offered a worried glower as she went to the door and gazed down the hallway, as though the boy would be playing there. "What's his name? You never said."

"Charles Stirling, of course." Claimed as such in the parish records, with no proof to show for it. "Chip, apparently—according to his mother's attorney."

"But you said nothing to him just now, my lord. Not even a simple good night."

He hadn't been able to find the voice for it. "It's not my habit."

"It very well should be." She was a raveled tangle of opinions that he didn't need just now. "If you are his father, then he needs to be acknowledged—if not as your legal heir, then at least when you meet him in the hallways."

As his father had acknowledged him? With the back of the hand, if at all? He wouldn't do that.

"And if I'm not his father?"

"All the more reason to treat the boy generously."

He didn't want her notions of him to count for anything, this compelling wife of his enemy. But they did; they were far more significant than he ought to allow. "The matter is a legal one, to be straightened out in court."

"That's your answer to everything, my lord." She crossed her arms over her chest. "Compassion as a commodity to be quantified and categorized."

Daft woman.

"Enough, madam. Your room is ready." Tired to his bones, Charles brushed past her into the hallway and to the next door. He opened it and gestured her inside. "We'll talk more in the morning. Good night."

She stayed in the doorway, stubborn to the last. "Come the morning, my lord, I shall be going home to my shop, as you promised. I have customers to serve and rent to pay to my landlord—who isn't a very generous man. If I don't meet my rent I'll be evicted, and then what will happen to my Stanhope?"

"Which is what, exactly, madam? Your cat?"

"My printing press, damn you. It was my father's. I have nothing else of his."

"Ah." Certain that he'd never sleep a wink tonight, Charles took the woman gently by the elbow and swept her into the chamber. "I shouldn't worry about that, madam. Everything in your shop now belongs to the Crown. The press, the ink, the paper. Along with anything else that my men find there in the morning."

Hollie held tightly to her anger, certain that she'd misheard the man, though her heart had taken off on its own trek and her stomach was reeling. "What did you say?"

"I'm impounding your Stanhope, as you call it."

"You can't. By what possible right?"

"By right of forfeiture, madam. A standard legal procedure that applies to anything that has been used in the commission of a crime."

"But not by me. By my husband!"

The near smile in his eyes was replaced by hardness, and in the clipped consonants of his rank, he said, "It matters not who committed the crime, only that the machine is unable to be used illegally."

"This is absurd; you're punishing the wrong person. I had nothing to do with my husband's crime. The printing press is mine, not his. It's never been his."

"It wasn't until you married him." He seemed to find some perverse satisfaction in that.

"What do you mean?"

"A wife has no rights of property after she's married. You're an intelligent woman, Miss Finch; you must have known that. Your husband gained it all when you joined with him at the altar."

Blast it all! She'd forgotten entirely, a simple fact of law that swamped her courage and stole her breath. "And so I lose everything because of something I have no control over? Whether Spindleshanks is caught, and tried, whether he wins his case or not—I'm to be punished!"

"Whatever happens from this point on, your printing press no longer belongs to you or to Mr. MacGillnock. You'd best get used to the idea, Miss Finch. And so good night."

"Ballocks, my lord!"

Hollie caught Everingham's arm as he turned to leave, but he was a bundle of rippling muscle and stopped only because he chose to turn back to her. "Nevertheless, madam, it is the law."

"And a convenient excuse to silence my press, just as you and your bloody Parliament would like to silence all printers and their presses."

"Only the seditious ones, madam."

"Which is all of them, sir—because, depending on one's viewpoint, sometimes the simplest truth looks a whole lot like sedition."

"The matter is settled."

"So am I to starve, my lord?" she asked, letting her bitterness spill into her voice. "Or do you expect me to ply my trade on the street corners of London?"

He frowned. "You must have family somewhere."

"None, as you already know. How do you expect me to live if you deprive me of the tools of my trade? I'm an innocent citizen. You have no right to keep me from an honest living."

"But I do from a dishonest one, serving the criminal element."

"With my husband at large and with a price on his head, I'm not likely to do that, am I?"

He paused overlong, drawing out the peril of her position. "I don't know, madam. Are you?"

It was exactly what she planned to do, though she certainly wouldn't let him know that. "I'm not a fool, my lord."

"Merely married to one."

Hollie could hardly find breath enough to speak. "You can't mean this, my lord."

"That's the price of sedition these days," he said, his eyes an unreadable midnight. "Good night, madam. Sleep well."

Chapter 6

Husbands!
 Those grasping, grumbling, overbearing creatures—especially the fake ones!

Mrs. Adam MacGillnock.

Could she possibly have been more naive? Giving away her freedom and the only weapon in her arsenal against Everingham, all in one witless, short-sighted act, trading a husband for her Stanhope. This brilliant idea had suddenly become a tree toad in a teapot.

Trust the earl of Everingham to turn it all back on her.

And now what?

Running away would leave her with nothing at all, no chance to deliver justice where it was so dearly needed. The only way to keep her

voice and to have any hope of learning the secrets of Everingham's commission, so that she
could warn the innocents of whatever grave
punishment was coming, was to stay here, close
to Everingham.

Which meant becoming a spy.

She wanted desperately to just climb into the
huge bed, to tuck herself under the silken sheets,
pull the covers over her head, and sleep for the
next three days.

But the thieving beast was in the next room,
gloating, believing himself the victor. And if she
didn't act immediately—make her bargain with
the devil—she would be homeless, penniless,
and without means to her campaign.

Resolved, Hollie tried her door, half-expecting
Everingham to have locked it, but the latch
opened easily.

She rapped twice on his door.

"Come."

Squaring up the ragged edges of her story,
Hollie entered his chamber. The chamber was
darker and more golden now, and Everingham
was nowhere to be seen.

There was only his scent and the breathless
feeling that she was being appraised from the
shadows.

"Dare I hope this means that you've changed
your mind, *Mrs.* MacGillnock?"

Hollie froze and searched for the low rumble
of his voice. What she'd first thought was a hunt-

ing trophy—a rampaging grizzly poised near the hearth—had moved slightly.

He stepped into the center of the room, where the light caught the deep crags of his face. Dear God, he was utterly, beautifully naked from the massive breadth of his shoulders to the top of his breeches. Naked and golden and powerfully muscled. So dreadfully handsome.

Hollie hadn't an ounce of air in her lungs, and a breath-stealing flush of something hot fluttered up from her chest. But not a whisper of it was fear; it was an unexpected, unbalancing admiration.

She ought to leave immediately and return after he was decently dressed. But she couldn't move. Even the carpet held her, tugging at her toes, making them dig into its softness, rooting her to the wool.

This was all quite improbable. She righted her nightgown, which seemed altogether transparent just now, too hot and too cool and far too clingy.

"Changed my mind about what, my lord?"

His voice was low and seductive. "About sharing my bed tonight."

Hollie closed her eyes to rid herself of the sight of him, all that raw and splendid power. But he was there anyway, in her mind, drawn even more sharply.

"I have . . . not." Not what? She opened her eyes, unable to recall his question, let alone the exceedingly important answer she ought to be coming up with instead of staring.

Something about his bed. About the silken counterpane and all those pillows. Yes, something about sharing—No!

The wily blackguard! "I've not changed my mind about sharing anything with you, my lord. Least of all your bed. I am a very happily married woman—"

"So you've said, madam."

"And I meant it."

"Then what are you doing here in my chamber?" He was casual in his stalking stride, his motion slowed because time had unwound itself. His breeches fitted him too well; the black doeskin caught the shadows and the golden light as it rode the long length of his thighs.

"I was . . ." He was . . . simply magnificent. Head to toe and all those remarkable places in between.

A dark pattern of sleek hair glistened across his chest and dove in a wide arrow into the top of his breeches, probably continued diving for some time, ending in all that maleness. The thought stirred up another whirlwind in her breathing, and spread like wildfire through her belly.

The earl had gone from bureaucratic inflexibility to sensuous stalking as he slipped his shirt back on, and a leonine grace brought him effortlessly across the expanse of carpet to stand a few feet from her, glaring down his nose.

"If you were trying to make an escape, madam, you should have turned left instead of right and gone down the back stairs."

Now that would be silly. Escaping him. This particular him. The rugged, rough-hewn, undulating crags and shadows of Charles Stirling.

"No. I was . . ." She was staring at him, just staring like a street-corner strumpet. And repeating herself when she ought to be forming a strategy.

"I wasn't running away, my lord. There's no point in that; where would I run to?"

"To warn your husband not to return to your little home above the shop?"

Oh, him. She had to remember to keep tabs on this imaginary husband of hers. But Everingham was real, and difficult enough to debate while he was fully clothed.

Though it took every ounce of her resolve, Hollie clasped her hands behind her back and went past him to the upholstered chair near the hearth.

"I'm sure my dear Adam will figure that out for himself. When he returns, he'll notice me gone, as well as the printing press, and have no reason to stay." She risked a glance at him and found him nearly dressed again, buttoned to midchest, rolling up his cuffs while he watched her. "I came in here, my lord, to try to reason with you."

"I'm a very reasonable man."

Reasonably pig-headed. "I'd like to know where you're taking my Stanhope."

"The Crown's Stanhope. It's coming here to Everingham for the time being."

Here! "How is it coming? Who's dismantling it? Please don't tell me you mean Summerwell."

Everingham leaned against the bedpost, looking smug and devilishly pleased with himself. "He's bringing it by cart. I assume he'll do whatever it takes to break it down appropriately."

Oh, no! "With a sledgehammer, I suppose. It's a delicate machine, my lord. He'll destroy it if he isn't careful."

This seemed to amuse him. "He won't, madam."

"And where will you store it when it gets here?"

"The stables, I assume. Or the carriage house."

Great heavens, no! "Then I have a proposition for you, my lord."

His eyes darkened again; he came away from the bedpost. "And that is?"

Hollie prayed that the man was as reasonable as he claimed. He was her only hope and her worst possible enemy. "I'd be grateful, my lord, if you would allow me to set up the Stanhope and use it, so that I can continue my ordinary business. Under your supervision, of course."

Charles held back his smile, because matters were progressing too nicely and she might deci-

pher his motives—just as he had deciphered
hers. This machine was vastly important to her, a
treasure she'd do most anything to hold onto. At
least he hoped it was so.

"Don't be absurd, madam."

"If my Stanhope lies around in your stables in
pieces, it'll be doomed to rust in the damp and be
useless to me or to anyone." She was an unwa-
vering advocate, pacing in front of him in flannel
that caught against her ankles and her calves,
that clung to her thighs and tempted him.

"You can't use your printing press, madam.
It's evidence against your husband, in case
you've forgotten."

"It can't very well be evidence against anyone
if it's stored away improperly, dismantled and
left without its signature."

"Which is?"

"Every press leaves its own mark. The imprint
of the platen, flaws in the type itself." She braced
her fists against her hips as she studied him. "Besides, I'm only being practical."

Entirely diabolical, Miss Finch. But he needed
her to convince herself that this arrangement was
her idea, not his.

"Tell me, madam: how can allowing the devoted wife of a dangerously seditious radical ac-
cess to her printing press be anything
approaching practical?"

"Well . . ." She plunked herself down on the
bench at the foot of his bed, tucked her hands be-

tween her knees. "Your commission needs the press assembled and working."

"Does it?"

"Yes, and I need to make a living."

She was as treacherously clever as she was beautiful. *May her husband rot in hell.*

"What's my guarantee against your conspiring with your husband to use your press against me?"

"I assume you'd be watching me every moment."

He'd watch her every bloody moment, if he could stand it, if he didn't succumb to his baser instincts.

"Besides, it's autumn, my lord."

"And that means?"

"The busiest time of year for me. I've got orders for all kinds of projects to keep me until well past winter. It's money that I'll need to keep a roof over my head when this horrible ordeal is finished and my beloved fool of a husband is caught and tried and hanged and I'm left a helpless widow."

Helpless. He couldn't imagine that.

"And if I agree to this enterprise, where do you plan to live while you're working here?"

"Oh! Well." Her eyes had grown bright and large with the scent of her success. "In the village, I suppose. Someone will take me in."

"It's eight miles from here. And I doubt you'll find a place there."

"I can sleep in the barn."

No doubt the woman would do just that if he allowed it. "That won't be necessary. The gate-house is vacant. It's small and hasn't been used in years, but it's watertight and warm, I'm told."

A wary look came to her eyes. "The gate-house? You'd allow that?"

"I would insist."

That drew a frown from her, the shadowy hint of suspicion. "Is there room enough for my Stan-hope? I need a large space with heat and—"

"I'm not a fool, madam." Or was he an utter and complete lunatic? To risk his strategy on a woman who enchanted him, who tempted him. "You can set up your printing press in my car-riage house in the courtyard. You work while I'm there, and you don't when I'm not."

"No." Now she was frowning again, shaking her head and all those curls. "It would have to be in the house."

Even better. "Why is that?"

"Out of the damp and the cold. For the ink and the paper, too. And I'll need somewhere with loads of light and room enough for drying."

"Your laundry, I suppose."

"The printed pages. The ink smears easily and needs a full twenty-four hours to dry."

He could see it all now, his silent house be-coming a printing shop and Miss Finch the mis-tress of it all. "The conservatory, then, under lock and key. I will approve every project before it goes out. Without negotiation, madam. Is it agreed?"

He watched a rainbow of doubt and hope cross her features, and was pleased beyond measure when she finally nodded. "Yes."

"Then good." He was now the keeper of Captain Spindleshanks's wife. No doubt a better keeper than the man she had married.

Which gave him no peace at all.

"What about my clothes?" She got bristly and aimed her clipped tones at him. "You'll excuse me, my lord, if I didn't think to pack before I left home."

"Summerwell has been told to bring everything—"

"Everything! I might have known that you meant lock, stock, and camisole when you confiscated my belongings. Am I to rent back my drawers from the Home Office?"

He kept his smile inside his cheek, imagining that item on the Privy Council agenda: "One pair of fancy drawers, leased to one Hollie Finch, wife of Adam MacGillnock, otherwise known as Captain Spindleshanks."

Lord. He hadn't the slightest idea how he would explain her to the Home Office.

"That won't be necessary, madam. I'll see that you have clothes in the morning."

"And a hot bath?"

"And breakfast on a tray."

Success seemed to stymie her, for she frowned

and cast him a wary look. "Then good night, my lord."

She glanced back at him over her shoulder as she swept through the doorway in a swirl of nightgown-clad curves and bare ankles.

She was the best kind of witness he could have imagined. Witness and temptation all rolled into one fiery-hearted champion.

If Captain Spindleshanks was any kind of a man, any kind of a husband, he couldn't possibly leave a wife like Hollie Finch for long without coming to her rescue. He would place watchers near the gatehouse and in the road.

It prickled his ethics some, but extraordinary measures were sometimes required to entrap an extraordinary criminal.

So he would bait his trap with the scoundrel's magnificent wife and lie in wait for the black-guard.

Chapter 7

~~~~~⌒⌒⌒~~~~~

Hollie awoke midmorning, buried to her eyebrows in a marvelously soft comforter, having spent the entire night dreaming of the man in the next room, dreaming of spying on him. Oh, what an astounding part of her dream that had been. And plotting against him, printing riddles on her Stanhope to confuse him, and whispering rhymes to charm him, and every word of it seditious and marvelously stirring.

She needed to find a way to continue her campaign against him in secret, to be close at his elbow when he sorted through the evidence he'd stolen from her shop. But she was fresh out of plans and not yet ready to face the man or to even open her eyes.

Yet she had the oddest feeling that she was being studied at close range. She peeked out from under her lashes, expecting a lounging cat or her frowning magistrate or Mumberton with her morning tea.

But it was the boy, Charles, kneeling on the upholstered bench at the foot of her bed, peering at her over the top of her counterpane like an elf in a woodland grove.

She couldn't help a smile. "Good morning, Chip."

His darkly lashed eyes popped wide in wonder. "You know my name?"

"Chip, for Charles, isn't it?"

"Yup."

"Mine is Hollie, for Holliway."

"Hollie? Like a Christmas greening." His smile was huge and lacked a few teeth.

"The very thing."

"I saw a deer out my window. He had pointy horns and he was eating the rose bush. Mumberton chased him."

Hollie laughed and sat up against the dense bank of pillows. "I'd like to have seen that. Where is Mumberton now? Have you escaped him again?"

Chip's ears pricked up, and he pointed to the doorway just as Mumberton came round the corner, loaded down with a hip bath, followed by what must have been the entire kitchen staff. They carried steaming water to fill the tub, thick towels, and a heaping breakfast tray.

"What's all that stuff for, Mr. Mumberton?" Chip plunked himself down on the bench, a little prince overseeing everything.

The man's shoulders sagged. "Ah, lad, you're supposed to be eating your breakfast in the kitchen. How the devil did you get in here?"

Chip stuck out his legs, pointed to his bare feet, wriggling his toes. "On these things, sir."

Hollie nearly laughed. "He's not bothering me at all, Mumberton."

But Chip had already zipped out of the room, leaving the butler to stare after him and swab his forehead with his sleeve.

"As I've told his lordship every morning and every night for the last three, I'm not a nanny. The lad is wild, and there's not time enough in the day to follow after him. I'm doing the best that I'm able."

"I'm sure you are." He was a dear old man, with bristling eyebrows and cheeks that pinked and a mustache that flicked from side to side when he was flustered—which seemed a constant state, no thanks to Lord Everingham. "The house will adjust to Chip in no time."

"If he stays."

What a sad thought—for father and son. "I dearly hope he does."

"God love us all." Mumberton rolled his eyes, righted himself from all this confessing, and stood at attention. "His lordship says you're to

have this gown and apologizes for his absence."
He dropped a pale blue dress on the bench.

"He's gone?" Vanished in the night? Please
God, dragged away to Westminster for a month.

"He's touring the grounds with his estate
manager. Till noon, he said. I'm to inform you
that it'll be this afternoon before the wagons ar-
rive with your belongings. Probably evening or
later before someone named Stan Hope arrives."

"My Stanhope. It's a printing press. And thank
you, Mumberton."

Mumberton continued with his prepared
speech. "In the meantime, his lordship says
you're to have breakfast and make use of the
parlor, while he—" Mumberton rattled off a
dozen instructions and injunctions from His
Bloody Lordship, none of which mattered in the
least.

Staying out of Everingham's clutches did matter, though. If that meant becoming a good little
printer, the innocent wife of the infamous Captain Spindleshanks, then she'd do it up with
bows and bunting and have him convinced that
she was everything he imagined her to be.

She'd start by arranging the gatehouse to her
best advantage, her only refuge against Everingham's prying. Ha! Let him keep her Stanhope
under lock and key; there were dozens of ways
to dodge around his wards and print whatever
she wished.

Mumberton finally left her to her bath, the

purest delight imaginable. The gown that Stirling had sent was a summer-weight spriggy
blue, though outside her chamber window the
morning was a drippy, foggy mess.

No camisole, no stockings, no shoes. Leave it
to a man to ignore everything but the obvious.

She struggled to button her gown at the back
but gave up after two buttons. She gulped down
her tea, then snagged her breakfast from the tray,
raiding Everingham's dressing closet for socks
and an oversized coat that smelled of his bay.
Then she found a pair of boots in the greenhouse
and set out to find her new home.

The new headquarters for Captain Spindleshanks and his obedient wife.

The gatehouse sat a few hundred yards below
the manor and, oddly enough, a quarter-mile
from the actual gate and the road.

But it was in full view of Everingham Hall. No
doubt that was the reason Everingham had sug-
gested it: so that he could monitor her comings
and goings.

And the comings and goings of her husband.

May the both of them meet a prickly end.

It was a thoroughly charming little house from
the outside: stone walls and a new slate roof, and
a wide covered portico which her carriage must
have passed beneath on her way in last night.

The thick, iron-bound door was unlatched and
swung easily into a small, richly paneled foyer
which then emptied into a good-sized parlor,

with plenty of windows to the southwest and a large hearth, and even a small kitchen beyond. She found an airy bedroom above stairs and plenty of light.

Perfectly lovely in too many ways. The cottage was the most wonderful place she'd ever seen.

Though the furniture was draped in sheets, which made everything appear a bit ghostly, the place was dust-free and welcoming. When she reentered the parlor with a mind to begin settling in, that feeling of being watched came again.

And again a moment later, when she was giggled at from beneath the wriggling sheet that covered an easy chair under the window.

Her new little shadow.

"Aye, me," she said grandly, creeping up to the chair and its little ghost. "I'm weary to my bones from my long walk." She yawned loudly and stretched. "I think I'll sit myself . . . *here!*"

She pretended to sit on the squirming boy, who screamed in delight and rocketed up to stand on the chair, all legs and arms beneath the sheet.

"I'm here! I'm here!" The boy was hiccoughing with laughter.

"Who be you, oh spirit of the gatehouse?" Hollie found his ribs with her best tickling fingers and he collapsed completely onto the chair.

"It's me!" He squirmed and laughed and tore

at the sheet, finally yanking it off his head. "Don't be scared, Miss Hollie! See, it's me!"

The boy was red-faced and sweaty, his hair sticking up in a hundred different places. Hollie gasped in mock horror and threw her hands across her eyes.

"Oh, oh! Who is me?"

"It's Chip! You remember from this morning." He leaped down from the chair and pulled her fingers away from her face. "It's me, Hollie! Meeeee!"

She opened her eyes to his gap-toothed grin and his apple cheeks and those dark, dark eyes. "Oh, Chip! It *is* you. You scared me!"

"I didn't mean to, but you scared me too!"

She couldn't resist brushing the jumble of curls back into place. "You know something, Chip? I sometimes like to be scared."

He giggled again. "Me too."

She loved having him here, but he needed corralling. "Well, now, young man, what are you doing in my house?"

"Your house? But you live in the big hall with my father."

It was no wonder he believed that. A new father, why not a new mother? "No, I live here, sweet."

He stuck out his lower lip and scrubbed shyly at the plank floor with the toe of his scuffed shoe. "Then you're not really going to be my mama?"

"I can't be, Chip." Though she wouldn't mind that one bit. He needed a mother to love him. A father would do, but his chances there looked dismal. "However, I'll be living here for a while. And you're welcome anytime."

"*Any* anytime?"

"Absolutely anytime." Hollie scooped the boy up into her arms, because he'd fit so well and he smelled of the fog and the wood-smoked morning. "As long as you ask Mumberton if you can come. Do you promise?"

"I do."

"Because I'll ask you that every time you come here. 'Chip, my good man, did you ask Mumberton if you could come to see me?' And you'll say honestly back to me . . ."

"I'll say yes. 'Cause I will ask. I promise." He squinched up his little face, worried to his bones by the rickety, changeable world around him. "But I didn't tell him this time, 'cause I didn't know I was coming here."

"This one time, then, I'll tell Mumberton that you helped me straighten things up." She set him down, and he clapped his hands together.

"*Can* I help you?"

"Are you a good sheet folder?"

"The very best." He rolled up the sheet he'd been tangled in and bunched it into her arms. "See! And I'm a good deer chaser too. I was following that big red one when I saw you come in here."

Country-raised, wild-limbed. What had his life been made of before three days ago? Four now. Oh, what a change a day could make. "So you must have deer where you come from?"

Chip scrunched up his brow. "I come from here now, Ringum Hall. Mr. Draskel, the 'torney, says I do."

Dear God, she hoped so. Prayed that Everingham wouldn't dispute the obvious, that Chip was his flesh and blood. There was no mistaking the fierceness of his little frown or the dark whorl at his hairline that raised his curls and sent them tumbling off in a natural part.

And if she had any doubt at all, Everingham himself erased it completely when he appeared in the doorway in the next breath. Father and son both frowning at her.

The man was dressed like a country squire, in rough trousers, a linsey-woolsey shirt, and a knobby wool jacket with sagging pockets.

Far more handsome now than he'd been in his linen and silk and far more dangerous.

Charles had expected the gatehouse to be empty and echoing, had thought to inspect it before he sent a cleaning crew to ready it for his reluctant new tenant, who ought to have still been beneath her counterpane, sleeping off the night's adventures.

But here she was in the gatehouse, dressed in a godawful long coat that looked damned familiar, wearing an over-big pair of muddied Wellingtons, her hair swept up into a loose tangle atop her head and fastened there with a stick of some sort, save for the wild curls that fringed her collar and made a halo around her face.

And the boy. Crowded up against her, caught inside the cocoon of the coat, his back pressed to her legs—clinging to her in terror or defending her from the ogre in the doorway, he wasn't certain.

He felt large and out of place, extraneous.

"Welcome, my lord," the woman said finally, tousling the boy's hair and picking up the wadded sheet that had fallen to the floor. "We weren't expecting visitors, were we, Chip?"

"Nope. Not that one."

That one. The little hooligan. He'd never in his life felt so thoroughly dismissed and certainly never by a creature who barely reached his waist. The boy caught the loose ends of the sheet and mirrored Miss Finch in her careful folding, his square chin in the air. A damning miniature of the one he saw every morning when he shaved.

Which was the problem. He hadn't the slightest idea how to be a father. He only knew his own had been unsuitable.

"I meant for you to remain in the house, Miss Finch, and wait for me—"

"For our meeting in the library, I know. But you were busy with your estate agent and I wanted to see the gatehouse, to settle in and be ready."

"You needn't do all this," he said, moving into the room. "I'll send the staff."

"We can manage this much, can't we, Chip?"

"Yup." The boy kept at his folding, his eyes averted now, when for the last three days Charles had felt them on him like a beacon. The surprise was that he felt the loss, felt an inexplicable emptiness.

"That is, if our plan fits yours, my lord." She was looking directly at him, her eyes more dazzlingly green than he remembered, a challenge in her stance, and the boy at the heart of it as she finished with the sheet.

This domesticity would keep her occupied, and would do the boy some measure of good—more than good, if he recalled rightly the motherly needs of a boy. "As you wish, madam."

She smoothed her gentle fingers through the boy's curly hair, bending down to his beaming, upturned face. "Chip, why don't you take all the sheets off the furniture and put them in a pile right there in the corner."

"The upstairs too?"

She smiled at him, and touched her fingertip to the end of his nose. "What an excellent idea."

The boy leaped to his task, knocking a table askew as he yanked off its cover, basking in her attention as he dragged the sheet to the corner and dumped it.

"I trust the gatehouse will do, madam."

Spots of rose defined her cheeks as she tucked

a stray strand of hair behind her ear and then sighed. "Actually, I swore that I wasn't going to admit it to you, my lord, but . . . it's quite lovely."

That pleased him for an instant, had him almost wallowing in pride, until he realized that she was doubtless imagining meeting her captain here in secret: a rendezvous, a happy marital reunion. In the bed upstairs.

Which left him wanting to renege on his offer and take her back to the house, to the chamber next to his. But that would only bring on a torment of its own. He swallowed back his untoward anger and said as evenly as he could manage, "You'll let me or Mumberton know if you need anything."

"Any sign of my belongings? I was hoping that's why you'd come."

"Not for a few hours." It wasn't until she was shrugging out of the huge frock coat that he realized where he'd seen it. "That's my coat, madam."

She clutched it against her chest. "And your socks."

"My what?" She slipped her foot out of the tall boot and showed him a long white sock drooping off the end of her toes, the cuff bunched down enough to reveal the angry bruise she'd gotten from the damnable shackle.

"Mumberton was busy enough without me bothering him about socks and such." She rucked the sock up her shapely calf all the way to her perfect knee and then jammed her foot back into the boot, prepared to do battle against the furniture, while the boy dodged between them on his errand.

"I suppose you stole those boots off my greensman while he was still wearing them."

"Do let me know if he complains, and I'll return them instantly." The genuine teasing of her smile stunned him, caught him in the gut, and filled him with a callow wanting. Wanting to sample her mouth and savor her laughter, to bury his face in her hair. And damned if she hadn't crossed the distance between them to stand just a foot from him, turning her back to him, sweeping up the scattering of curls off her fine shoulders, and exposing the ivory column of her neck, the snowy shell of her ear.

"Buttons, if you please, my lord." The back of her dress was gaping but for two tiny buttons. "I could only reach a few of them."

A whole line of open little buttons exposing her bare back.

Her absolutely bare back.

Bloody hell, Mumberton had found the dress but forgotten a set of small clothes. This insubstantial little gown was hardly more decent than her flannel nightgown and certainly no barrier to his imagination. No wonder she'd borrowed his coat and the boots and his stockings.

Hell, that's just what he needed. To be carrying this image with him all day and well into the night—her breasts unbound inside her bodice, just beyond the muslin, just beyond his hand.

Far beyond that, if he had any sense, any decency at all. He hadn't slept well last night, wondering how this ruse was going to play out, wondering if she longed for her coward of a husband. Had she lain awake praying that he would scale the walls of Everingham Hall and rescue her? Most of all, he'd wondered why the thought of her being married at all had set his blood to boiling.

He fastened the buttons as swiftly as he could manage, given their pea size and his large fingers, trying not to brush the downy silk of her skin in the breach.

"There."

"I'm obliged, sir."

And I am standing on quicksand, aroused and wanting you, madam.

"May I send for food from the village? There's little in the kitchen." She brushed past him in her scent of peach and vanilla and laid a folded sheet on a side table. "You can mark it against my account."

Her account! "You'll take meals in the house." The barked order came out of nowhere and drew a suspicious frown to her mouth.

"That's not necessary."

"It is, and you will."

She hesitated, her hand rounding against her hip, defining too many lush curves for a misty soft morning in a secluded cottage. "Does this mean that I'm your prisoner after all, my lord? Doomed to obey your every whim?"

It was plain to him which of them was doomed in this inequitable arrangement between them. "It means, Miss Finch, that you'll starve if you don't come to dinner in the hall."

She blinked at him and looked to the boy across the room, madly rolling up a sheet. Her smile was fond and unfeigned, her gaze gentled from its usual wariness.

"Well, Chip, it seems as though you and I'll be taking our meals together with his lordship in the hall."

The boy smiled. "Good, Hollie! We'll pretend that you're my mama!"

Doomed, indeed.

Chapter 8

Charles spent the rest of the early afternoon with his estate agent, an autumn ritual that he'd once detested for the way it tied him to the inscrutable harvest accounts, to the bushels per acre, the rents and tithes and the leaseholds. He'd feared the accounting most of all for the disorienting array of facts and figures that flew through his head before he could capture them.

But he'd long since mastered his dread as well as the complexities of the accounting, and in recent years he'd come to enjoy the process, looked forward to the scents of the estate and the textures of the changing seasons.

He'd even started making excuses to spend more time at Everingham Hall and less in London.

What he dreaded now were the cartons and crates from Miss Finch's shop, stacked everywhere in his library. Each one was filled with an indiscriminate collection of bottles and banners and scraps of fabric and stacks of paper. The work table looked just as daunting, with neatly indecipherable piles of placards and letters and newspapers that would finally and forever bring Spindleshanks to his knees.

With some help from the man's uncompromising wife.

Blazing hell, what was he going to do with it all?

And with the woman standing in the midst of it like a defeated but dangerously determined general, surveying the scattered remains of her beloved army.

At least she was now more fully dressed in a gown of her own, stockinged and slippered, and wearing a nearly shapeless, ink-stained muslin apron that went from her shoulders to her ankles. The color was high in her cheeks, a dazzling light in her eye. The effect made her look as though she were halfway through an exceptionally healthy pregnancy.

The astounding fantasy that she was with child and that he'd planted it there made his heart skip and roll.

"My husband isn't going to like this intrusion into his business, my lord."

He couldn't have asked for a stronger dose of reality. She wasn't his; she never would be.

"Your husband isn't meant to like anything about our transaction, madam." He touched his fingers to the blocky printing on one of the placards on the table and tried to shrug off the uneasiness that settled over his shoulders.

The trick would be gaining her cooperation in a way that she would never think to guard against. He was plenty practiced at it; with any luck Miss Finch would be too engaged in her own trickery to notice his own.

Too caught up in her defense to notice that he couldn't read a word.

"Your men picked up everything willy-nilly and just dropped it into boxes."

Sedition, high treason, and all, Miss Finch. He took a breath and cleared his head. "Nothing damaged, I assume."

"It's too soon to tell."

"I wouldn't want the evidence ruined. The path to your husband's whereabouts is in this room somewhere. Make no mistake, I'll find him."

She snatched a leaflet off the table and wagged it at him as though it meant something to him. "Well, then, my lord, here's something that will certainly help you locate his hideout. 'Putney's Cheltenham Salts. By appointment to His Majesty King George, for the relief of bilious livers and dropsical dispositions.' "

Charles kept his silence as the woman flicked her way through the stacks on the table, ticking off titles as she went, sniffing at him as she found another to read.

"Ah, now this might be just the evidence you've been looking for: 'Stove grate radiators—for ornamental comfort and everlasting heat. Fenders, fire-irons, and patent baths.'" She tapped at the engraving. "That's it, my lord. Find this stove grate radiator and you've found Captain Spindleshanks.

"Oh, and let's not dismiss this blasphemous page from *The Handbook of Song Birds*. Note the civilly disobedient woodcuts." She had worked her way around the table to his elbow, pointing to four delicate, fine-lined engravings on a single large sheet of thick paper, the top two panels upside down. "I need hardly explain to you that this nested starling was designed to incite the heart of any weaver to rise against his master. Sedition, to be sure. And due to my customer in just two weeks."

She was marvelous to watch, dancing with her words to distract him from his investigation of her bloody beloved Adam. He took the page from her when she offered it—a marvelous display of intricacy. A common nuthatch in every detail, down to the faint lines of the small feathers at its eye.

"Who is your customer for this?"

"The Dunsmere Avian Society. For their

Christmas volume. I have another hundred copies to print and bind."

A disorienting art, this printing business; different rules from those he was used to. "Why are these two upside down from the others?"

"This was drying, my lord, when it was packed. And ruined here where the ink smeared across the wing."

"My apologies."

She glanced sharply up at him, doubt in her eyes or surprise that he could apologize for anything. "Yes, well, I was still to print another set of birds on the reverse of this page. Two sides of a sheet of paper folded twice for a total of eight pages, four per side. Upside down, because of the deckling on the edge."

"Which is . . . ?"

"When the pages are cut in half and assembled correctly, the uneven edges appear consistently at the bottom and the right edge and the cleanly cut edges across the top and inside the binding."

She was very good, if this was truly her work and not MacGillnock's. Though the business had been her father's.

"And you printed this on your Stanhope? Just you?"

"You still don't believe me! The Tuppenny Press is mine. See." She stuck out her hands, flipped them palm up. "These are the hands of a printer. Ridged with ink, smelling of linseed. Inspect them if you will; you'll find all the proof you want."

Charles slipped her hand inside his—selfishly, for no reason but the chance to lace his fingers between hers.

Long fingers, strong and beckoning; neat fingernails, healthy half-moons, clean, trimmed, and unmistakably inked. Her delicate wrists were still chafed from the handcuffs.

"Not linseed-scented, madam." Peaches and warm summer days. Though he shouldn't be noticing another man's wife. Especially this particular wife.

"The printer's brand, my lord. A handful of ink. It's probably in my veins."

"And does it flow as readily through your husband's veins? Is he a printer?"

Hollie couldn't reply; her heart was still stuttering from the man's singular touch, the lightning and its afterglow that skipped across her skin and pooled low in her belly. Worst of all, she couldn't recall what she'd told him last night, what—if anything—she'd said about her husband's job when he wasn't out being the dashing Captain Spindleshanks.

Should Adam Gillcrest be a printer? No, not Gillcrest, *MacGillnock!* Or was he a scholar? Or a newspaper reporter from New York? Yes! In America, where the press was free and uncensored. She opened her mouth but shut it again quickly. She'd told him that her Captain Spindleshanks was from Scotland.

"My husband is an accomplished printer." And she was becoming an accomplished liar. "He's every bit as good as I am. Better, I think. Though I might be seeing him through the eyes of a loving wife."

Everingham studied her in silence, a tic of impatience at the corner of his mouth. "What was the last item Adam MacGillnock printed in your shop?" He was good, this commissioner of inquiry into the massacre in St. Peter's Fields, surprisingly insightful for a peer of the realm. "Is it here?"

"Why?"

His eyes narrowed, deepening the demon look of him and reminding her that she couldn't let down her guard for a moment.

"Because I asked, madam. Because I am conducting an investigation into his crimes."

"I don't recall what projects my dear Adam was working on." She escaped to the boxes that lined the wall on the other side of the table, on the lookout for anything that would point directly to her.

Like Captain Spindleshanks's costume! The hat and the coat, the wig! Oh, lord, was it here somewhere, just waiting to be discovered?

"My husband spent so little time at home, my lord. And when he was at home . . . well—"

Everingham growled suddenly and picked up the page of starlings. "Not this damn bird book?"

"No, that's mine."

"And this?" He grabbed a handful of loose paper from the table and came toward her, causing her to sit down hard in an upholstered chair.

Hollie looked down at the first page in his hand and suffered a moment's panic.

"The Old and Wicked Corruption . . ."

Dear God, her notes. Her raw, unfettered, seditiously radical thoughts, laid bare for anyone to read. Page after page of helpless sorrow and private rage and probably high treason.

And a trail that led directly to Spindleshanks.

To her.

Unless she appeared to purposely betray her beloved husband once again. Hardly a noble heart. Because she would never do such a terrible thing to the man she loved.

"Read it, Miss Finch."

Needing to be free of his influence, she ducked under his arm and pretended to scrutinize the paper in her hand, trying to decide how to explain it to him.

"The Peterloo Massacre!!!!" it read, with all those points of exclamation that she always hoped would snag her reader's attention. "It's only an idea for a publication, my lord. I never printed it."

"This is *your* hand?"

Now he'd know the ebb and flow of her handwriting. But he'd have learned it soon enough; bits of herself were strewn about everywhere in his library. "It is."

"Read," he snapped.

She opened her mouth to tell him to read it himself, but he had turned his back and was picking through one of the boxes.

Please, God, don't let him find the costume! Spindleshanks would have taken it with him.

She watched him in his constant prowling and tried to read. " 'Containing an eyewitness narrative of the events which preceded, accompanied, and followed the fatal meeting in St. Peter's Fields, 16th August, 1819.' "

"What the devil is this, madam?" He was studying a small type block. The frame was still intact, its letters and slugs locked in place. He looked up at her, frowned in great suspicion, and held the block out to her.

Her heart skidded to a stop, overtaken by a horrible memory of sabre and blood and chaos. "It's just an obituary."

Her father's.

"This is?" Stirling ran his thumb across the letters, then held it up to the late afternoon light streaming through the tall windows. He shook his head and then shot a stormy glance at her. "It's nonsense."

"It's a type block, my lord." Hollie joined him, rescued the dear composition from his paw before he could accidentally dismantle it. "It's used to compose a section of type before the whole piece gets locked into the skeleton." She hadn't had the heart to knock it down, to resort the letters into the type boxes.

"You can read this?" He lifted her hand and peered even closer at the block of upside down, backward letters.

"The printer's habit, my lord. Reading backward and upside down and all in a jumble."

"Go ahead. What does it say?" He folded his arms against his chest and leaned against the table beside her.

"It's just an obituary."

"Read it."

He would know too much about her then. She took a wobbly breath. "It says, 'Robert Finch. Publisher, printer, beloved father—' "

"Finch?" He startled her with the fierceness of his question, with the concern in his eyes. "This is your father's?"

"A keepsake."

"Go on."

She didn't want to. Though he couldn't read the text as well as she could, it would take him only a moment to cipher his way through the backward and reversed letters. And then he'd know everything for himself, all the circumstances of her father's death, her motives and her methods.

So much for her life as a spy in the earl's camp.

" 'Born the 14th day of July, 1771, son of a wool merchant. Died the 16th day of August, 1819—' "

"*When* did you say?" She'd rushed through the date, but he'd recognized it anyway.

" 'Died the 16th day of August, 1819 of fatal injuries sustained on St. Peter's Fields at the hands of the Manchester Yeomanry.' "

He was quiet for a very long time, his fine mouth an undefinable line. "Why didn't you tell me of this?"

Feeling oddly guilty, Hollie turned away to a nearby box and carefully replaced the type block. "Because my father is my private business."

"The hell he is, madam." He wrapped his warm fingers around hers and turned her, his eyes as opaque as the midnight of his hair. "If Robert Finch, your father and the father-in-law of Captain Spindleshanks, was in Manchester with the rest of the radicals, if he met his death there that day, then it damned well is my business. You've made it so."

Hollie tried to pull away, but he'd trapped her against the table with his impossible height and his ferocity. "My father wasn't a radical, sir. He was a newspaperman. He was there to report the news."

"I don't care who the devil he was or why he was there. He was killed in the rioting." He laid his fiery words against her cheek, the barest brush of his breath at her hairline.

"He was murdered, my lord. Bled to death on

the field, his shoulder slashed through by a soldier."

He said nothing, then finally nodded. "His name wasn't on the list of the dead."

"And it wasn't a riot. It was a massacre, my lord. But I'm sure that the reports from your commission will lead you to that same conclusion once you've studied them carefully. Impartially."

He pulled away. "Damn the report, madam. Your father shouldn't have been there."

"Oh, and why not? It was his job, as it was of every other newspaperman in the country: to record and publish the speeches. A peaceful gathering of citizens that became a bloodbath. My father shouldn't have died."

"He wouldn't have if he hadn't been there."

"He was in Manchester to record Henry Hunt's speech, to report the events of the meeting as they unfolded, nothing more."

"Hunt and his cronies were preaching an end to the government. That is against the law."

"That wasn't the purpose of the meeting."

"My God, woman, there were sixty thousand people on the Fields, looking to make mischief."

"They merely wanted to petition the government by legal means to reform the election of members to the Parliament. How can merely discussing a subject ever be wrong, let alone illegal?"

"It will always be so when that discussion poses a danger to the peace of the community."

"Ballocks, my lord. The men came to Manchester to hear the speakers. That's all. They were purposely sober and orderly and dressed in their Sunday clothes, because they were tired of being called unkempt and unorganized."

"They had been drilling like soldiers on their various village greens for weeks."

"Unarmed, and ordered to remain so by their leaders."

"Then they marched in columns into the city, exactly like a militia. And so they were met with the same."

"Dear God, Everingham, they marched there with their children and their wives beside them, maintaining order all the way! Hardly the act of men intending mayhem. And for no reason but arrogance, the magistrates brought down the militia on them."

Hollie suffered a familiar and sobering chill, a bell-clear memory of the screams of terror, that remorseless vision of the horror on the field littered with the wounded and the dying and the dead, the soft ribbons and the small shoes.

"Children were killed, my lord, and their mothers. How can you possibly excuse that?"

Everingham glanced away to the window, then found her eyes. "An unnecessary tragedy of the worst kind, madam. Made more so because the Riot Act was read and wasn't obeyed."

Hollie tried to match his steadiness, regretting her honesty, her temper most of all. She had to act like a spy if she was going to be one. "It damn well wasn't read, my lord."

"It was indeed read, according to my sources—"

"Damn your sources and your spies and your informers, my lord commissioner!" So much for calm. "They are wrong. If the Riot Act was read, then nobody heard it. I know this for a fact, because I—"

I was there, she'd nearly said. But she didn't know where that would take him in his barbaric logic. And her heart was still aching and too full of memories. She could feel his gaze on her, shifting impatiently along the bridge of her brow and settling on her mouth.

"Because you what, madam?"

She swallowed back the tears that clogged her throat and prayed that he wouldn't suspect. "Because I know dozens of people who were there at the time, who saw everything."

"Your husband among them, I imagine? Your dear Adam?"

"And others who were outraged that their government would send troops into a crowd of innocent citizens." She grabbed for a breath that was meant to clear her head, but it came out a convulsing sob, which only made her angry. "But of course, you'll never read a word of their testimony in your files, and so it will never make it into your official report."

A shadow crossed his resolute features, and

for an instant she could almost believe that she'd made inroads into his thick skull. He straightened.

"You know nothing at all of the Home Office inquiry, madam, or the findings of the commission."

"I know that what I've read so far in *The Times* is nothing more than a quick jig meant to distract the public from the real truth."

"Whatever you have read, it can be speculation only. I've submitted nothing to the press, and I won't until the inquiry is complete."

"Don't bother, my lord. Your information is but a mockery of justice, concocted by unscrupulous, mercenary spies who were hired by the Home Office and paid for their violence. Tainted testimony collected from informers and scallawags and the murderers themselves. Let's not forget the commendations for bravery that Lord Liverpool and his lot made to the magistrates and the Manchester Yeoman Cavalry for courage under fire. Bah! For using swords against an unarmed crowd."

"It takes far less force than a sword blade to deal a fatal blow. A stone. A cudgel."

"Not a single stone was thrown, else there would have been a hail of them, and the soldiers would have surely reported such wounds by the dozen. But such injuries were impossible."

"Why is that?"

"Because every stone and stick had been deliberately gathered from off St. Peter's Fields and from the streets for the two days before. The magistrates ordered their attack against a defenseless crowd. And when the field cleared, my lord, the dead and the dying were strewn about like the leavings of a market festival. There were bonnets and shoes and people and . . . my father—"

She stopped because she was sobbing, because he was lifting her chin and searching her face, his dark brows pulled together, an unfathomable look in his eyes.

He said simply, softly, "You were there."

Hollie stopped breathing, tried to look away from him. But the terror had already dropped into her stomach, churning her thoughts into useless circles. He'd come so close to the truth in so little time. She'd just handed it to him.

Some kind of spy.

Charles could see the truth of it plainly in her eyes, in her sorrow, and in her panic, as well as in the denial that perched on the glistening bow of her mouth. The truth shifted his world, tilted his balance, because there was more than this inside her, probably more than he was prepared to know.

"And if I was there, my lord? What then?"

Bloody hell, she was one of them: an improbable radical. Her plots and schemes, her impossible opinions that she shared with her hero husband, were treacherous currents that would swamp her.

"Is that where you met him?" Feeling a thorough cad, he gave her a handkerchief from his pocket. "Your husband?"

Confusion crumpled her brow, then she heaved a huge sigh and dipped her head as she wiped at her prim little nose. "No, not then. He came along afterward."

He could imagine that scene. Adam MacGillnock riding up on his white horse, scooping the innocent maid onto his saddle and riding off with her.

"Your whirlwind romance," he said.

"Of sorts."

For no reason at all, Charles's heart gave a mad leap. *Of sorts.* Hardly an overwhelming passion. Merely admiration, perhaps. Gratitude born of her grief and the unscrupulous man's ready shoulder to cry on.

Not that her private affairs mattered to him in the least. And yet he felt the loss of her heat when she unfolded herself from him and slipped away to the wall of boxes, the leavings of her life.

"Will you arrest me now just because I was there?" She grabbed a piece of green flagging from the box, shook it out, and pretended to study it.

"Where exactly were you when the rioting began?"

She huffed and the banner fell open to a scramble of letters. A single undulating unintelligible word. As jumbled as his pulse and his intentions, as the things she'd told him that he'd never heard before.

"If you mean when the cavalry charged, then I was standing below the hustings alongside my father, listening to Henry Hunt orating about the importance of reforming the House of Commons. I saw as much as anyone."

He'd committed the map of the event to memory, knew exactly where she had been. In the thick of it, the little fool, near the path of the hussars. The thought made his stomach reel. "What were you doing there?"

"What I always did for my father. I was taking down the speeches, Hunt's commentary on the absurdity that a large town like Manchester, with its huge population and all its factories and industry, hasn't a single member of parliament to represent its interests."

"That was your job—collecting speeches? From where?"

"Anywhere: petition meetings, rallies, debates, Parliament."

"You collected speeches from the press gallery in Parliament?"

"Regularly."

"Since when?"

She shrugged. "I was eight or so when I started in the Commons. Twelve or so in the Lords."

And he'd never noticed her?

"And your father allowed you to do this? To

record Parliament in session? I can't imagine a worse occupation for a child."

"He encouraged me while I sat beside him. Afterward we compared notes, and Father would write the speech, and I would set the type. Just like the press corp from *The Times*, only a much smaller operation."

"So you were one of the reporters in the gallery?" He could imagine her leaning over the railing, scribbling madly, doubtless wanting to leap down and lead the debating herself.

"And I will be there again, sir, as soon as I'm free of this nonsense and back to my newspaper."

"And to your husband."

She lifted her gaze to him for a brief time and then dropped it. "If he lives."

He hadn't the slightest idea how to reply to that. The subject had gotten off track. And he had a dozen places he needed to take it.

He was almost relieved when a tap came on the door, then Mumberton's voice. "My lord."

Charles opened the door to the man's incessant bowing. "What is it, Mumberton?"

"There are two gentlemen here to see you, sir. Are you in to them?"

He was expecting no one and damn well didn't need to be entertaining guests just now. Not with the wife of the dangerous, elusive Captain Spindleshanks standing in the middle of his library, a witness to the rioting, a victim of its tragedy, and chockful of her own radical notions.

"Who the hell is it, Mumberton?"

"Sir John Watford and Lord Bowles."

"Blast it all." Two of the commissioners.

"They indicated that they weren't expected."

"Yes, yes, I know." No doubt they'd heard that he'd arrested Spindleshanks and wanted a report. Impeccable timing, as usual.

He wondered if she would know their names. Her husband certainly had reason to dread them, and nothing seemed to escape her notice. A paleness had gathered around the fine rose of her mouth, though it wasn't fear; it was more like a determination that matched the fire blazing in her eyes.

Yet she said nothing, this chatterbox who could talk the salt out of the sea, who had his head spinning with her soft scent and her wayward sensibilities, and her unsettling, unexpected words.

Those gathered-up stones on the field.

And she had said something else that had struck him soundly in the breastbone—something about the children in St. Peter's Fields.

They marched there with their children and their wives beside them.

He knew very little of children, but he couldn't imagine parents putting their sons and daughters in harm's way.

Which made him suddenly wonder where the boy was. Because Mumberton was here in the library and therefore not playing nursemaid.

And Christ, he wasn't ready for this confrontation with Watford and Bowles, hadn't formed a coherent strategy. The evidence was scattered and unread, Spindleshanks still on the loose, the man's wife now his star witness.

No, not his witness. He was using her blatantly, a bewitching lure to draw out her worthless husband.

Mumberton waited in his overly patient way, fingers laced at their tips, rocking up on his toes and then down again.

He couldn't very well send Watford and Bowles away without some word of Spindleshanks's apprehension. They'd come the two hours from London in a jouncing coach. He had to meet with them. The news of the impending arrest must have spread through the Lords and Commons like a field afire.

There would be clamoring for blood and retribution once they knew he'd caught the radical's wife; calls to punish her for the man's crimes.

Charles scrubbed his fingers through his hair, wondering how this day—this entire bloody week—had gone so very wrong. "I'll see them now, Mumberton."

"In the east parlor, my lord? And a tray of tea?"

"Yes. I'll be there in a few moments."

Mumberton bowed his way out, closing the

door behind him, leaving Charles alone with Miss Finch.

She hadn't moved a muscle, still held the folded banner across her arms as though awaiting his judgment.

He'd seen despicable things in the prisons where radicals were kept. He deplored the unlivable conditions and had spoken out in Parliament against prison abuse. The stories of women raped and degraded by the wardens were more than just rumor.

He couldn't take the chance.

Despite her bravado and her cunning and that razor-sharp tongue of hers, she'd be no match for a lecherous jailor with a hungry cock. She was too marvelous a beauty—the sort that even wise men lost their judgment over.

Yet he sure as hell couldn't trust her here on her own, with such powerful evidence against her damnable husband at her fingertips. He'd doubtless return to find the last scrap of sedition piled in the garden with the new-raked leaves, rising up in a great conflagration, and the woman fanning the flames with her skirt.

"Come, madam." He motioned toward the door, but the woman didn't move.

"You're not taking me in there."

"You'll sit quietly, madam. Speak only when spoken to."

"Not even then, my lord. You can't do this to me."

Hollie held her ground. Watford and Bowles were two of Everingham's commissioners, enemies of the people. He was going to just hand her over to them on a platter. Maybe she'd said too much about the massacre after all, and he'd realized that Adam MacGillnock was nothing more than a figment of her imagination.

"You'll come with me, madam, else I'll carry you in."

Certain that Everingham was willing to and capable of carrying her all the way to London if he had a mind to, that he would take great pleasure in dropping her in a heap before his fellow commissioners, Hollie shucked out of her apron and marched along behind him, her dignity intact but her world shattering to bits.

Chapter 9

The east parlor was a long, ornately galleried hall with an archipelago of chairs and tables and settees, scattered islands of gilded mahogany and brocade, and to-the-ceiling windows richly draped in velvet.

She recognized the two men immediately. Sir John Watford, squinting at her past the billowy smoke from his pipe, the younger, Lord Bowles, rising from a settee and coming toward her with a predatory cast to his eyes, his voice oily.

"Well, I say, Charles! Who is this lovely young woman?"

This is Captain Spindleshanks's wife, gentlemen: shall we jail her or just hang her here from the chandelier?

No need to coddle the Stanhope, no need for

119

his staff to finish cleaning the gatehouse. Or for him to suffer her opinions on child rearing.

He stood like a storm cloud gathered behind her, the steamy heat of him collecting in the folds of her skirts, sifting between her buttons. He touched her there, at the small of her back, his broad, bracing hand slipping around the curve of her waist as he nudged her farther into the room. A lordly gentleman to the very last.

"Lord Bowles, Sir John, this is—"

Mrs. Captain Spindleshanks. Hollie nearly blurted out the name herself.

"Miss Finch, gentlemen. Miss Holliway Finch. She's . . ."

Not MacGillnock? She waited for the man to denounce her as her husband's proxy. She wanted to kick Everingham's shin for putting her through this lingering torture, but then the rogue said, "Visiting for a short time."

Visiting! Shackled and dragged here, imprisoned in his gatehouse.

"I say!" Bowles beamed at her, leered as he made a leg. "Who is she really, Everingham?"

"Miss Finch is my . . . ward. Temporarily."

His ward? What the devil was the man thinking? She spared a quick glance up at him, but he just stood there glaring thunderously as Bowles took her hand in his and bent over her fingers.

"Delighted, Miss Finch," Bowles said. "How very nice to meet you. Quite a pleasant surprise for once, eh, Watford?"

"Indeed." Watford stuck his thumb into his waistcoat pocket and peered at Hollie across his slumping spectacles. "Good to meet you, Miss Finch. I pray you'll enjoy your visit."

"She will," Everingham said.

Watford pulled on his pipe and lifted a brow. "Well, then, Everingham, you know what we've come for. You did catch him, didn't you? That rotter Captain Spindleshanks."

Hollie resisted the pressure of Everingham's hand at her waist but moved forward into the room, his prisoner still.

"Where did you hear that his arrest was about to happen, Watford?"

"From Sidmouth himself, of course. Said you'd gotten a tip from a useful individual, that you had a fresh warrant and had sent out your bailiff to apprehend the bastard." Watford smiled apologetically and bowed. "Begging your pardon, Miss Finch."

Hollie wanted to clock the man on the head, but she curtsied slightly instead. "And given, my lord."

"You're visiting the earl from where, did you say?" Watford's brows climbed precipitously, pumped to their arcing height by the working of his mouth.

"Lately of Lancashire."

Bowles poured himself a cup of tea. "The deuce you say! Then you've no doubt heard of this Spindleshanks fellow. Perhaps you've even seen him or his handiwork."

"What handiwork would that be, Lord Bowles?" Hollie bit the sides of her cheeks to keep from saying more.

Bowles snorted as he stirred his tea. "So you haven't told the lady of the man's crimes, Everingham. All that balderdash about our commission's inquiry into that mess at Manchester being corrupt. Imagine."

"Yes, imagine," she said, ignoring Everingham's growl behind her as he led her to a chair.

He bent to give her one of his threatening scowls. "Please, Miss Finch, do take a seat here."

"Yes, but did you capture him, Everingham?" Watford asked, "Our informant was correct, wasn't he? We've bloody well paid him well enough."

Spies. Miscreant mercenaries. Though she was one of them now—but on the side of right and justice.

"My bailiff went to the right location, Watford." She could feel Everingham's gaze on her neck, at her ear, as though he were whispering there. "Unfortunately he was too late."

"The devil you say." Bowles sat on the nearest chair. "He got away, scot-free?"

Hardly. If she were free, she'd be standing at her press printing another editorial against Everingham and his bootless Peterloo Commission! But here she was, dangling from tenterhooks, wondering why Everingham hadn't hauled her up by the scruff of the neck and tossed her to these dogs.

The great earl merely said, "I suspect that he was warned off by someone. Escaped down the back stairs."

"Damn those village types for their gossip. Tight-mouthed bastardy to the end. Did you get a name?"

Hollie chanced a look at Everingham's unreadable profile.

"It's MacGillnock," he said finally, though he couldn't possibly have imagined that her heart was slamming against her throat. "Adam MacGillnock."

"What the devil kind of name is MacGillnock?"

"Scottish, it seems. My bailiff did collect a substantial amount of evidence at the scene. Which will be sorted through and analyzed."

"At least there's that much and a name. Worth the money, I'd say. Sidmouth will be pleased. But damned if I wasn't hoping Spindleshanks would still be here and I could spit in the bastard's eye."

Try it, Watford. I'll spit back.

The man jabbed the air with his pipe. "He needs to be stopped before he can print another word of sedition. Makes us all look like complete fools."

"Mark me, Watford, I'll catch him. It's just a matter of time."

And she had so little of that, so much to do before Everingham tied up his report and Parliament acted on it.

"I'm for jailing them all, starting with that bloody James Wroe at the *Observer*. Fair enough punishment for calling the damned incident Peterloo. A slap in the face of Wellington, a great warrior."

"Fortunately this Spindleshanks fellow has put the noose around his own neck for you, Everingham. Couldn't find a better confession than all those broadsides of his."

"Was that his great crime, Lord Bowles?" Hollie asked, tucking her gaze well away from Everingham's glower.

"Treasonable, in my opinion, Miss Finch. Printing inflammatory broadsides and other illegal and illicit materials is a crime against the king's peace, as it should be."

"Ah, you mean that charging the Home Office and the king, and even Lord Everingham here with corruption isn't allowed in the press?"

Bowles blustered, "It damn well isn't. But don't worry your pretty head about it, my dear. They're soon to be squashed for good and all, eh, Everingham?"

For one lunatic instant Hollie expected Everingham to pounce on Bowles, to show that he wouldn't be a party to squashing innocents. But he only tightened that muscle in his jaw, and his eyes narrowed and darkened to coal.

"Make no mistake, Bowles, the man will soon be caught and tried on evidence he created himself."

Bowles chortled and clapped his hands. "Why bother with the expense of the trial, I ask?"

Watford pounded a fist on the table. "Hang him straight away you find him, Everingham! Right there in the town square. Sidmouth would be grateful to have this Spindleshanks episode over and done with before the report comes out."

"Due process, Watford. I don't want to make a mistake that might acquit him."

Watford leaned back and crossed his pudgy fingers across his girth. "Can't have these damned reformers raising up the lower order with their outcries for a change of government. Voting rights for the masses! Ha! Makes them believe themselves better than they are, and we all know what that leads to."

"Anarchy," Bowles said, raising his cup of tea. "Bloodshed. Revolution. Nip it in the bud, I say. These are dangerous times."

Hollie's blood was at a full boil. She wanted to bolt out of her chair and scream and rail at their idiocy, but there was too much danger, too much to lose, too much to learn.

"What do you know of the children, gentlemen?" Everingham had been quiet, watching the two men as though he'd never seen them before.

Children? Had he said that? Her ears were still ringing with outrage.

Yes, he'd said something about the children in his dangerously quiet way.

She had often watched the man's stalking power as he made his parliamentary speeches, as he breathed his fire and ice, imagining that he would smell of brimstone if she ever got close. And here she was, even closer now, as he touched the back of her chair for a thrilling instant and then moved away. But it wasn't brimstone that beguiled her nose and made her sniff at him in secret, it was lime and laurel and soap. It was woodsmoke and autumn and the fog that still dampened his boots.

The man was imperious to everyone, quick to temper, readily frustrated, but ultimately reasonable. And try as she might to make herself believe otherwise, she had never once felt in danger from him, though he'd shackled her and stolen from her and made her want him to love his son.

His touch was ever emphatic and hot and too generous.

And now here he was, the great earl of Everingham, head of the Peterloo Commission, asking softly about the children.

"What children are these, Everingham?" Watford asked.

Charles had remembered this from Miss Finch's tirade earlier, a new detail that had snagged on his thoughts and hadn't settled right. Still didn't.

"The children in St. Peter's Fields that morning. What do we know about them?"

Watford tapped his finger on the edge of his saucer as he pursed his lips in thought. "Two dead, I believe."

"Two." Charles's stomach clenched. He turned away from Watford's sterile accounting and found Miss Finch staring open-eyed at him, on the brink of admiration, it seemed, her eyes as bright as emeralds, her lips damp from her worry and so intimately inviting.

"Why is that, Watford?" he asked.

"What do you mean, Everingham? Why are they dead? I suppose because they got in the way of the rioters. Happens with a mob like that. Illiterate, unwashed."

Bastard. Charles's anger flared sharply, fueled by Miss Finch's gasp and a deep outrage he'd never felt before, that made him wonder again where the boy was and whether Mumberton knew.

"No, Watford, it doesn't just happen. What I want to know is why there were any children at all on the field that day."

Watford shook his head, casually threw out his hand. "Who knows?"

"What are the ages of the dead?"

"I don't know that either."

Charles had memorized every detail of the day in question, at least those details that he'd been informed of. But he hadn't heard a single statistic on the dead or the wounded or the children, hadn't considered their numbers of any importance until now.

Until Hollie Finch had stuck her nose into his life.

"What about the women who were killed, Watford?"

The man shook his head. "Whores and prostitutes, I imagine—"

"Damn it, Watford." The man started backward a step, but Charles gripped the back of a chair rather than wrap his hands around Watford's thick neck. "Don't imagine anything about anyone or anything until you know for certain. That's why we're here: to find out. How many of the women who were killed were wives of the men in the crowd?"

Watford blinked and sputtered, "Damned if I know."

"Someone knows, Watford. But there's nothing of this in the official file. I want you to find out why there were children on the field that day."

"I don't know that it matters, does it?"

Charles dug his fingers deeper into the back of the chair. "And I want to see a full accounting of the dead and the wounded. A casualty list. Have either of you come across such a document?"

"I haven't." Watford shared a shrug with Bowles, setting Charles's teeth on edge in that momentary exclusion from their exchange. How often had he missed just that sort of communication?

Bowles answered with another shrug and fiddled at the lace edge of his neck cloth. "I surely haven't seen anything like that either, Everingham."

He'd been a lax commissioner, uninterested in the outcome. He'd learned from long experience that questions begat answers in many different forms, some that he couldn't control when the papers flew and the ink flowed.

But Miss Finch had asked, and he hadn't a good enough answer to give her. He had more questions now than he'd had only this morning. There was a dark danger lurking here in the not knowing.

"Then find out why," Charles said. What else hadn't he been told, what other detail had slipped past him?

"Yes, but . . ." Bowles bristled as though Charles had demanded that he swim the Thames beneath Tower Bridge. "Where the devil would we get this information from, Everingham? The estimates say there were more than four hundred wounded. They're probably scattered to the four winds, hiding out from the law."

"I suggest you begin your search with the authorities in Manchester."

Miss Finch snorted lightly and then coughed quietly into her fist to cover up her dissension. He regretted her being privy to the shortcomings of his inquiry. It was more ammunition for her husband, if the man ever managed to slip past him. But it was too late now.

"Try the hospitals nearby, Bowles. The doctors. The magistrates, the locals. Ask Nadin or that Major Trafford!"

"Who?" Bowles stood, shaking his head, both the Deputy Constable and the commander of the Manchester Yeomanry forgotten or dismissed long ago. "And to what end, Everingham? We're nearly finished with the incident. Why stir up more work at this late date?"

Charles stared at the man and wondered at the unfamiliar taste of disgust on his tongue and why he'd never noticed it before. "You'll do it, Watford, because I'm telling you to."

Watford's face went crimson to match his waistcoat, a newly-minted baronet yearning to sputter his objections at an earl. Yet Charles knew the man would remain silent; the ranks between them were too great. He and Bowles had both been pleased to be seated on Charles's commission, chosen by Sidmouth because Charles hadn't cared at the time who sat.

Why the devil he cared now baffled him completely. Except that his own name would be attached to the report, and it suddenly seemed vastly important that he know exactly what he would be signing.

"Well, then, my lord Everingham, I'll do just that."

"And you'll report back to me immediately."

"Of course." Watford tented his fingertips together in a light, entirely unnecessary bow.

But it brought Charles a sense of order again, of everything in its place. Except Miss Finch—who had behaved herself remarkably well, considering.

"Then we'd best be leaving, Everingham," Bowles said, then held out an envelope to him. "Oh, yes, Sidmouth wanted you to look at these."

The writing on the outside of the envelope blurred, anger and dread stirring the ink together into a whirlpool.

Charles snatched the envelope from the man. "What is this?"

"Sidmouth didn't say. Only that he wanted you to see them before you met with him next week."

Charles dreaded these unguarded moments: documents presented to him without preamble or explanation, reminding him of the full measure of his paucity.

He had an office full of papers that he couldn't read, files and boxes packed with decades of reports and estate records and tax assessments—and yet the papers might as well have been blank.

No matter, he would trick Bavidge into reading Sidmouth's papers for him, bluster and bruise his way through the ordinary business of the day, as he always did.

Just read it, damn you, boy! His father's insults still clung to every letter, to his every effort to make sense of the ordinary.

The word is cat, Charles.
Yes, Father.
It's a bloody three-letter word, you stupid clot.

It wasn't his father's blows on his back that had hurt so much as the disdain that had always dripped from his father's curses—he'd failed the man who ought to be proud of him.

But he'd learned later that the heir to the earldom of Everingham could do as he pleased in school. He could taunt and terrorize and buy his way into academic success. He hadn't taken an exam on his own since leaving the nursery. And even there he'd made it difficult for his teachers to catch him long enough to instruct him. Because instruction meant testing and writing, and that was a terrifying world that he didn't understand.

He'd transformed himself into an utter hellion at home, gone through governesses and tutors like wine through a sieve until on his ninth birthday his father packed him off to school for good. The old man had died twelve years later to the day, and Charles gained his majority and the earldom with his infamous reputation intact.

But that wasn't him at all, the rakehell and the bounder. He longed for quiet and softness and home. A wife who wouldn't notice that he couldn't read. Or a wife whom he could trust with his secret shame.

And a son to make it all up to one day.

He'd eventually learned that he wasn't stupid. On the contrary, his mind was quicker than most.

He'd developed an unfailing memory for everything he'd ever heard. But still the doubts remained and could rob him of his confidence in
an instant.

Worst of all, he was forced to trust people who
couldn't always be trusted. As he'd relied on
Watford and Bowles and the other commissioners to do his reading for him regarding St. Peter's
Fields, to bring the information to him already
digested and ready to act upon.

They never had a clue that he was using them
in this way, and he'd convinced himself that this
method wasn't unusual for men of his station:
that popes and government ministers, heads of
state, kings, busy men everywhere, used their
clerks and colleagues in the same way.

But what if it wasn't good enough? What if it
had never been?

"Now, if you'll excuse us, gentlemen." Charles
walked to the door and motioned to Mumberton,
who was standing just outside in the hallway. He
was obviously not minding the boy; where was
the child?

"Napping, my lord," Mumberton said when
Charles hissed the question at him, and Charles
felt an out-of-proportion sense of relief.

Bowles and Watford both pledged their efforts
to Charles's list of casualties and gave their best
wishes for the capture of Captain Spindleshanks,
even as the young Bowles bowed again over
Miss Finch's hand.

Charles waited while Watford clucked over the woman as well, waited even longer while Mumberton led them from the room, waited through the end of his patience before finally turning to Miss Finch with every intention of setting the complicated matter of her husband's capture in motion.

But she was standing at the tall bay window, bathed in the late afternoon brightness, far more a homeless waif than the wife of a radical reformer.

A radical herself, and so very proud of it.

"It's no wonder, my lord, that your commission is in such a tattered state. If those are the best men you could find for the job, then we're all in trouble."

Bloody hell, if the man's wife had only been bitter and foul-breathed, disgruntled or scoffing. He could have managed that quite well.

Instead, she was a handful of sunlight, and he hadn't the slightest idea what to do with it, with her. Or with the memory of the perfect fit of her waist against his hands, the buoyant shape of her breast. The gentleness in her eyes when she looked at the boy.

He'd set a perfect trap. Now he hoped to hell he wouldn't catch more than he'd bargained for.

Chapter 10

"I have no intention of standing here defending my commission to you, Miss Finch"—though he'd certainly found a gaping hole in his process of sifting through information.

A bloody chasm.

But she was shaking her head at him as though she'd gained a sudden insight, her laughter a rueful yet sumptuous sound.

"That's because your commission is completely indefensible. If your files are as sloppy as your investigation, my lord, then you haven't a chance of justice. And neither have I."

"You?"

She sniffed. "My husband, of course. If you catch him."

"*When* I catch him, madam. And it matters not

what you heard in here; my commission is not threatened in the least and not a subject for debate. Are you listening to me, Miss Finch?"

"Oh, yes, my lord." Hollie had been listening very carefully to Everingham and his commissioners. To the carelessness and the disregard for the unforgivable consequences of not tending to the details.

What do you know of the children, gentlemen?

She'd listened in awe to that question too. So simple in the asking, yet fundamentally powerful and rife with hope, if it was truly the way Everingham's mind worked. A concern for the innocent children. A sense that a parent wouldn't endanger a child.

No matter that he had completely ignored his own.

Are you a good man, my wicked earl, in the guise of a heartless villain?

Are you irretrievable?

Or reformable?

She dearly hoped so. For Chip's sake. For the other children. Even the worst calamities had opportunities within them, like the chance to change the man's thinking, like finding herself living here among the wolves.

Like Sidmouth's letter to Everingham. He'd tucked it unopened into the inside pocket of his coat. A tricky spot to steal it from while he was wearing it, but not impossible. She needed to discover its contents and to use them.

But how? She couldn't very well seduce the man, to strip him of his coat and rifle his pockets. He believed that she was married and seemed bound by an admirable code of honor.

The letter would doubtless end up in Everingham's office or library—perfect places for a careful spy to plumb the secret files of the Home Office. Then she would make them public and find public justice for her father.

And to guarantee an impartial review of the massacre to prove that she had been spreading the truth, not sedition.

There was so much work to do.

Hoping Everingham would follow her, Hollie brushed past him and started for the door. He was after her in a shot, hooked her arm to stop her, and turned her.

"Where the devil do you think you're going?"

"I want to be absolutely sure that the so-called evidence you have collected from my dear Adam's alleged crime is catalogued by me and then sealed, not left exposed in the middle of your library."

"For what possible reason?"

"To keep the evidence from being tampered with by spies, informers, thugs. Ask Lord Bowles. Now *there's* an upright man of honor."

"I can assure you, madam, that the evidence is safe with me and my commission."

"Ha! My marketing list isn't safe with the likes of you, sir." Hollie shrugged off his grip and started down the corridor toward the library. "I insist that it all be catalogued and sealed, then given over to a third party, so that the evidence can't be added to or subtracted from or the text altered to implicate my husband—or me—in crimes trumped up for the sake of the Home Office."

The man followed and then beat her stride and met her in the doorway. "You're in no position to be giving orders to me, madam. Least of all in the disposition of evidence. You obviously know nothing about the workings of a trial."

"Oh, I've sat through enough trials for sedition and high treason to know that nothing is safe or sacred in the hands of the government. Least of all evidence that might prove my dear Adam innocent."

"Whether you care to believe it or not, I am conducting an honest inquiry into a very serious matter."

"Ballocks."

"Are you calling me a liar, madam?"

"Only if you're of a mind to take it that way, my lord."

He began that growling sound in his throat, which made her stop and listen instead of dashing past him. "Let's get one thing straight, madam. You may question my politics and even my title if you wish, but never question my integrity. Ever. For you will find me dangerously short-tempered on the matter."

"I shouldn't worry about it, my lord. I don't think any the worse of you for your shortcomings."

"And what exactly are my shortcomings?"

Not your eyes, my lord. He had very fine eyes, dark as midnight and always questing where they shouldn't. But she couldn't very well say that.

Or mention that he had possibilities.

"You, sir, have inherited the natural penchant of your class for lying to suit your politics and your purse. Though I doubt you can help it from your lofty height."

"Meaning?"

"Just that you project your own changeable ethics onto the heart and soul of the average working man, and thereby believe him as lacking as yourself."

"Lacking what, exactly?" He folded his arms across his chest, scoffing.

"Certainly lacking interest in discovering the absolute truth. Any truth will do, if it closes the books on a thorny matter of justice."

He laughed his derision, as she'd so often heard him in Parliament. "Your gall is boundless, madam."

"And you, sir, wouldn't know the truth about the Peterloo Massacre if it was clinging to the end of your watch fob. Because you don't want to know. If you did, you'd keep the inquiry open until you were thoroughly satisfied." She crossed her arms, taunting him for his own good. "And you're not satisfied, are you?"

It took him too long to recover from the question, and he dodged it badly. "That's quite enough, Miss Finch. My investigation is nearly complete."

"It can't possibly be." She'd just have to work on him, wear him down, one drop at a time. "You haven't interviewed *me*, my lord."

His brows drew together for an instant, and then he laughed again. "Ah, and your account of the day's events would be unbiased? From your viewpoint below the hustings, where you must have nearly been trampled."

"I'm an eyewitness. A trained journalist. A very good and impartial one. I was there, my lord."

"So was your husband, madam."

"I didn't know him then."

"And your father."

God, the memories were fresh and raw. And hit her like a blow to the heart.

Everingham paused, then expelled a weary breath that made his broad shoulders droop, as though he was ashamed of pressing that particular advantage. "I mean only that your testimony would be tarnished by your loss."

"Not tarnished, my lord, just made sharper. I lost my father, not my objectivity." At least she hoped she hadn't lost it, hoped she wasn't losing more than that—the gapingly safe distance she'd felt between herself and Charles Stirling. "Show me your evidence, sir. Let me read the depositions and the interviews and study the maps and the statistics, and I shall gauge your integrity then."

He paused, as though he were actually considering it. "Not possible."

"Afraid of what I'll find, my lord?"

"Madam, the information is confidential and must remain so. This is a matter for the Home Secretary and the Chancellor and me. Not for common knowledge, to be broadcast to the public by the press or by some radical scoundrel in a moth-eaten costume."

"Secret information compiled by your secret committee from secret witnesses. Of course."

"As it should be. The facts in a case like this are easily distorted."

"By which side?" Hollie crossed her arms. "Go ahead, sir, ask me a question. Any question at all."

He studied her for a long time, then leaned back against the desk, folded his arms across that massive chest, and asked the only question she couldn't possibly answer.

"Where is your husband, Miss Finch?"

Charles loved watching the woman: the play of hot emotions on her mouth and in her breathing, the crackling fire of her independence, the impertinent arc of an eyebrow.

"You'll have to look around you, my lord. He

could be anywhere. Anywhere at all."

She spun on her heel and left him for her precious sea of placards and handbills and song birds.

His life had been changed irrevocably in the last hour. For good or ill, the woman and her opinions had altered him.

Because on top of all the rest, she'd brought him face to face with the disquieting conclusion that he might be completely in the dark, his position of power threatened by his greatest fear: that there might be more in the commission's files than he had been told about and much less than was necessary. Whether purposely or not, the men who reported to him filtered every fact and statistic through their own prejudices before he learned of it, leaving him with a suddenly prickling conscience and the very real menace of having the report found to contain false and misleading facts, convenient logic.

When he finally signed and submitted the report on the debacle at St. Peter's Fields to the Cabinet and then to Parliament, the official record of the events and the results of the findings would bear his name. He couldn't risk not knowing the facts, all of them, from every side, whether overlooked or deliberately hidden or merely misinterpreted.

Though how he was going to master the problem without revealing his inability to read was another matter.

For the moment he would employ the tactics he'd always used: wholesale intimidation and imperious bluster. He stood beside the bulwark of his desk and watched Miss Finch pick a piece of paper out of a small box.

"Read it, madam."

"Are you sure, my lord?"

"Read!"

She flicked him a wry smile and read unabashedly, "One pair of ladies drawers . . ."

What the bloody hell was he going to do with a woman like that?

Chapter 11

Try as she might, Hollie had no luck retrieving Sidmouth's letter from Everingham's pocket. He wore his coat all afternoon as he stormed his way through the remains of her shop, wore it all through their nearly silent supper with Chip, and then he disappeared into his office with Bavidge afterward while she bundled his son off to bed.

With the library locked down tightly and her Stanhope not yet delivered, Hollie was left with absolutely nothing to spy upon or do but to wonder again where her very incriminating Spindleshanks costume had gotten off to—because it hadn't been in the library, thank God.

She hurried off to the gatehouse and breathed easier when she found the costume stuffed among the clothes that Summerwell had delivered in an ungainly heap on the sofa, still the lumpy bundle she'd made of it after escaping Rennick's mill.

She spent a few hours unpacking, grateful that Everingham's invisible crew had supplied her new home with fresh bedding and linens, candles, and a few supplies for the kitchen.

She raised a toasty fire in the hearth and a pot of tea, and had just settled in to catch up on her reading when she heard a tiny knock at the door.

No doubt it was Everingham come to check on her, to see if she was entertaining her husband.

But the face that peered at her from her doorstep was small and sweet and too near the ground. "Chip! What are you doing here?"

He was nearly blue with the cold, his little limbs quaking. "I-yai-yai c-couldn't sleep."

"And so you came all the way here in the dark?" She rescued him with a blanket, bundled him in it before he could take another step. "Across the cold, wet grass."

"I-yai wanted t-to hear a s-s-story." His shivers came in great, teeth-rattling waves.

"Ah, and you thought you'd find one here?" Hollie took him to the fireplace and rubbed his back, covered his head with a towel, and held him close.

"Oh, y-yes, Hollie. I think you have l-lots of stories. With all your p-p-papers and things."

He couldn't keep doing this, sneaking off to

see her. He and his father needed to find some measure of compromise together, else the boy might wander off entirely one day.

She caught his chin and his droopy, tear-stained gaze. "Chip, my good man, did you ask Mumberton if you could come to see me?"

The boy sniffled and shook his head, dropped his cheek onto her shoulder, and whispered against her collar, "I couldn't find him anywhere."

The poor man had probably crawled into a nook somewhere for a good forty hours of sleep. "What about his lordship? Your father. Did you ask him?"

"I forgot."

Hmm. "But he was there?"

More nodding against her shoulder. "In his library. I sneaked past the door."

"Oh, Chip, why?"

The boy snuggled against her and then stilled. "He doesn't like me."

"He does." He *must*. Hollie kissed his cool forehead and held him tighter. "He's just not used to having you around yet."

"I'm not used to him, either, Hollie, but I like him."

I nearly do too. Though it seemed a dangerous thing to do, when she meant to be spying on him and stealing from him and running as fast and as far as she could. "You just keep on liking him, sweet, and he'll soon come around to your side.

In fact, I know the perfect story about this sort of thing."

He sighed, settled deeper into the blanket. "I told you so."

"It's about a very sad king, who had a monstrous spell cast upon him by a council of evil chancellors."

"Uh, oh." His little forehead puckered, etched with lines that fretted and swooped exactly like his father's. "What happens to him?"

"That's the happy part. A little prince comes along and sets the king free." Hollie scooted her chair close to the fire and pulled him deeply into her lap, then wove a story for the boy while she warmed him for the long, icy trek back to the Hall.

"Have you had any schooling, Chip?"

He turned in her lap. "Mrs. Lassiter taught me to spell my name. Watch me: C-haitch-ipp!"

"That's very good, Chip." At least something of his learning had stuck with him. "Who's Mrs. Lassiter?"

"The cook at Bagthorpe Manor."

"Is that where you lived with your mama until you came here?"

"My mama died before I could remember her. I lived next to the kitchen till the Bagthorpes had to give their house away and I came here."

Dear God, what a lonesome little heart. "Did Mrs. Lassiter teach you how to spell anything else?"

"She mostly chased me out of the kitchen. Is that how you spell my name too, Hollie? Like Mrs. Lassiter did?"

"I think I'd be more likely to spell your name, C-H-I-P."

He screwed up his face. "I should spell it that way too."

"It certainly will help if you want to get your point across."

"Is that how he spells it?"

He. Charles Stirling the elder, the supposedly wiser. "That's exactly how he would spell your name, Chip." If he would only take the time.

"Then tell me how it goes again, Hollie. I forget."

She spelled Chip's name slowly, and he repeated it again and again until it became a rhyme and a song and then another story. Until he was as warm as toast and mumbling, sinking down her lap into a gentle snooze.

"It's time to take you back to your bed, sweet, before Mumberton misses you."

"He won't." He snuggled his arms around her neck.

"I wouldn't be so sure of that. You're a very missable fellow."

And that made him smile.

"Dammit, Mumberton, what do you mean the boy's gone? Just . . . go find him." Charles had sent Bavidge away from the office for the night and didn't like the alarm that had suddenly shaded Mumberton's eyes. Didn't like it at all.

Mumberton blinked. "But I've already looked everywhere, sir—the pantry and the east tower lookout and the chapel. That's what I mean: he's gone."

"Blast it all, Mumberton, you've lost him again." Charles stood and stuffed his arms into his coat, certain that he knew exactly where the boy had gone. And who he'd gone to see. At least, he hoped so. "Never mind, Mumberton. I'll take care of it myself."

"You, my lord?" Mumberton's expression of worry became a grimace of utter horror, as though he believed Charles would dunk the boy into a cauldron and bring it to a rolling boil when he found him.

"Me, Mumberton." Charles left his office with his butler trailing after him.

"Yes, my lord. But he's just a lad, remember. And a bit unstrung from his recent upheaval. It's to be expected, sir, all this wandering about. Please, sir. You wouldn't use a strap on him. . . ."

Charles halted in midstride, and Mumberton had the good sense to stop blathering.

"Bloody hell! As though I would ever strike a child." He had enough scars himself to last a lifetime, straps and buckles and the heart-bruising sting of the back of his father's hand. He snagged his cloak from the hook at the side entrance and slung it over his shoulders. "Go to bed, Mumberton."

"But—"

"Whatever you think of me, Mumberton, I'm not a monster." He lit a lantern from the flame of the sconce and watched it flare, his hands shaking more than he'd expected.

"Of course not, sir."

"And by the way, Mumberton, you're right that you're no kind of nanny. You keep losing him. I'm quite certain that I can do better." Keeping track of a small boy couldn't possibly be that difficult. Yet the night was dark and steeped in foggy shadows. And the boy could be anywhere, could have lost his way.

He started off toward the gatehouse, Miss Finch's Refuge for Seditious Radicals and Runaway Boys. He prayed the boy hadn't gone wandering out in the fields and valleys.

Good God, there were mole traps out there and poachers and chalk pits and quarries and that old copper mine.

He was nearly running down the drive when he heard the crunch of gravel in the lane ahead of him and stopped sharply to hold his lantern to his shoulder.

She came into the pale wash of light like an angel, her long cloak flowing around her ankles and plain boots, her hair loose and streaming against the dampness, and her arms ripe and full of boy, leaving Charles spent with relief and confusion and a lingering fear that the boy would never really be completely safe, anywhere. No matter the loving embrace that held him.

"Look what I found, my lord." The boy was a dangling of thin arms and lean-muscled legs sticking out from her encircling cloak, a mass of dark curls nuzzled against her neck.

"Mumberton lost him again." It was a cowardly dodge when he knew where the responsibility lay, when that fear of an unnameable loss still prickled his scalp.

She snorted softly and whispered, "I think all of us are a bit lost these days, my lord."

She hitched the boy higher on her hip and started past him toward the house, her burden far too great for her to carry.

"Stop. Please." Weighted with so many doubts, his heart thunked as she stopped and turned and waited until he managed through an oddly constricted throat, "I'll take him."

She narrowed her eyes at him, testing him, interviewing him for the position of father. "He's asleep, my lord, and I promised him I'd tuck him into his bed."

"You'll never make it up the stairs, Miss Finch."

She sighed heavily and nodded her reluctance, no doubt expecting better from him—or worse, since he just didn't know how to be a father.

He set the lantern on the ground and collected the boy onto his shoulder, much like wrestling a day-old lamb into a bushel bag, with a lot of soft murmuring against his ear and wriggling and re-arranging, knobby knees poking into his ribs. The boy finally settled against his chest, lighter than he'd imagined and warm, yet as heavy as a sack of golden wheat.

He couldn't think of a thing to say as he started off toward the house, following the woman and the lantern. A powerful urge to protect the boy surged inside him like a winter tide along with the need to keep him warm and molded against his chest. More difficult to credit was a deep and unsubtle melancholy that the boy's legs were long and his feet were hitting him in the knees, a sorrowful measure of irretrievable days that made his throat close over and his eyes burn.

"I don't mean to be an attraction for him, my lord."

But that was her greatest transgression—for both father and son. He was being suddenly rushed toward a blind cliff. "He has to learn his place."

"Have you told him where his place is, my lord? Because if he doesn't know, then he can't very well be expected to stay put, and he's liable to go on looking elsewhere until he finds some place that suits his little heart."

She had the right of it. Running elsewhere, anywhere, always looking for that soft place to fall.

She stomped ahead of him, leaving her trail of crunching gravel and bobbing light, then hurried up the steps to the side entry, where Mumberton was peering with his long face through the window beside the door.

She held a muttering exchange with his butler, patted his hand, and sent him on his way down the dark corridor.

"Mumberton was worried," she said, as though he himself hadn't been.

"Don't put yourself into the middle of this matter. You don't belong." He was doing the best he could, was trying.

"I'm already there, my lord." She shuttered the lantern and left it on the side table, then turned her glare on him as she hung her cloak on a hook. "So are you. As in the middle of it as you can possibly be. He's your son."

"Why, because Bagthorpe's attorney says so?"

"Because he looks exactly like you. You've noticed, else you'd have sent him packing the moment he crossed your threshold, attorney and all."

"I haven't time to be a father."

"You should have thought of that before." She hurried up the back stairs, hitching her hem to her ankles.

"Before what, madam? Before Draskel left the boy on my doorstep?"

"No, my lord." She stopped on the second

stair above him, her stormy green eyes level with his. "Before you lifted his mother's skirts and took your pleasure with her."

Stunned by her bluntness, staggered at the bent of this conversation, he shifted the limp weight of the boy to his other shoulder. "What did you say?"

She raised her brows at him, put one hand on her shapely hip. "That's how children are conceived, my lord. Or did no one ever take the time to tell you?"

"I know very well how children are conceived," he whispered, trying not to waken the boy.

"Then you know where he came from." She ran her fingers through Chip's hair, sifting the soft curls past Charles's cheek. "And you also know what you need to do about him."

She flounced up the stairs and away from her astoundingly out-of-place lecture and hurried directly into the boy's chamber. She was straightening the mussed covers and the pillows when he arrived.

"I'll take him now." She reached into Charles's cloak and lifted the boy away from him as easily as if she'd done this every day of his short life.

"Time to sleep, Chip. You're safe. I'm here." Then she hummed a little melody and the boy was fast asleep, buried to his cheeks in the blankets, looking so very, very small. Easily breakable.

And smiling from the gentle kiss she placed against his forehead. "Good night, sweet."

He couldn't imagine the bliss of it, couldn't recall his own mother ever entering his room to say good night, let alone to tuck him under the covers and sing a bedtime song.

"He likes you," she whispered, when she stood and caught him staring.

"Who does? The boy?" Nonsense. He'd given the boy no reason to.

"Chip is his name. You could at least try to call him by something besides 'boy.' "

"I'll call him what suits me." But he had blustered too much, and she shushed him, hooked her hand around his elbow and drew him out of the room. She closed the door quietly, taking one last, longing look, one that he'd have given the world to have awakened to each morning.

"No wonder he's terrified of you, my lord."

"Terrified? You just said he liked me." And that had felt very good—good enough to ache a bit when she stole the pleasure back from him.

"A perfect example of the very insecure place you've put him." She started down the stairs in her determined way, trailing her startling accusations behind her.

"He actually told you that he was terrified of me?"

"He didn't have to; it's plain to me. It must be as plain to you."

"If he's claiming that I've struck him—"

"He said nothing of the sort. He hasn't got a dishonest bone in his body, and you wouldn't do such a thing, my lord."

"I damned well wouldn't." It pleased him vastly to know that she understood that much about him.

"But much worse than frightening him, my lord, you ignore him. You never say a word to him. Like tonight at supper: you sat like a stone at the other end of the table."

They'd been a full ten feet away from him. Besides, "What the devil does a grown man have to say to a six-year-old boy?"

" 'Hello' makes a good beginning."

"I've bloody well said hello. And more than that! I've said . . . well . . ." He couldn't really think of anything he'd said directly to the boy. To Chip. But he'd said plenty.

"You're the parent, my lord. It's your responsibility to make it right. What did your father talk with you about?"

Charles snorted. "He didn't."

That stopped her, softened her voice and her patience. "But if he had, my lord, if he'd been the very best father in the whole world, what would you have talked with him about?"

This was completely beyond his experience. "He wasn't anything like the very best father."

"Well, then, you'll have to make do with your imagination."

"Meaning?"

"Find out what Chip likes to do and ask him about that."

"He certainly likes to run away from me."

She grabbed his sleeve and held onto him. "Then, sir, I'll give you this hint: he seems fascinated by the deer on the estate."

Perfect. Damned precocious, in fact, that the lad should be interested in game at his age. "Good, then I'll take him hunting."

"Dear God, no, my lord." She released him, and her shoulders sagged. "He thinks the deer are pets that live in the garden. Please don't shoot one in front of him; you'll lose him for sure."

"There, you see? I'm at a loss." He couldn't believe that he was standing in his hallway with this woman in her nightgown once again, asking her advice on the ways of sons.

"Ride with him, then. Show him the stables."

"I doubt he rides."

"Then teach him how. A simple smile and a soft word—any word at all—will win his little heart forever. He wants to love you. I adored my father. And there was never a question in my heart that he adored me back. It's just that simple."

He watched helplessly as her eyes welled with sudden tears, which glistened for an instant before sliding down her cheeks. Ah, that he could ever be loved so well!

"Come, madam. I have something you'd like to see."

She wiped at her cheeks with her sleeve. "Where?"

"This way." He caught her gently, meant only to turn and guide her down the stairs, but like a man not in his right mind, he slipped his arm around the compelling warmth of her waist and held her too closely, stealing the momentary fit of her against him, the scent of her hair and the moonlight beaded there.

His pulse thrummed with the heat of her, with the shape of her, with the very real possibility that he was about to dip his head and pull her close and close his mouth over hers.

Just a taste to satisfy his curiosity.

Hollie thought for an astounding moment that he was going to kiss her; he was close enough and wound tightly enough, his breathing as unsteady as hers, a fire banked in his half-lidded eyes. The heated hardness of him blazed through her nightgown and burned her bare flesh, that stealthy male part of him, his vitality.

And, oh, my, if she wasn't thoroughly ready to be kissed by him.

But he closed his eyes and measured his breathing as he stepped away from her, raking his fingers through his dark hair.

"Your deepest pardon, madam," he said wryly. "I've a wholly more proper objective than that. Come."

Chapter 12

❧❧❧

"Where, my lord?" Not that Hollie cared a whit where he planned to go. Her imagination was still captivated by the possessive strength of his fingers as he led her down the back stairs, the unexpected gentleness; she was willing to follow him through the dark byways of Everingham Hall and out into the fields and furrows if he had a mind to go there.

They passed into the pale, moon-blue shadows of a room made of glass walls and iron framing.

The conservatory. And in the middle of the midnight emptiness, the hulking upright of her father's press leaning at a hard angle against its base.

"My Stanhope!" A lamp flared behind her, and

then another moved close as she touched its familiar strength, her chest flushed with pride and hurt and anger. Her eyes went suddenly hot with the stinging grief that still ambushed her at the worst possible moments.

"I thought you'd like to know that it arrived this evening. With all its parts, Summerwell assures me."

The type cabinet and the inks, the brayers and a few of her father's precious set of stereotypes too, his dear words founded in iron and so rich in memories.

"I won't know until I put it all together if everything is here." She wrapped her hand around the platen handle that was sticking out of a box at a wry angle, cradled her fingers into the grooves worn there by her father's. Too wide for her own, but dear and familiar. "Thank you."

"I trust the room will do."

Hollie caught her threatening smile with her teeth. Another miraculous site, seeming to be purpose-built for her needs. "I confess, my lord, that it's fashioned right out of my dreams. It's large, and the floor made of slate. The windows are tall and grand. Doors opening to the fresh spring garden, to clear the air of the ink and linseed. Daylight will doubtless stream in from absolutely everywhere. I hate to admit it to you, my lord, but it's perfect."

He smiled at her as he set the lantern on the

press's fat iron base, and lifted the rounce barrel by the handle. "You learned to operate this contraption from your father?"

"Learned my trade on this very press. From my exceedingly patient father."

"It looks like a bloody siege machine."

She laughed, and he smiled at himself, easy and enchanting. Oh, how could the man possibly have become even more handsome than he'd been earlier in the day? He'd come out of the mist like a prayer in his midnight trek to find his little son.

"A daunting beast for a little girl to conquer, my lord, but I wouldn't change a moment of my life. I suspect that Father taught me the printing business in defense of his own work. I learned to read while watching him."

He shifted his head, sharpened his focus. "You taught yourself to read?"

"Father helped, of course, but I was determined, because I was a very busy little body and I wanted to know everything he was saying to people in the papers he printed. I gobbled up every word I could get my hands on. I still do."

"Only now you print them for yourself."

"The proudest moment of my life was the day I set my first composition for an issue of the *Tuppenny Press*. It was a present for my father's birthday. I was very proud."

"How old were you?"

"Seven."

"Blazes, woman, you were but a babe. Reading and writing and composing for a newspaper?"

"They come naturally to me, words do—if you haven't already reached that conclusion." She knelt down and opened a canvas bag, then groaned. "Oh, blast it all."

"What is it?"

A whole bag of typeface. "Dumped into a jumble, of all things!"

"Is it broken?" He dropped on a knee beside her, an inescapable presence, casually looking over her shoulder as she reached inside the bag and drew out a few letters.

"Not broken. Just a muddled pile of vowels and consonants."

"These bits of metal are?"

She managed her pulse and her breathing perfectly well when he cupped his hand beneath hers and reached into her palm to pick up a letter—those startlingly big hands of his that could be so gentle.

"It's the Roman type I was using for the *Song Birds*." She absorbed the heat and the brush of his fingers, the whispering drape of his sleeve against her wrist. But it was his unguarded curiosity that awakened a restlessness in her, the stillness of him that left her breathless and wanting to shape her hand against his cheek. "They ought to be in their separate boxes in that type case drawer."

He dropped the letter back into her palm, wrapped his fingers around her hand, and held it. "Fixable, I assume?"

Dear God, the man shouldn't be so unbalancing or so hard-muscled. He should have kissed her and gotten it over with. Now her heart was setting up such a racket she could barely hear his question.

"Fixable? Uhm, yes, of course. With a few hours of sorting." She stumbled to her feet with the heavy bag of type and was rescuing its case drawer from where it was leaning against the box of ink and linseed oil when the weight of the bag vanished from her fist.

"Where does this go?" Everingham lifted the bag as though it contained only a few pennies.

"Here." She patted the scarred and ink-stained worktable and set the case drawer beside the bag, stumbling over the simplest words under his gaze. "Thank you."

What was she to do with this grievously impossible intimacy growing between them? With the exotic scent of him, which blended so well with the dear and familiar scents of linseed and indigo and varnish. The man who had tilted her world so radically, who tilted it more with every passing moment.

So terrified of his little son. So sure that she would want to know that her Stanhope was safe.

The sudden and reluctant champion of the fallen children on St. Peter's Fields.

Her jailor, her possibly redeemable earl.

No, no; she shouldn't be thinking in this direction. He was one of them. Her enemy. And she was here to spy on him, not to make up preposterous excuses for his out-of-character behavior.

She dodged around him and went to her Stanhope, patting its solid shoulder. "I can put the press together myself, but it's a lot easier with another person. May I borrow Summerwell or Haskett?"

"Borrow them? Good God, madam." He closed the distance between them in his easy stride, giving the Stanhope an appraising study and then shifting the caressing heat of his gaze to her. "You've taken up residence in my gatehouse, you've commandeered my conservatory, my coat, and even my socks. Next you'll be wanting my cook."

"Only her recipe for Devonshire Cherry Tart. Putting the press together will take the best part of a morning with two people. May I borrow one of them, please? After all, they took it apart."

"No."

The ogre once again. Good. She knew exactly how to handle his growling, unreasonable stubbornness. "Well, then, I'll just assemble it myself. I have done so before."

"What I mean, madam, is that I can't spare any of my staff. I'll help you with it myself."

Hollie canted her head, certain that she didn't hear him rightly. "You, my lord?"

"Yes, me."

The woman looked thoroughly skeptical, as though she believed he was unable to perform the most menial task. Charles blew out a snort and wondered how the devil he'd suddenly gained this reputation for inertia as well as his butler's assessment that he was a child eater.

"Why?" she asked, in that blazingly stubborn way of hers.

"Because, Miss Finch, I want to clearly understand the innermost workings of this Stanhope device, so that I'll know when you're trying to wheedle your way around my edicts."

"Ha! I don't wheedle."

Because wheedling required patience, and the woman lacked that particular trait. Resentment of him she had in abundance; it flared in her eyes before she went back to putting the remains of her life in order.

He'd spent most of the evening with Bavidge, developing the strategy for Captain Spindle-shanks's trial *in absentia*. No matter which way he considered the matter, it still went against his ethics: first using the blackguard's wife to lure him out of hiding, and then bringing him to trial without charging him to his face.

Not that he could have avoided the situation. The Privy Council had insisted on some movement in the case before the arrest warrant had been issued and would want it more firmly now that the arrest had gone wrong, if only to incite the man to show himself.

As though Hollie Finch wasn't draw enough for any man. Good God, he'd nearly kissed her.

"Which of these parts of the machine is the most important?" he asked, while she straightened and frowned.

"They're all important, my lord, or they wouldn't be part of the workings."

"Yes, but which part can't you print without, once it's all assembled?"

She planted a fist against her hip. "That would be the devil's tail, my lord."

Minx. He knew that flicker of defiance, her word play. "Which is what, exactly?"

"This." She lifted a long-handled, dog-legged lever that must have weighed a dozen pounds. "The handle. It works with the coupling rod to press against the toggle lever, which then presses the platen into the paper, which picks up the ink off the type from the bed below."

"I see." He didn't completely, but he soon would. "Just so that you don't get any ideas, Miss Finch, this devil's tail will remain in my possession."

"That goes without saying, my lord." She handed him the lever, dipped him an insincere curtsey, then went back to the heap.

"What are you doing, woman?" She was trying to lift a huge iron frame of some sort, teetering on her feet. He reached out and caught the frame before she tumbled over.

"It's in the way of the base."

"It'll keep until the morning. Come, I'll walk you back to the gatehouse."

"I'm perfectly capable of making the trip on my own."

"Not in the dark."

She sighed deeply. "If it pleases you, my lord."

She stalked off to the side entrance, grabbed her cloak, then stalked ahead of him, out into the night in her gravel-crunching silence, but he followed her right into her warm little parlor.

"There's something else you need to know, madam." Though he wasn't looking forward to telling her. "It's about your husband."

She turned a quizzical look on him, then harrumphed and went back to raising a fire under the kettle in the hearth. "Have you caught him already?"

"It's a matter of his trial. Just letting you know a point of law."

"What now? Have you been ordered to shoot him on sight? Is that what Sidmouth's letter contained? The one that Bowles brought today?" She watched him with an uncommon amount of interest.

"Not that, madam." Charles braced himself for her anger. "This particular process was already in motion. Once the warrant was issued for the arrest of Captain Spindleshanks—whoever he turned out to be—then the law allows that an inquest and a trial could follow any time afterward."

She narrowed her eyes at him, as though daring him to explain. "But you have to catch him first. Right?"

"Wrong. The law doesn't require a defendant."

She stood. "Since when?"

"Among other things, suspending habeas corpus allows a criminal to be tried *in absentia*."

"Let me understand this, my lord." She clamped the lid on the kettle and threw off her cloak as though she were preparing for a battle. "The Home Office can bring a man to trial, can find him guilty and sentence him to death, without him being present in the court to defend himself?"

"Exactly."

"And you're planning to do that to . . . to my husband? To Captain Spindleshanks?"

"The inquest is scheduled for three weeks from now."

"Whether you have him in your prison or not?"

"That's it."

She paled, balling her nightgown in her fist, fearing for this man she'd married, her hero. "But how do I . . . he . . . how does he defend himself?"

Charles waited to answer. "He turns himself in."

Hollie was sure he must have heard her heart pounding. She drew away from him to the hearth again, breathless at this sudden race for her life. Tried and convicted before she had a chance to defend herself. "This is madness!"

"It is one of the tools of justice, a remedy of law."

"It's that very large stick that the Home Office calls a state of Alarm. Another cudgel for controlling the public, inflicted on the populace to keep us in line whenever the Cabinet gets a little edgy. I hardly need to explain it to you."

"Indulge me, Miss Finch." The earl lounged back on the settee, gestured for her to continue with those able hands of his. It was like entertaining a very hungry lion in her parlor.

"First of all, when that great pudding, Lord Liverpool, decides to—"

"Great pudding?" He smiled.

"The Prime Minister is a slothful, shapeless bag of curdle and whey."

He laughed broadly, disarming her entirely. He probably shared her opinion of the man. "I believe I'll keep your opinion of the Prime Minister secret when next I see him."

"I don't need your protection, my lord."

That only made him smile all the more. "Do tell me more of this monstrous 'Alarm,' madam. What does the Great Pudding do then?"

"He announces to the public that the Home Office, by way of your friend Lord Sidmouth—that other great pudding—has learned of a dangerous threat to the peace of the nation."

"Your husband, for example."

"And other horrifying tattle and talk of plots against the Cabinet: machine breaking, revolution, anti-parliament meetings, seditious pantomimes." That drew up the man's brow. "But of course, Sidmouth purposely withholds the source of this information from the press."

"So that it can't be turned into panic through the politics of fear."

"No. So that it can't be verified."

Everingham stilled, his amusement gone. "And then, Miss Finch?"

Hollie plunked herself down on the ottoman in front of him. "Then this heap of unsubstantiated information is sent off to secret committees in the Lords and Commons, like the secret committee that you head, my lord. Which you then are chartered to examine for truth, as you are doing now, from which you will write a report of your findings to the House. Correct?"

"To the letter."

"Except that the government will then take your findings and use them to enact some cruel and punitive legislation against the people it's supposed to protect. Like the suspension of habeas corpus: a travesty of justice that allows a man to be tried for his life *in absentia* so that the Home Office can strike a killing blow against the press and public assemblies before anyone can protest."

"That's not the intent."

"Well, that's the result. And mark me, sir, that's just what will come of your Peterloo report."

"If an act of Parliament is required to quell the unrest, so be it."

"And when you learn that your commission has made one tremendous error after another and innocent men have been transported and imprisoned and even hanged, no one will be condemned for the misjudgment—because by that time, Parliament will have passed an act of indemnity absolving the ministers and their agents from culpability. It's a devilish stratagem, my lord."

"I say again, I will not issue a report until I am satisfied."

"I plan to be there in the gallery when it's read, my lord, when Lord Pudding tries to explain himself in Parliament. I'll collect his speech and Sidmouth's—"

"And mine?"

"Yours in particular."

"What of my other speeches, madam? Have you ever collected one of mine?" The man was trying his best to look nonchalant as he leaned forward again on his elbows, but having no luck at all. She wanted to smile but held back.

"Hmm . . . Everingham . . ." She tapped her cheek as she pretended to remember back to some unmemorable time, to some unremarkable speech.

He'd always made her spitting mad with his thick-headed politics, but she'd loved his voice, the way it echoed off the chamber walls. Worst of all, he always trod the borderline of being correct: a shove to the left and he'd be one of us, she'd always said.

He was watching her steadily, waiting for her answer. "Well, have you?"

Hollie sighed for effect. "I suppose I must have. Yes, I have."

The man was trying to hide his smile, but it was there in the corners, fighting for purchase. "You must have an opinion of me and my speeches."

"Well, naturally, my lord, since you are a pig-headed Tory, your speeches are just so much wallowing in what Tories are bound to wallow in." She waited for his growl, but he seemed amused at the moment, so she continued, "It's just that I always enjoy your—"

"Enjoy, madam? I'm flattered."

"Enjoy as in appreciate your speeches for the way you—" The way your dark eyes scanned the gallery, as though you were looking for me, as though you wanted me to understand you.

"For the way I what?" He leaned closer, his breath as near to a kiss as she'd ever gotten.

"Well, the way you speak without notes, my

lord. Off the cuff in a very . . ." That pesky blush came again, spreading up from her chest like an indictment.

"In a very *what*, madam?"

"In a very compelling way."

"Compelling?"

Passionate. Oh, but she couldn't say that. She was paying too much attention to his mouth, the shape of his words on his lips.

"When you speak, the others in both Houses seem to stop their chattering and actually listen." Bits of fog still clung to his coat in tiny diamonds; she stopped her hand just as she would have reached up to brush them from his broad shoulders.

"They listen, madam, but you don't, do you?"

"I don't what?" It was then that she felt the gentle tugging, his fingers wrapped in the ends of her hair, idling there. No wonder she was having difficulty following his questions. He was too large for her parlor, too grand for her life. He smelled of the forest instead of the cold chambers of Whitehall, of woodsmoke and leaves and hard-worked leather instead of his wealth and his title.

His breathing had become deep and steady, breaking softly against her cheek. His eyes held hers, stealing her breath when he traced the line of her lip with the pad of his thumb as though he might actually kiss her this time.

And then without a hint of warning the man blinked suddenly and stood. "Bloody hell."

"What is it?"

He scrubbed his hand around the back of his neck, took her hand, and raised her to her feet.

"I think I'd best go, madam, before I forget myself altogether. Before I forget the greatness of the divide between us."

Hollie stood in her little parlor and watched him go, felt her spirit winding out the door with him, like a silken ribbon caught in his pocket.

"Oh, my Lord Everingham, you have no idea of the impossible greatness of that divide."

Chapter 13

~~~∽◯◯∽~~~

Charles's house looked vastly different to him in the clear, crisp light of morning. The halls, the library, his office—settled, civilized. The carpet, the books, the brass upholstery buttons, all of it—entirely comprehensible. And he was in control once again.

Not a hint of the heady temptations of the night before, no flashing eyes to distract him from the business of the day, none of her challenging opinions that made him think of nothing but the rosy bow of her lips.

His sanctuary belonged to him again save for the faint, trailing tendrils of her scent that had followed him into his office and hung above the inkwell on his desk. He caught himself sniffing at the air like a simple-minded hound. Watching the door for her smile.

Hell and damnation, he'd nearly kissed the woman last night. Twice. Another man's wife!

He should have left her at the gatehouse door. He would keep his promise to help her assemble her damned Stanhope, then he'd spend the rest of the day on his much-needed inspections of the estate.

"Your pardon, my lord." Bavidge's knock at the office door startled him.

"Yes, yes, come, Bavidge." Charles couldn't help his bellow, couldn't hide his irritation as Bavidge entered, his arms overloaded with files and the day's business.

"Three letters for you to sign this morning, my lord. From last evening's dictation."

"Yes, yes, bring them." Charles yanked his chair from his desk, sat down and took up his pen. He hated this part of the day. The endless signatures, the blindness that overtook him as his dutiful clerk put the first of the letters on the blotter in front of him. Bavidge's clear, precise script, familiar and life-saving yet shattering at the same time—because it was all chicken scratching—and awaiting Charles's signature.

He jabbed the pen into the inkwell and scrawled his signature at the bottom of each of the letters. "See that these get to Sidmouth today."

"Yes, my lord. Anything else?"

He'd been about to wave Bavidge away for the

remainder of the day when he saw a carefully folded letter tented against the lamp.

"Wait, Bavidge." He picked it up, sending a light waft of perfume past his nose. Her peach and vanilla. His heart leaped, slid around like a schoolboy's. "Take care of this first."

Anticipation drew sweat from his brow as he handed the letter to Bavidge and tried to relax in his chair, shuffled papers as he prepared to listen.

No doubt another inflammatory diatribe against him. Peterloo, the boy, her husband's trial—the subject could be most anything.

"It's from Mrs. MacGillnock."

"Yes, yes. Go on. I haven't got all day."

" 'My Lord Everingham, Regarding . . . ' Oh. Well." Bavidge stopped abruptly.

"Regarding *what*, Bavidge? Get on with it."

Bavidge's sudden blush should have warned Charles, but the man cleared his throat and then continued, " 'Regarding last night's . . . indiscretion between—' "

"Bloody hell!" Charles lurched to his feet and snatched the letter from Bavidge, damning himself for being so utterly stupid, for trusting the woman. "I'll take care of this. Leave."

Bavidge gurgled something as he backed up sharply into the side table, rattling the prisms on the lamp. "Yes, my lord."

The man's neck and the tips of his ears were a hot crimson. He lunged for the door.

"Indiscretion!" Holy Christ, he'd nearly kissed

her. Bloody hell, he'd been two heartbeats from doing more than that.

But he hadn't, damn it all! He'd gathered up every last shred of his honor and left the woman unkissed.

Yet here she was putting the whole of it in writing. An indictment against his unforgivable behavior, for tempting the bounds of decency.

Blackmail, surely. Her insistence that she be able to air her grievances in exchange for postponing her husband's trial.

He took a moment to right his thoughts, drew a steadying breath, then glanced down at the page, willing it to make sense for once. A fruitless activity, as always. The ink swam as it always did, as it ever would. And the blindness shuttered his heart.

Nonsensical lines and poetical curves and delicate swirls of various thicknesses. Gibberish, all of it. Damnation, if he could only pound the words into his head, he could understand her meaning.

That was the frustration of it. This knowing that Bavidge had read some of her words, that Bowles could and Watford, and the man who delivered the dry goods to the kitchen could, yet *he* couldn't. He gripped the page between his hands and tried.

God knows, he had always tried.

You're a fool, boy.

He had squinted and steadied his breathing and searched for patterns among the scrawling: a clam shell, a butter churn, a bulbous nose. But never words.

He focused on the top line, a single word. Probably, though he couldn't be completely sure, "Charles." His name, drawn lightly, cleanly in her easy hand, and all the words that followed in their graceful dance across the page were created by her just for him—to read, to understand her thoughts.

Anger at him, more instructions on his parental duties, or that hint of haughty amusement? He'd never felt so cut off from the world.

From *her* world.

"Bloody hell!" He passed Mumberton in the corridor. "Where is she?"

"Conservatory, my lord."

Waiting for him to help her put together her accursed printing press. Charles growled and doubled his pace down the hall.

He would have barreled into the room, but she was sitting at a small table at an angle to him, bent over a sheet of paper, a short stack of the same piled at the corner. She was tapping her lower lip with a pen, her chin tipped to the window, her mouth forming silent words. She must have found the perfect sentiment just then, because she smiled in triumph, dotted the air with the point of the pen, and then dipped it into the inkwell.

Breathtaking, distracting. He would force himself to keep a better distance from her.

Taking a long, defensive breath, he strode into the conservatory, stood over and slightly behind her, then dropped her own note across her hands and the letter she was scribing.

"What the devil do you mean by this, madam?" He straightened and moved away from her, fearing the scent of her perfume would distract him from his purpose. He needed all of his faculties if he was to employ his usual strategies.

She seemed not at all surprised to see him as she turned halfway in her chair and asked easily, "What do you think I meant, my lord?"

He'd long ago learned ways of coping with his deficiency. He used trickery, deceit, quick maneuvering with his associates, and common, ordinary autocratic blustering with his underlings. But Miss Finch wasn't taking the bait, and he had no idea of the subject matter—only her allusion to last night's bloody indiscretion.

He pointed again at the offending page, flicked the corner. "Explain yourself."

She huffed, raised a winged brow. "I thought I had, my lord. Quite clearly."

"Not clearly enough by half." He was skilled at turning the problem back on the reader.

"I assumed you'd agree with me on the entire matter."

"I—" Hell and damnation, what was she talking about? He hated this swimming blackness, feeling his way blindly, more than anything.

"Yes, my lord?"

"I think, madam, that we need to discuss the matter. Here and now."

"What part of my letter bothers you?" The bloody woman could have been a lawyer with all her double-talk.

My lord Everingham, Regarding last night's indiscretion between—and *then* what, madam?

He needed another, safer tack. He lifted the letter again, leaned over her shoulder, and fitted it between her fingers.

"May I remind you of what you wrote here?"

She turned slightly in the closer cocoon of his arms, brushing the top of her head against his chin, tempting him to nestle a kiss against the scented bounty of blond. But that was the subject, wasn't it?

"Why are you so angry, my lord? I didn't blame you, because we both had a part in it. Or are you merely shocked at my openness?"

Bloody hell, he'd like to be shocked. Or angry. Or delighted.

"Read it for yourself." He clamped down on his desire to shout as he tended to do with his staff. The tactic worked on them, though it always caused Bavidge to quake and Mumberton to run for the nearest corner.

The redoubtable Miss Finch merely set the pen into the holder and frowned up at him. "I meant only to apologize for my part in last night's—"

"Apologize?"

She caught her lower lip with her teeth just long enough to dampen it. "I really should have stopped you. I am, after all, a happily married woman."

Great God. "No, Miss Finch. I'm the one who stepped over the boundaries. It won't happen again."

"So you're not angry about our little indiscretion?"

"No. I'm not angry." Aroused then, aroused now, but not angry.

"So is it my request that angers you?"

He shoved away from her, the air knocked out of him. What bloody request?

He'd learned long ago to stick to short sentences when trapped in a dark corner. He stepped away from her to the windows, needing less distraction if he was going to survive this lopsided interrogation.

"Explain yourself." Here was the safety he respected: distance, putting the onus on her to explain herself. He turned, in charge once more, and clasped his hands behind his back as he took a thoughtful step toward her. "If you're seeking my approval in the matter, Miss Finch, I'm afraid you'll need to be more clear in your details."

She cocked her head and peered at him as

though he'd grown a second nose. "I just wanted to know if I could have a few rags for the Stanhope."

"Rags?"

She scrubbed her hand along the base of the printing press. "It's gotten full of grease and ink on its trek here. It must be cleaned before it can be put together, else everything I print will have smudges."

Good God! The great and terrible subject was rags.

He expelled the stifling breath he'd been holding back, nearly laughed in relief, nearly reached out and kissed the woman, because she was standing too close again, impatient as always. This woman he wanted but couldn't have.

"May I, my lord?"

He smiled because he'd survived once again, because it felt damned good to be standing in the shimmering daylight of his conservatory with Hollie Finch in her practical, ink-stained apron. "You may have all the rags you want, madam."

"Good," she said in her businesslike way. And he would have been just fine for the rest of the day if she hadn't reached up and smoothed her cool fingers between the wool of his waistcoat and the linen of his shirt, if she hadn't pulled gently on his neck cloth. "But I'm sure you'll want to take this off first."

"My neck cloth?" His blood rose like a tropical tide, filled up his chest and then flooded his groin, became a keenly throbbing erection and a deep need.

"And your shirt."

Christ, she would be the death of him. "Before what, madam?"

A rosy impatience tucked itself into the corners of her mouth. "You insisted on helping me assemble the Stanhope, my lord. I'm only warning you that the very first thing you'll learn about ink is that it's indelible."

Oh, but not nearly as indelible as you, my dear. Not nearly.

Chapter 14

~~~₀~~~

"**W**hat is this thing, Hollie?"

Hollie was tying off the drying line when Chip sped past her and grabbed hold of the upright in a hug.

"It's a printing press, Chip." Barely so. She and Everingham had worked for the better part of the morning putting it together. She'd only needed him to help move the large iron pieces; she knew the smaller fittings as well as she knew her own hands. But he had stayed at her elbow, wedged his opinions and his questions into every joint and spring and lever, efficient and orderly in his assault on the Stanhope.

The man had eventually emerged the arrogantly masterful, ink-stained victor. All the parts were back in their proper place, but he'd been a sore test of her patience.

And her heart. He had a wilfully distracting effect on her pulse and her focus—the bay-fresh scent of him, the midnight of his hair, the sinuous brawn of his arm muscles when he stripped down to his shirtsleeves. The glistening streak of ink across his jaw where he'd scrubbed with his knuckles in his battle with the platen spring.

He was a contrary man who filled her with profoundly contrary feelings. The powerful earl and the pressman. His scowling darkness and his reluctant smile, the way he'd fitted Chip so snugly against his broad chest when he'd carried him through the fog.

Not least of all, his maddening deference to her marriage vows. She'd have been well and truly kissed last eve if not for his blazingly misplaced honor. Not that she ought to be allowing him liberties, but just once, she would like to succumb to a bit of that potent appeal. One kiss. Maybe two.

That would be enough.

"What's it do, Hollie?"

The man's precious son was a different sort of distraction altogether, making her yearn for a warm hearth and a home full of voices, all the dear and everyday things that filled her dreams when she forgot that she was a radical reformer bent on spying. Which she'd done little of in the last two days.

"The press prints ink onto paper, Chip." She bent and kissed the top of his head, left a bit of her heart there.

"Ink and paper like you write with?"

"In a way, it writes all by itself."

"It does? What does it print, then?" He ducked beneath the print bed to push and poke.

"It prints almost anything, Chip. Pictures and newspapers and books. Like this one." She held out a copy book of letters and numbers and turned to the front page. "See: 'An apple is red.'"

"Does it say my name in there too?" He flipped through the pages with his quick little fingers.

"Not yet." But it definitely should. Hmm . . .

But he'd already gone to the type cabinet. He had the top drawer open and was peering at a letter pinched between his fingers. "What's this? There's lots of 'em here!"

Hollie chased the little whirlwind, who was faster than his father but no less distracting and invasive. "Those are letters." She picked a C out of its cubby and put it into his small palm. "Here's the first letter of your name. C for Chip."

"C-H-I-P!" he recited without a pause as he inspected the letter carefully, then peered into the type case. "Are all my letters in there? The H an' the I an' the P?"

"Every one of them. Would you like to see?"

"Oh, yes!"

This was the magical part, the thrill of printing. All the pieces coming together into the whole.

Amazingly, Chip stood stock-still at her elbow while Hollie dabbed the letters of his name one by one against an ink ball, then carefully imposed each onto a small sheet of newsprint. When she brought her hand away, Chip whistled.

"Does it really say Chip?"

"It really does." An idea came to her with the force of a miracle: the perfect way to keep the boy occupied while his father learned a bit of fathering and Mumberton got a bit more rest. "How would you like to learn to read more than just your name?"

Chip's chest broadened, nearly popping the buttons on his vest, his eyes alight. "I'd like that more than strawberries."

"Would you be willing to work very hard if I help you at it?"

"You can do that, Hollie? Teach me to read all the words in this box?"

"More words that you can imagine, sweet." She kissed the top of his head, and he shied her a smile.

It seemed a perfect plan, schooling the boy while she had the chance. But Chip's face suddenly slid from utter delight to wide-eyed dread as he looked past her to the only man who could bring on such a dire face.

Everingham. Standing in the glass doorway to the garden, his linen sleeves once again pristine white, his fisted hands cleaned of ink. The afternoon light filtered through the door, catching his profile perfectly, limning his fine nose and the brow that she'd nearly kissed last night.

Chip backed up against her, the paper with his name stamped on it crunching up in his hand, catching his father's startled attention.

It was difficult to say who was more terrified at the moment, father or son.

Everingham's scowled deepened, and Hollie was just about to clout him good with the leather ink ball when he shifted his shoulders and then strode purposefully into the room to stand in front of them, his hands clasped behind his back in a stern-browed and terribly overly fatherly way.

He rocked back on his heels and said to the open-mouthed boy, "What's that in your hand?"

Chip jumped, then scooted backward into the folds of her apron and onto her shoes. Not exactly the approach she would have taken, but at least the man was making an attempt, this wayward lord of hers.

And that made her heart flutter madly, tickling absurdly across her ribs.

"It's just my name, please, sir," Chip whispered.

Charles felt like a big-booted ogre. Bloody hell, Miss Finch was right: the boy was utterly terrified of him! And for not a single reason in the world. He met the woman's militant stare head on, and something in it sent him scrambling to recall her advice.

Something about . . . about . . . something. Hellfire!

"Show me," he said, which roused still another frown out of the woman and fretted the boy's forehead. Perhaps he'd barked it. "Please," he added.

The boy remained sheltered in the skirt of her huge apron, his gaze flicking out from under his dark brows while he slowly unballed the crinkled page and finally held it up, tucked under his nose.

"Chip has learned to spell his name, my lord."

The boy had, apparently. He then rattled off a short string of letters and then stood as still as a lead soldier, waiting for another order from him, another word.

Something encouraging, because it was marvelous indeed; it caught at his heart and his pride. Only six, and the boy was spelling.

"Excellent," Charles said, with an emphatic nod that ought to end the matter. A fine word. None better for a son to hear from a father. But all he got for his effort was more wary staring from the pair.

Miss Finch at last made an extravagantly patient sound in her throat. "Excellent, indeed, Chip. Why don't you take the paper and show Mrs. Riley what you've learned? She'll like that."

"She will, Hollie. And she won't run me out of the kitchen."

The woman's eyes sparkled as she smiled fondly at the boy. "She might even find you a sweet."

"Can I come back here an' help you then?"

"Please do."

The boy flew out the door without a backward glance, and Charles was left to face the woman who'd made a profession out of sitting in judgment on him.

And yet she had a smile caught up her damp eyes. "He's a very quick study, my lord."

Unlike me. That sense of pride surged again, and his stomach calmed with relief that the boy wasn't cursed as he was. "Is he?"

"A very sharp mind—like his father's. But he needs someone to teach him regularly. I assume you'll hire a governess for him soon, but in the meantime I'd consider it a great joy if you'd let me teach Chip to read."

A joy? Painful old memories filled his chest to the brim, and a sudden fear that she knew somehow of his failings. That she was plotting an even more clever blackmail against him. He tamed his heart, but his question came out sharply. "Why?"

She snorted lightly, as though he'd asked why the boy ought to be fed.

"Because he doesn't know how, because no one's ever tried to teach them. Apparently the Bagthorpes' cook told him once how to spell his name. Miraculously, he remembered most of it. But he needs more than that. And he's certainly ready for it."

"He'll be schooled soon enough." *If he stays.*

Though he'd begun to notice the ill-fitting quiet when the boy wasn't in the room. Just as there was without Hollie.

"But what's the harm in starting now, my lord? I'd love to be his teacher for a time."

Charles turned away from her eagerness, making an unfocused study of a bolt in the upright. "What makes you think you could teach a boy his age how to read?"

"I was already reading at his age, whole newspapers. I can teach enough of the basics to give him a good start."

But could you teach a grown man, Hollie?

"How would you do that?" The question slipped out of him like a confession, as though she'd cast a paralyzing spell over him, cracking open a window of hope that he couldn't quite close.

"His letters to begin with. How to sound out the parts of the words so they make sense. And how to love them." She made this magic of hers sound so simple, so orderly and possible. As though the letters didn't dodge and change at random, weren't forever shifting around on the page, tricking him, tempting him to believe in them as she did. "You've seen that he's eager to learn. I know he'll try."

As though she understood what trying meant. "Bloody hell, woman, it takes more than a bit of trying."

God knew he had tried and tried, and he had failed every time.

A lazy bastard, that's what you are, boy. Stupid. Ill-gotten. No son of mine.

"You're right. But I'll make it as simple for him as possible. I'm not an ogre. Please, my lord."

He wanted to say no, to shout it to the heavens, because he wanted no part of it, because even now his stomach was churning with a cold memory of recrimination and the shame of failure.

I raised a fool, damn you, boy!

Yet Charles had sworn that he would never treat a child as he'd been treated. And what would it hurt for Miss Finch to teach the boy how to spell a few words?

"Where would you do this teaching?"

She'd been hanging on the edge of his reply, ready to pounce should he refuse. His question softened her brow, and her voice went charmingly humble all of a sudden.

"In the gatehouse. After supper."

"You've got this worked out, haven't you?"

"It's a simple thing, my lord. I think the world of my new little friend." There it was in her eyes: the reach of her heart, the way she'd already enfolded the boy, the challenge she'd issued for him to do the same. A motherly sort.

And then he wondered if a babe was even now growing in her belly, wondered when she and her cowardly, inattentive husband had last been together. If the man was even now skulking around the estate, looking for an entry point.

By God, how could he not be tearing up the countryside for her, for all that heady passion, for that astonishing smile, the scent of her hair, the silk of it?

"Do I have your permission, my lord?"

Christ, anything to keep her out of trouble while she waited to be rescued; anything to keep himself from following after her like a besotted fool. "You'll conduct these lessons here in the conservatory, where I can keep an eye on you."

She laughed gently. "Are you afraid I'll corrupt your son with my radical leanings?"

His son. "I'm utterly terrified."

"You should be." She was obviously pleased with herself, with him. "I'll need chalk and a free-standing chalkboard and a few small ones."

She started scribbling on a scrap of paper, so dreadfully free with her words.

"Give Mumberton your list."

"Oh, and one more very important thing, my lord." She stuck out her hand. "I need the devil's tail. You've hidden it somewhere, and I can't work the press without it, remember."

How could he possibly forget? "Will after supper do, madam?"

"I suppose it must, my lord."

Hollie kept her smile to herself as she watched the man leave through the garden door without a backward glance. Let him think he held the key to Captain Spindleshanks's seditious tracts. He didn't realize that it wasn't just the press that was important.

The words were made with letters.

And there were great handfuls of them in the bag she'd taken off to the gatehouse. With a chase and a print block smuggled there in her huge apron pockets, she could compose to her heart's content in the privacy of her bedchamber, and then steal a moment with the Stanhope when Everingham wasn't looking.

He was a vigilant man, but she would have to be more so. More devious than she'd ever been as Captain Spindleshanks. And if Charles happened to be her target, then so be it. The fault was his, because the truth was in his power and he chose to ignore it.

But the idea of deceiving the great earl of Everingham wasn't sitting as comfortably as it had a few days ago.

He wasn't supposed to be gentle or aching or anything but unremittingly wicked. He certainly wasn't supposed to be redeemable.

Deceiving Charles Stirling was getting easier by the hour. Deceiving herself, her heart, was becoming impossible.

Chapter 15

◦◦◦◦◦◦◦

"**T**hat big hunter's in his stall, m'lord, champin' for a hard workout."

"I'll give him just that, Carlson," Charles said, taking Briscoe's bit and bridle off the peg. He was pleased that he'd only sought out Miss Finch in the conservatory twice that morning. That he'd stayed with her in the gatehouse last evening only long enough for two proper cups of tea. God knows he'd wanted to stay much longer, and for far more than tea. But he'd resisted, had gone back to his cold cell and a monkishly ice-cold bath.

Hellfire! "How does the rest of the stock look, Carlson?"

"Every one of them fine and out to their pasturing, sir."

"I'll take a look while I'm about." Charles left the tack room and walked down the corridor of empty stalls to the windowed end of the western row. He'd be gone most of the day to view the quarry road at Wheelwright and to mark out the site of two new dower cottages at Grompton.

If Miss Finch needed the devil's tail for her song birds, she'd just have to wait till the evening.

Briscoe wickered softly to him and tucked his nose under Charles's hand. But the horse had an odd, skittish look about him, his eyes wide, his ears flicking and flattening in a way he'd never seen before.

"Hold yourself, Briscoe. You'll be out of here and running free in a moment."

Briscoe took the bit as though he wanted to be long gone from the stall.

"Woah, there, boy." Charles stroked the sleek neck and slipped the bridle over Briscoe's ears. He would have led him out into the corridor but for the sudden sun-gilded rain of straw cascading from the loft above, followed immediately by a scraping sound—something larger than a cat. He shut the stall gate and eased out into the aisle.

"Who's there?"

The rain stopped, and the sounds. The feed was in from the fields, stored in the loft for the winter. There shouldn't have been anyone up there.

"This is Charles Stirling, whoever you are. Come down here at once."

The stillness lengthened. And then, "I can't, sir." It was the littlest voice he'd ever heard, squeaky with a fearfulness that made his stomach lift and then fall like a stone.

"Chip?"

The quiet and the rain of straw came again, landing on his shoulder and Briscoe's rump. "Yes, sir."

The boy was not ten feet over his head, able enough to talk, hardly in mortal danger, yet Charles's heart was racing at a full gallop. "You can't get down?"

"Nope."

"Are you hurt?"

"No, sir."

"Stuck on something?"

Silence from the straw again, and then came a teary admission. "I'm scared."

His heart gave a leaping loop that sent him to the post ladder. "I'm coming right up, boy."

Charles made the floor above in three bounds and came face to face with the woefullest little fellow he'd ever seen.

"Hello," Charles said simply, because Hollie had said it was an excellent place to start.

"Hello, sir."

His next impulse was to instruct the boy on how to get oneself down out of a loft; turning around and hanging on with one's hands, and trusting one's legs until they found purchase on the first rung of the ladder.

But the boy's face was a mask of hopeless terror. And Charles wouldn't have wanted to hear that from his own father at the tender age of six. He'd have wanted to . . . well, to fall into his father's arms and feel that nothing in the world could hurt him now.

"It's a way down, isn't it, Chip?"

The boy snuffled and nodded. "A long way."

"When did you climb up here?"

"Right after breakfast."

Three hours ago. "Hungry again?"

"Yessir."

"Let's get us down from here, then. Can you hold onto my neck?"

The boy scanned his face, skeptical at first, then resolute.

"I'm pretty sure."

"You'll have to scoot forward a little and get up onto your knees. I won't let you fall."

Chip caught his lip with his teeth and pushed himself to his knees. "Like this?"

"Exactly. Very good, Chip."

With nary a grunt of warning, the boy launched himself forward and gripped Charles around the neck in a stranglehold, scrubbing his teary cheek against Charles's eye.

"Well, yes, Chip," he said calmly, thankful that he'd been holding onto the post. "That'll do fine."

The boy clung to him like a limpet as Charles eased him over the side and climbed down the ladder with him. Chip clung to him even after that, until Charles knelt all the way to the ground and let off his passenger.

Charles remained on his knee as the boy backed up against the stall door and fixed his eyes on him in that terrified silence.

Repairing the short distance seemed vastly important. "What were you doing up there?" A stupid question. He was a boy; boys climb around in haylofts. "Never mind, Chip. Just tell someone next time."

"You, sir?" He scraped at his nose with his sleeve.

Charles stood and nodded. "That would be fine." More than fine, he wanted to add.

"Because I don't think Mumberton could come and get me as good as you did, sir."

A zinging kind of pride filled up Charles's chest and stung the backs of his eyes. "Mumberton tries his best."

"I know, sir."

Charles cleared his throat of a restricting lump. "So you weren't scared?"

"Maybe at first."

Briscoe chose just that moment to reach his huge head over the stall door and breathe a snort against the top of the boy's head, rocketing him across the aisle and sending his arms around Charles's legs.

"He's big!"

"He's an old softie." He wasn't, but the boy didn't need more terror, and Briscoe *was* even-tempered. Charles patted the little shoulder, marveling at the miniature construction of bone and muscle, the vulnerability. "Ever been on a horse?"

"No." With a whole lot of head shaking.

"Would you like to ride?"

Chip gasped and pointed to the hunter. "On him?"

"I'll keep hold of you." Charles reached into his pocket and pulled out a lump of sugar. "Give him this, and he'll be your friend for life."

The boy looked skeptically brave as he extended the sugar on his palm, ready to yank his hand away. But Briscoe gently nibbled at it with his lips and a snort, and Chip squealed in glee.

"What's his name?"

"Briscoe."

"What does he eat for breakfast?"

"Oats. Now let's find *you* some food before we go."

All the way into the stable yard, into the plowed fields, and along the edge of the limestone quarry, Chip asked an unending flood of questions, offered bits of boyhood wisdom, and showed a fearlessness that nearly brought Charles to his knees in terror.

"Let's go show Hollie what we can do!" Chip's

little heels popped against Briscoe's back, his legs too short to reach the horse's flanks.

Feeling suddenly skilled at fathering yet nervous as hell, Charles led the hunter and his charge around the corner to the front of the manor, prepared to show off to Miss Finch.

"Looka there, sir!"

A vaguely familiar flashy black coach sat in the drive. A footman perched on top, and the two horses were matched bays.

Lord Bowles. Bloody wonderful.

He was standing on the front steps, talking with Miss Finch. Dressed to the nines and gushing over the woman.

Charles would have gladly gone another month without a visit from the blustering young lord, but there was a report to compile, answers to find. He owed the woman at least a nod toward the facts she'd offered.

"Hollie, look at us!" Chip was waving both arms at her from atop the horse. A magnificent smile lit her face as the noonday sun spun its gold into the strands of her unbound hair.

She waved her arm, and Bowles turned, shielding his eyes from the glare. Then he left Miss Finch and met Charles at the base of the stairs, his hand extended.

"Afternoon, Everingham. I say, who is this young man?"

Charles looked to the woman at the door,

knew that she had heard Bowles's question, just as the boy had heard it. "My son, Bowles. Chip."

Charles could see the instant, erroneous, connection that Bowles made. The woman waiting for them on the stairs and the son obviously born on the wrong side of the blanket. But the man had the sense, the survival instinct, to leave the rest of his questions unasked, piled up for the gossip mill to sort through and pass judgment upon.

Charles caught the full force of Miss Finch's approving gaze against his chest. She'd not only heard Bowles's question, she must have heard his own answer.

The boy was his. A simple fact that had begun to crowd his lungs with sunlight, that tattered his breathing when he looked into the little face.

Bowles sounded taken aback. "Well, I say, then, Lord Everingham. Very good, Very good. And I've brought you news from Sidmouth."

Miss Finch hurried down the stairs. She winked at Charles as she took the reins out of his hands, and sent his head spinning with the stunningly intimate brush of her fingers against the inside of his wrist.

"I'll take care of Chip, my lord."

The boy was already leaning down toward her from the saddle, his cheeks crimson, his dark curls lifted by the breeze. "We rode everywhere, Hollie."

"You look like a brave warrior up there, Chip. I want to hear all about it." She flashed Charles another heart-swelling smile, then led the boy and the horse away.

Her acknowledgment of his progress in the art of fatherhood set well and deeply in his chest. It seemed important here in the harshly examining light of the day, with Bowles looking on and his son twisted around in the saddle, grinning like blazes at him, for her to know that he wasn't a brute, that he'd taken her daunting advice and had found it priceless.

Charles dragged his attention from the woman and his son and the rump of that great, patient beast of a horse.

"Come in, Bowles. I haven't got all day."

At least, he hadn't time for the blustering young lord who followed him up the stairs and into the huge house, which was fast and firmly becoming the home it had never been.

Because of you, Hollie Finch, and your indelible heart.

Chapter 16

❦❦❦

"His name is Briscoe, Hollie, and he lives right there in the stables with the other horses." Chip slid down off the hunter and into Hollie's arms.

"Briscoe looks tired and hungry," Hollie said, distracted from Chip's bouncing joy by her blazing curiosity about Everingham and Bowles's message from Sidmouth.

She'd wanted to race down the steps and embrace them both when she heard Everingham introduce Chip as his son; wanted desperately to know how they had managed to find each other. But she'd kept her joy in check and let her heart fill with admiration for the contrary man.

"Carlson's gonna feed Briscoe some oats." Chip patted the horse on the flank as the amused stableman uncinched the girth and lifted the saddle off.

"I think it's time we go feed *you*, Chip. Do you like oats?"

He laughed and scrambled out of her arms. "I like oatmeal cakes!"

And he was off across the stable yard on his lean little legs. Hollie followed him to the kitchen and ate a dinner of bread and butter and soup with Chip, then carried him up to his bed when his eyelids began to droop.

He was snoozing softly before his head hit the pillow.

Now she would join Everingham's impromptu Peterloo commission meeting. Casually, as though she'd stumbled upon it. And she nearly did just that, barely missing Mumberton as he was coming out of the kitchen with a tray of tea.

Tea! "Is that for his lordship, Mumberton?"

"It is indeed, Mrs. MacGillnock."

"I'll be happy to take the tray in to him and Lord Bowles. You're a very busy man."

"But not nearly as busy as I was a few days ago, ma'am. I'm very grateful that you've taken charge of the lad."

"A pleasure, Mumberton." Hollie took hold of the tray with determined hands, praying that she wouldn't have to wrestle it from him. "No trouble at all."

"Thank you, then, Mrs. MacGillnock." Mumberton released the tray with a rattle of cups and saucers, then went on his shuffling way back to the servants' hall.

Feeling like a sneak thief, Hollie notched her chin into the air and hurried off toward the murmur of voices coming from inside Everingham's office.

They were squaring off across Everingham's desk, Everingham's face stony, Bowles obviously trying to explain himself.

"No one could say, exactly, Everingham. No word from Trafford and apparently that fellow Nadin wouldn't talk. Seemed uncommonly stubborn."

"I don't care how stubborn the man is. If the men under his watch dismounted after the mob had dispersed and then stood about while the dying and the wounded were writhing on the field, then someone in authority must have been there to attend to the casualties. Someone local, to record the names and the injuries."

"Apparently not."

"Where were the damn magistrates?"

Hollie didn't hear Bowles's answer for the thundering roar in her ears as the command was given: *Take their flags!* The horses surged into the people, and then the groans and the screams and the confusion began. She'd grabbed her father's hand in the first wave, but they were separated in the second. And he fell beneath the slash of a sabre in the next. She swam through the crushing panic to find him, to hold him as he lay dying.

But she wasn't on the field at St. Peter's. This was the office of Charles Stirling, and the great earl was looking at her, his brows drawn in dark suspicion.

"Yes, Miss Finch?" he asked abruptly.

Feeling thoroughly exposed, she slid the tray onto the side table. "I thought I'd give Mumberton a hand with the tea."

Everingham's glower turned to flint, and his frown deepened. "Lord Bowles is just leaving."

"Alas, I am, Miss Finch." The carnal interest had returned to Bowles's eyes, to the pressure of his hand as he bent over her own. "A long journey back to the City, I'm afraid. Perchance we'll meet again."

"Come, Bowles." Everingham caught the man's arm before Hollie had a chance to answer and marched with him through the doorway, leaving her alone in the office—with the table spread with papers from the Peterloo files.

The treasure trove she'd been seeking since she arrived nearly a week ago.

Bowles's voice still rang out in the hall above Everingham's thunder. She hadn't long, didn't want to be caught snooping. She sloshed herself a cup of tea and then sauntered to the far side of the table, against the windows, putting the table and its treasure between her and the door.

She sipped her tea and read swiftly and watched the door, never touching a single sheet of paper. Oh, what a great lot of hocus pocus it all was, smoke and shadows and official prevarication! Depositions from magistrates and merchants and mill owners, articles from *The Times*, letters and testimonials, sworn affidavits. One-sided poppycock.

And nothing from Sidmouth, at least, that she could see. Her fingers itched to shift the papers and read more, but Everingham could walk in at any moment—

"Worth the reading, madam?"

Hollie glanced up at him over the rim of her teacup, at the animal grace of him in the doorway, schooling herself and her heart to take the dark midnight of his eyes and his accusation in her stride, chiding herself for letting her attraction to him wedge itself into her spying. Yet she was plagued suddenly with the unreasonable suspicion that he'd left her here with his files apurpose, not to catch her with them, but to spark a debate.

Thoroughly unreasonable, given his thunderous staring.

"Interesting, my lord, but nothing more than I had expected. One side of the case only. And Joseph Nadin refusing to talk doesn't surprise me in the least."

"Why is that?" he asked easily, pouring a cup of tea for himself.

Hmm. Was her stubborn commissioner at last making a stab at interviewing her?

"Ask anyone in Manchester. The Deputy Constable made his fortune there as a thief-catcher, a man known for arresting innocent people because he's paid £2 and a Tyburn ticket for every person convicted of a felony. God knows he'll die a rich man."

She couldn't read his silence or the perilous ease of his posture.

"As for Trafford and the other men of the yeomanry, they were hardly professional soldiers, merely cowardly publicans, watchmakers, insurance agents, farriers. Each with too much to lose to offer the truth in a sworn statement, and none of them friendly to the idea of reform."

Everingham idly picked up an affidavit from the disarray on the table and lifted his eyes to her from under those silky black lashes that stirred her pulse. "You must have seen the ambulance carriages brought in that afternoon to convey the wounded to the Manchester Infirmary."

"Only hours later. In the meantime, the town was patrolled by the troops, the streets were nearly empty, and the shops closed because everyone was terrified of enraging the yeomanry to more violence. Did Bowles find you a casualty list?"

"No. Apparently there's no such item available at the moment."

But there was; the Peterloo Relief Committee

was collecting the information to give aid to the families of the fallen. It was volatile information, not to be trusted to anyone in the government.

"Did Bowles verify that the marchers came with their wives and children and fathers?"

Everingham dropped the affidavit onto the pile with the others. "Which makes the marchers all the more foolish than I'd first imagined. Manchester was a powder keg, a dangerous place for anyone, let alone children. I don't care what their intentions were. And now it seems, madam, that your Captain Spindleshanks has made another appearance."

"Has he?" Absurd, of course, the costume was safely hidden in the attic of the gatehouse. But she ought to at least look worried in a wifely way. "Oh, no! My Adam? When?"

He eyed her from beneath his brow, as though she already must have known this. "The night before last."

Impossible. She was already here at Everingham by then. "Oh, where, my lord? Is he well?"

He hadn't blinked. "In the north, outside a mill in Yorkshire."

The Leeds Reformers. She had intended to put in a fleeting appearance there this week to rally support for the victims of the massacre. But it wouldn't be the first time that Captain Spindleshanks had been the subject of a well-placed rumor. She'd been seen riding at midnight along the Liverpool road when she'd actually been in

London at a suffrage convention. This was no imposter, just the active and convenient imaginations of her supporters, with a bit of help from the press.

But Everingham could think whatever he liked. She laid an anxious, wifely hand across her bosom. "Dear me, he wasn't caught, was he? Adam isn't in jail?"

"He's not. It must be difficult for a devoted husband like yours to choose between making a costumed appearance in Leeds and coming to rescue his wife."

She hadn't meant to snort and dared not look at him. "I don't think I need rescuing, do I?"

"I don't know? Do you?" He was crafty and dodging, this earl.

"Why haven't you told your commission members who I am?"

Charles had been waiting for that question, though he still hadn't formed a satisfactory answer. "You would only distract from the facts, madam. A temptation for the Privy Council to overreact."

A temptation of another sort for him. That cascade of hair that sought his hands when she stood too near him. The gleam of green in her eyes as she took another proper sip of tea.

"So you admit that Liverpool and his Cabinet have their faults?"

"Would, madam, that we were all as clearsighted as you."

She bunched her brow into a frown, then set her teacup on the tray. "I have work to do, my lord. On my Stanhope. And you have the devil's tail."

"Where's the boy?"

"Chip is sleeping. Little boys need a lot of that."

"Merely a pause in the day when they can store up more energy."

She bit her lower lip. Whether hiding concealed a smile or a sharp retort, it charmed him, inflamed him. Her little sigh nearly drove him to cross the distance between them and claim some of that neglected, unappreciated passion, spent so generously on a wastrel husband who didn't deserve her.

"You made him very happy today, my lord."

Not nearly as happy as you made me.

"Charles," he said. "My name is Charles. Please use it. 'My lord' makes you sound like a servant."

"Ah, that's right, I'm your prisoner." She raised a challenging brow, daring him to deny it. "Will you be coming to the conservatory anytime soon?"

"Soon will have to do. I have work of my own."

"Of course." She flounced out the door, taking the sunlight with her. And the sweetness of the air.

Leaving him to wonder at the mildness of her

reaction to the news about her negligent husband, who was apparently unconcerned that his wife was being held against his arrest.

Perhaps all wasn't well at the MacGillnocks' home.

An hour later, Charles found Miss Finch standing in front of the tilted shelf in the type cabinet, looking ripely pregnant in her billowing apron. She was pinching pieces of metal type out of the cubbyholes and then sticking them from right to left into a long, slotted piece of wood that was corralled inside a contraption much like a small, three-sided picture frame.

"What's that you're doing, madam?"

"Getting ready to make a registration test." Her fingers moved from the bins to the little frame like lightning. "One of a dozen adjustments I need to make before I can start on the song birds."

"What does that say?" It was oddly easy to ask the question, when he had always been so careful not to show his vulnerability. But few people could be expected to read the type with the skill of the lovely printer, who had a streak of ink on the bridge of her nose.

She held the frame still and read from its confounding landscape. " 'Woodlark. Smaller than the skylark. Voice trilling, sings while airborne.' " She glanced up at him, her eyes luminously green. "And that's all I've gotten so far, my lord."

"Charles."

"Yes. It's a facing page for the woodlark etching . . . Charles." She smiled up at him, then shoved an escaped tendril of hair off her brow and went back to her composing.

"You're very quick at that, madam."

"Hollie," she said without looking at him.

He caught a huge smile inside his gut, a bloody bonfire. "You're very quick, Hollie."

She made a proud little *harrumph* in her chest. "I can compose a full page of print in less than an hour. As long as the copy is mine and I'm composing on the fly."

"For the late-breaking edition of the *Tuppenny Press*?"

"Ha! I've beat *The Times* to the street in my day." She turned all that elemental brightness on him, then set down the block she was working on and pulled seven large letter-blocks from one of the drawers, hiding them from him.

"Now what?" he asked, utterly fascinated by the magic in her hands.

"A surprise." She quickly stacked the seven letters side by side onto a stick that had a channel cut down its center. She transferred the letters into a block, then locked it into the center of a much larger plate that had a border of some sort, and cinched everything down in the bed of the press.

"The chase," she said, placing a sheet of thick paper into the leaning frisket frame.

He'd never seen a press actually printing anything. The Stanhope was an unwieldy, woebegone creature to assemble. But her movements were like an intricate dance, as familiar to her as breathing, exotic and excluding to him.

"It's very quiet just now," she said, glancing up at him too briefly and then going back to her dance. "Chip must still be asleep."

"He is. I checked." He'd meant only to glance in on the boy, trying to gauge the next wave of battle, but he'd stayed to marvel. Loose-limbed and flushed and breathing steadily.

She smiled that knowing smile of hers, catching him in the heart: a great, thumping wallop of admiration and gratitude and something else that he'd rather not examine.

Because it involved too much hope and too little honor.

She hummed as she inked the leather balls on the marble-topped inking table, pounded and rolled the pair together in a steady rhythm, then inked the letters, folded down the frisket onto the bed, and slid the whole platform easily beneath the bulk of the huge machine.

"Now I need the tail, my lord," she said, with a smile tucked into the corners of her mouth. He brought it to her from the table and she screwed it into the fitting. Then she pulled it sideways with the full might of her shoulders and arms.

He hadn't been able to resist bending to watch

the platen press against the paper; his curiosity strained toward what she was printing.

This *surprise*.

Bloody hell—something she would make him read.

The slate floor beneath him began to shift, and his heart slowed with his pulse, making it difficult to breathe.

"When I'm working with one or two other people, I can manage two hundred copies of the *Tuppenny* an hour."

He wanted to make excuses and leave her, but he couldn't manage a step as she reversed her dreadful, fascinating dance.

He stood rooted to the ground, watched her brows knit as she leaned over the bed and carefully peeled the paper off the inked form. Then she held it up for him to see.

"Charles," he said aloud.

He said. Because he'd read it.

His name. Clearly, unmistakably. He'd never seen it so plainly before. He didn't know the letters or the sound of them, but—great God, had he actually read the word? Or did he just recognize the shape of it?

"Well, Charles?" She was still holding the piece aloft, still smiling patiently beside it. "What do you think?"

His heart was rocketing around inside his chest. He hadn't any breath to answer her; it was tangled up in a shout of joy that he didn't dare let loose, caught up on the tremendous desire to beseech her to print another word for him. And another.

He wanted her name this time. Desperately wanted to know what it looked like.

"Hollie."

She quirked her head. "Yes?"

Caught. Distracted.

"Fascinating," he said.

"Endlessly." She smiled, walking away from him to the window, where she held the page up to the light, inspecting something across the flat surface. "Addicting, I think."

He followed her, his enchantress in her inky muslin apron, battling to keep himself from capturing her waist and turning her, from carrying her into his arms and kissing her. "What are you looking at?"

She reached up and pointed to the arc of letters that made up his name. "I'm checking the sharpness of the type as it touches the paper. Do you see there?"

He bent his knees so that he could see the flat of the sheet from her vantage point, chastising himself for seeking the scent of her. "Why is this important?"

Hollie could hardly keep from sighing, had to work to keep her hands steady. His chest was so warm against her back, his mouth so near her temple, his words hot against her ear.

"Well, you see, Charles, the kiss has to be just right."

His would certainly be. A perfect kiss. A simple thing to turn slightly and touch her mouth to his chin, to sample the sheen of his afternoon beard.

"The what, Hollie?" he asked, his question brushing past her cheek, one hand on her shoulder, the other on her waist, hot-palmed and huge, the searing heat of him invading the weave of her apron, seeping right through to her chemise, spreading down her back and into her drawers.

"The kiss," she said breathlessly, "shouldn't be too deep or too light."

It was difficult to recall exactly how they'd gotten onto this subject. Even more difficult to think at all as he turned her toward him, and hovered over her in his possessive way.

"Just deep enough, Hollie?" He tilted her chin so that she was forced to look directly into those midnight eyes, the eyes that came to her in her dreams. "This kiss you speak of?"

Yes, oh, please do. And for as long as you wish.

Then she realized the depth of her error and stumbled backward a step into the Stanhope, which only made him catch her around the waist.

Oh, my, his hands were warm and broad, his thumbs meeting low on her belly.

"That's what it's called, my lord. Sir. Charles. A kiss." She took a deep breath and rattled on, so aware of the contours of his hands and the fit of his hips against her. "The kiss impression, actually. The depth of the letter imposted against the paper. It's very important."

"I imagine it would be."

"Oh, yes." There wasn't a single inch of her that wasn't blushing and on fire. Glowing beneath his hands. She stepped out of his startling trap and escaped to the drying line hanging across the room.

"May I have one?"

His rumbled question turned her on her heel and stole her breath with the smoky fog of his gaze, the hard-muscled, heated scent of him. She'd been banking on his honor, his restraint— because it appeared that she had none.

"A kiss? You forget, sir, I'm a married woman."

"It," he said, his eyes sharper than before. "I meant, may I have it? The sheet of paper with my name on it."

Ah. She pegged it on the line. "The ink hasn't dried yet, and it's impossible to get it off anything it stains. Can it wait until later?"

"If you think it best." He started toward the garden door, then turned back, so very tall, so different than she'd always believed. "Oh, and Hollie . . ."

"Yes?"

"Believe me, I'm not likely to forget the state of your marriage."

"Neither am I, Charles."

Which made her want to cry.

Chapter 17

His library seemed different tonight. The lamps giving off more light, the room feeling occupied, almost friendly. He'd never given the books housed inside the wire-hatched cases any more notice than a paper-brocaded wall. They merely took up space and defined his title and his class: a label for the room, as the oven labeled the kitchen.

Now the books seemed to be whispering to him.

Making promises.

His tidy desktop had been merely a piece of furniture, with a silver inkwell that dried up regularly, unused, a blotter without blots, pristine pointed pens that never needed replacing. Its edge was marked with half-moons where his heels dug in when he was pretending to relax and read.

CHARLES.

The picture of his name was still clear; black letters on ivory. And Hollie's warm smile.

His throat closed up; the sting of hope and gratitude seared the backs of his eyes. He'd given up trying so long ago. And yet he'd actually read the word this afternoon! He was certain of it.

And here it was. She'd put the page on his desk sometime in the late afternoon, displayed it squared to the corners of his blotter, the edges deckled, as she called them.

Surely he could copy the printed lines.

I'd love to be his teacher for a time.

She'd promised to make it simple enough for the boy.

And for me, Hollie? As simple as this? His hand shook as he opened the lid of the inkwell; his breathing quickened in a familiar kind of panic as he picked up the pen. He'd learned long ago how to scribe his signature, but that had quickly become an unreadable slash, resembled nothing like the original letters.

His name, lost to him.

Until now.

The paper lying in front of him was as daunting as any had ever been. But these letters were large and strong and printed by Hollie.

Her smiling surprise for him.

A bloody huge surprise. A challenge. A tiny miracle that no one would notice but him. He dipped the pen into the ink, put the nib to the paper, and drew the first letter of his name. A simple curve.

C.

The result was shaky and gobbed with ink at the end of the stroke. But readable—and heart-pounding because he couldn't recall the name of it.

He took another steadying breath, dipped the pen into the ink again, and tried the second letter, unable to recall its name either for the ringing in his ears. Simply two short lines crossed with a hatch. His palms were sweating; a trickle of pure terror and sizzling hope ran down his back.

He inked the nib again, ready to try the next letter, when he felt someone watching him intently. The tingling across his shoulders, the prickling fear at his scalp kept his eyes riveted to the pen barrel.

Hollie. It had to be. She'd come to spy on him on her cat feet.

One glance at his chicken-scratch efforts and she'd know exactly what he was doing, what he was trying to do. She would use the information against him in her next breath.

He grabbed at the dozen well-rehearsed defenses scattering around inside his brain as he braced himself for the battle, as he looked up and into the eyes of his accuser.

But it was his own face looking back at him, his much, much younger self.

"Chip." The boy's hair was a darkly curling jumble, one side mashed by sleep, his eyes twinkling.

"I can write my name, too." That huge, heart-tugging smile was missing another tooth.

"What happened to your tooth?"

Chip stuck his tongue into the gap. "It came out in the kitchen. Hollie and I were sharing an apple and there it was! Didn't hurt at all. Can I show you how I write my name?"

A moot question, because Chip was already climbing onto his knee and grabbing the pen out of his hand.

"This is a big C," he said, his tongue working as he wrote just below the first letter that Charles had scribed. His hair smelled of apples. "Hey! My C's just like yours."

His own attempt had been larger, a bit more precise. Not bad, actually.

"H is the next one." Chip dunked the nib into the ink with an astonishing eagerness and dribbled it across the pristine blotter and onto the page.

Charles remembered relentless dread, not the boy's boundless, unsettling joy, his driving sense of discovery. "When did you learn to do this?"

"Last night. Hollie showed me. She's my teacher now." He whipped around to grin up at Charles, his eyes brighter than before as he pointed back at the page. "Look, sir! My H is like yours too!"

H. Aitch. The first was a sea, like the ocean.

He watched the boy finish off two more letters. "This one's an I," he said, "and this is a P. Chip!" He turned again on Charles's knee.

"Chip."

"But it's really Charles. Like yours. Can you write 'Charles' for me, sir? Right here."

Holy Christ! But the boy had already shoved the pen into Charles's hand, inking his palm and his wrist. His usual defenses rose up around him like a flock of voracious ravens, blue-black wings brushing at him, obscuring his vision.

He was about to stand up and bluster at the boy, to distance himself from the threat, when Hollie appeared at the side of the desk, his guardian angel, and peered down at the untidy page of letters.

"Your name's there already, Chip," she said, leaning down and bracing her elbows on the desktop, her mouth just inches from his own, her lashes brushing her cheeks. "See: here's 'Charles' at the top."

She lifted her gentle eyes to Charles, neither accusing nor suspicious, just pleased, sharing a moment with him, making him wonder how long she'd been watching.

"There it is!" The boy pointed to the name. "I can write that!"

Charles watched over the top of the boy's

head, following the unsteady but determined stroke of Chip's pen, watching the ink spreading between his little fingers, as his amazing son scribed the name they shared.

You can do it, boy! He wanted to say that aloud, had desperately wanted to hear it from his own father. But the encouragement came instead from the sublime woman at his elbow in her softly ripened voice.

" 'Charles,' " she said. "Oh, Chip, that's very good."

"I am good."

Charles thought his coat buttons would burst.

Hollie wanted to kiss them both: Chip for his huge grin and his curling hair and for the little stick horse he was now drawing in the corner of the paper while he sat wriggling in his father's lap. And Charles because he seemed enormously enthralled by his son's progress, and because he . . . well, he was just ultimately fine and good.

He tilted a private smile at her that simply melted her heart and sluiced it down into her belly like summer honey, that made her pulse skip along lightly. And all that lightness made breathing a bit difficult.

She was about to suggest that she and Chip take some time to do a little reading lesson while the boy was focused when she noticed a letter from Sidmouth sitting with others, leaning against the lamp base.

It was probably just ministerial blathering. Charles received so many letters from the Home Secretary every day, there were enough messengers to Everingham Hall to warrant a full-time traffic warden.

But Charles was Sidmouth's advisor, and any punishment against the press and the people that might be brewing in the Home Office would surely cross his desk before it was presented in Parliament.

But she could hardly just steal letters off his desk and slip them into her apron pocket while Charles watched his son drawing pictures or rifle his files in the middle of the day. A midnight raid would have to do. Crawling in through the window, if necessary.

"Is that a horse, Chip?" Charles was peering at the little drawing.

"It's Briscoe. See his white sock?"

"There you are, my lord!" Mumberton rushed through the library door in his shirtsleeves and danced a little jig in his impatience. "It's Carlson, sir; he says the foal is coming."

"What's a foal?" Chip dropped the pen and whipped his head around to his father.

"It's a baby horse, Chip," Charles said evenly, tousling the boy's hair as he lifted him off his lap and stood him in the chair. "How long, Mumberton?"

"Sounds like right now, my lord." Mumberton shuffled off down the hallway.

Chip's eyes were saucer-wide. "Carlson's bringing a baby horse to the stables? Can I go see it, sir?"

"Well, Chip, that's. . . ." Charles raised a worried eyebrow at Hollie, a wordless consultation.

Should I take him, Hollie? was his question. *Is he old enough to understand?* The man was certainly doing his best, and Chip was a bundle of curiosity.

"Chip and I'll both come along with you. If that's all right, my lord?"

"More than all right, madam." He smiled and gestured toward the door.

"Come on, then!" Chip grabbed Hollie's hand and dragged her past Charles, leaving her the briefest glance at the jumble of envelopes leaning against the lamp, hoping they would stay put until she could find the opportunity to read the ones from Sidmouth.

Hoping most of all that Charles would forgive her when she was finally gone, when he finally learned what she had done.

The stable yard was awash with lantern light and scurrying grooms. She knew very little about horses, but this seemed like far more excitement than an ordinary foaling would require.

"Briscoe's the sire, Hollie," Charles said, shrugging out of his coat, his eyes straying to Chip, who was clinging to the fence rail. "His foal will be worth a great deal someday."

So are sons, Charles, she wanted to say. But it

seemed that he was coming to that notion on his own.

It was the most natural thing in the world for Hollie to reach out and take his coat from him while he rolled up his linen sleeves to the elbow. The wool was still warm, smelling of his day in the fields.

She stayed with Chip in the lantern-lit stable yard until it became clear that the mare was going to deliver in her own good time. It was after ten when she finally got the boy well storied and tucked into his bed.

The lamps were still blazing in the stable yard when she skulked down the hall and into Charles's library. Snooping. Spying. Betrayal was nearer the feeling that slithered through her limbs.

There was one letter to Charles from Lord Liverpool and three from Sidmouth. The last of them sounded a tocsin in her heart—a clear threat in the offing.

. . . but my colleagues have remained unconvinced of the imperious and urgent necessity of adopting this measure, which would meet and overcome a danger greater than any to which the country has been exposed since the accession of the present Royal Family to the throne.

"What measure do you mean, Lord Pudding?" she whispered.

What were they planning? And what did Charles know about it?

She'd have to keep her eyes open for letters from the Privy Council. When details of this only measure arrived, she'd copy it and see that its message was broadcast before the hammer could fall.

Hollie doused the candle and left the library, her heart as heavy as lead.

Chapter 18

Charles had convinced himself that his treks down to the gatehouse sprang out of duty to his investigation. The fact that he did it every night after the main house was quiet, after Chip was tucked safely into bed, was merely a measure of his determination to catch Captain Spindleshanks in a dangerous moment of weakness: creeping up the drive to finally rescue his wife, scurrying from shadow to shadow, cloak and tricorn and long hair blowing in the night breezes.

But the deeper truth was utterly transparent to him: he was in danger of losing his heart to another man's wife.

Hollie Finch MacGillnock.

Mrs. Captain Spindleshanks.

Hell and damnation.

There was something so unsettlingly right and natural in their evenings together and in their days, in the nimble way she debated him. He craved her slightest touch, admired her bull-headedness and her idealism, adored the way she nurtured his son as though the pair were flesh and blood.

And yet he couldn't act upon this madness. It went against everything honorable that he'd schooled himself to become. He couldn't relax his guard for a moment, else he'd find himself slipping his arms around her, because she fitted too naturally inside his embrace.

There was too much at stake to risk that kind of contact, and it had all begun to feel too much like a courting dance.

The thought that troubled him the most was that Adam MacGillnock had become a rival with the deck stacked inevitably in Charles's favor. Once the man was indicted and tried—whether in person or *in absentia*—and his fate was decided by the judge and jury, Hollie Finch might be a free woman.

Would be free. And then what, if he was the agent of the man's destruction?

There was something unsavory and unjust in the power that he held over MacGillnock. Which was the reason he had to step away from the man's wife before it got that far.

And yet here he was, setting his trap, not wanting it sprung.

His heart rattling around inside his chest, he followed the gravel drive, trying not to hurry, trying not to think of the future.

But as he rounded the line of trees, he stopped. The gatehouse had far too many lights blazing tonight, and smoke dancing out of the chimney.

Feeling like a burglar, a bloody Peeping Tom, he took to the silence of the clipped lawn till he reached the front door beneath the portico. There his heart dropped into his stomach.

A man's voice, muttering low tones, and then hers, thoroughly pleased and lilting. No clear words; only easy banter between a man and a woman.

Christ, this was it: the end of his illusion that Hollie was unattached and neglected. Hollie and her devoted husband, who'd left her hanging out to dry while he gallivanted all over the countryside, using his wife as cover.

Not that he was any better than MacGillnock—stooping to subterfuge and spying like a jilted swain. Angry to the marrow, prepared to survive the pain of catching the pair of them in a lovers' embrace, Charles slipped through the door and into the hall, then went directly into the main room, his heart hardened to coal, prepared to tackle the coward as he leaped for the window.

He wasn't at all prepared for Hollie standing

in the middle of her parlor, holding up a document of some sort and surrounded by a half-dozen of his staff.

They were staring at him, their startled faces flushed with guilt and horror.

Hollie's glare was just as sternly condemning. "Can I help you, my lord?"

He opened his mouth, but the only thing that came out was an accusing, "What the devil is going on here?"

"I'm explaining the Magna Carta."

To his staff?

"I was just reading to them that 'No man shall be seized or imprisoned, or stripped of his rights or possessions, or outlawed—'"

"Miss Finch."

Hollie had recognized the man's voice and his outsized mood even before she'd turned toward the doorway. His face was as thunderous as she expected; she probably ought to have informed him that she'd offered to teach a few of his servants to read.

She would have said as much just then, but he was so devilishly handsome, his hair so moon-dampened. "Will it wait till morning, my lord?"

"It bloody hell won't wait, Miss Finch." He took his time approaching her, slipped his long fingers around her upper arm, and then turned his back to her terrorized class, shielding her from the dread in their eyes, surrounding her with the riotous scent of him.

"What is it, my lord?"

A muscle flickered in his cheek. "What the devil are you teaching, madam?"

"It's a reading lesson."

"A lesson in sedition, you mean. Straight from your radical philosophies."

"From the Magna Carta, my lord. Hardly sedition." She held up the folio sheet for him to see, which only made him frown. "The foundation of the English Constitution."

"I know damned well what the Magna Carta is—"

"Translated, of course, from the original Latin."

"Translated by whom? One of your husband's radical cronies?"

"By me. And printed on my Stanhope some time ago." When he didn't move, when he continued to stare at her, Hollie offered him the folio. "If you suspect my motives, then you can verify it for yourself."

He snatched the page from her and studied it fiercely, his eyes never lighting long enough anywhere to read a word of it. He finally grunted, and his breathing became less ragged. He scanned her face, a hitch in his brow.

"What happened to 'cat' and 'dog,' Miss Finch? Why confuse them with this ancient and inscrutable legal document?"

"It's only inscrutable in the whole. The parts are very simple. Cat and dog are here too, my lord. And lots of other words. Hundreds of them, ready to be used anywhere, just as I had been saying when you entered."

"Balderdash."

The lout must be thinking that she was trying to subvert his staff. And he'd be exactly right. "I was just reading my favorite section—"

" 'No man shall be seized or imprisoned.' I'm sure you were." The man had such a remarkable memory for words. And yet he always seemed so averse to them. Sometimes they outright angered him, no matter the subject, as though he believed they had some power over him.

Which they did. Knowledge was the root of power. And she had every intention of spreading it around wherever she met ignorance and intolerance and stubborn earls.

Hollie stepped around the heady wall that was Charles and found a half-dozen pairs of eyes riveted to the man standing behind her. He'd stunned the entire class with his visit, though probably not for the same reason that her heart began pounding whenever he came near.

The gardener's assistant looked ready to bolt, his mouth hanging open. It would take her the rest of the session to regain their trust.

"Which of all the words in the Magna Carta do you like best so far, Clyde?"

"Me, miss?" Clyde flinched but stood up slowly, hunching his lanky frame as though he were afraid to be seen by his lordship. "My favorite word?"

"Of all the words you've heard so far tonight." Charles was still a heated, growling force behind her.

"Well, I guess that would be this one." Clyde nodded toward the top of the page. " 'Dub-lin.' "

Hollie heard Charles's snort, felt him peering over her shoulder as she searched for the word. "Ah, 'Henry, Archbishop of Dublin.' Why Dublin, Clyde?"

The young man smiled with all his teeth. " 'Cause my da come from there when he was a boy."

"I've got a favorite word, Miss Finch." Katie, the young girl from the scullery, hung halfway out of her chair, waving her arm in the air.

"What is it, Katie?"

The girl shot to her feet and screwed up her brow as she spelled out, with great drama, "T-H-E."

"The."

"Yes."

"That's your favorite because . . . ?"

"It's everywhere, Miss Finch!" The girl stabbed the page a half-dozen times. "Here and here and all around. All I gotta do is learn all the ones in between."

Charles felt a great welling in his chest, something akin to hope and anger and adoration for

the woman who lighted this dark world of theirs
with her patience. He was holding too tightly to
the copy she'd given him, crinkling it.

"What's your favorite word, my lord?"

She was looking right at him, earnestly waiting for him to play along with her eager class,
while the ink danced and mocked him, while he
struggled to recall the words in the Great Charter
so that he wouldn't look the fool. He knew the
document well, another feat of memory that had
saved him in his youth, but she had scrambled
his concentration again.

She could ruin him, would surely do so if she
ever got the slightest notion. But now it was coming back to him: the coping, the cunning of the
classroom.

He steadied his breathing and said with non-
chalance, "I suppose my favorite word would be
'forever.' "

The delight that swept across her face made
his heart skip like a fool's. "Why that particular
word, Lord Everingham?"

*Because it makes me think of you, makes me wish
beyond reason.*

"Because it's the very last word of the last arti-
cle of a damned long document." Even as his
reply left his lips, he regretted saying it because it
made her sigh.

"Well, then, would you care to sit and observe,
my lord? We're almost finished for the evening."

A classroom. It should have chilled him, but it

was so unlike the sterile attic room of his childhood and the strict, echoing halls of his schooldays. And these were Hollie's eager students, still watching him in terror, ready to skitter out the door, completely unaware that their teacher was a miracle to him.

"I'll stay for a time, perhaps."

Sit, boy. You won't learn till you sit.

He'd done his best to thwart his teachers, to keep them from knowing the worst of his fears.

But this one said in her natural kindness, "It means a lot to them to have you here, my lord." Her eyes gleamed at him, made him feel wanted and worthy.

He found himself whispering too close to her ear, drowning in her scent. "And you, Hollie?"

But she only smiled, then suddenly shied away from him and went back to her seditious charter.

Fear pinched at the base of his neck as he edged around the perimeter of her make-do classroom with its motley collection of chairs and leaned against the mantel.

The wide eyes that followed him blinked away when she spoke again, and her students went back to their studying, following her quick change of reading material.

"Lark," she said, and then she spelled it, wrote it on the chalkboard.

They spelled it back to her easily, eagerly, the gardener's assistant, the young woman from the scullery, the eldest boy of the rag and bone man from the village, and other familiar faces.

He found himself following along with them under his breath, his heart slamming hard against his ribs.

Because she was magnificent to watch, to hear, and because he understood.

"Hark," she said, then wrote the word on her standing chalkboard and spelled it aloud. And then, "dark" in the same way. And then "park."

The simplicity of it. She carefully replaced the first letter each time. Only that. He didn't recall the names of the letters as they went past but watched in amazement as the others in the words stayed the same.

Ark. And in her magic, she'd made four words of it. Lark and hark and dark and park.

Hark, the lark in the dark park. He found himself grinning madly, nearly laughing aloud.

"Excellent, class."

And then it was over, a door slamming shut on a dark dungeon after that one tantalizing moment of pure daylight. He cleared his throat, and her students fled as though the woman had invited a dragon into their midst.

She reentered the parlor, clearly satisfied with herself and their progress. "That went very well."

"You asked me for permission to teach Chip. I said nothing about starting a dame school in my gatehouse."

"I didn't think you'd mind, Charles." She used

his name softly as she folded up the easel and leaned it against the wall. "Everingham Hall will profit from the lessons—though this is thoroughly selfish of me. I couldn't resist making new readers for the *Tuppenny Press*, if I ever get the chance to start it up again."

"And if you don't?" *Because I can't let you, Hollie.*

She nudged a ladderback chair under the table. "Then they'll have to read all about reforming the Parliament in *The Times*."

Charles followed her lead and righted a few of the chairs. "Ah, and if you were the Prime Minister, what reforms would you institute?"

She sniffed as she picked up the strewn pages of her lesson. "Very well, my first would be to enact a secret ballot."

"Voting in secret?" He should have known she'd have opinions beyond an ordinary woman's. Because she wasn't anything near to ordinary. "A man should be confident enough in his own character to vote in the clear light of day."

"Unless that man has a landlord or a master who threatens him or his family or his family's fortune if he doesn't vote the way he's directed. You can't say that doesn't happen."

No, he couldn't. He didn't practice coercion himself, but secrecy was no way to vote one's heart. "What else do you propose to your Parliament, madam?"

"Universal suffrage."

"Now there's a foolish notion."

"For both men and women."

He laughed as he added a few logs to the guttering fire, reveling in the domestic peace between them, trying not to imagine a lifetime of nights with her. "You can't possibly mean that, Hollie. Giving women the vote—"

She leveled a finger at him, shaking her head as she came toward him. "Don't, Charles."

"Don't?" He opened his hands as she backed him against the small desktop, knowing it best for both if he hid his urge to smile, better still if he kept his hands from reaching out to span her waist as they were aching to do.

"I know that scoff only too well, sir." She fitted herself perfectly between his knees, and the temptation struck him breathless. "I've heard it all from the day I was born, even from my own father. It's male and hairy and it's universal and it's ballocks."

"Hairy?" Charles bit the edge of his tongue before continuing. "The vote belongs in the hands of citizens of property and income and learning."

"Which immediately excludes women, doesn't it? No matter their education or their class, because women obviously haven't the sense to own property." Her lovely cheeks grew crimson in her outrage; that fine, slightly inky finger was leveled at him again. "Yet women have the sense to clean this same property and to manage it and secure it from theft; they pay the bills, make repairs, they raise their sons on it, while their husbands go off to work for the day and then stop by the public house on their way home, completely unaware of what it takes to manage a household."

Hollie nearly lost her balance when Charles said softly, "Touché, madam."

Unswayed, she shook her finger at him again, because he had to be teasing her. He was a man, after all, though not an ordinary man in the least. "Don't mock me, sir."

"I wouldn't dare, Hollie." He stood and straightened, nearly too tall for the ceiling and hopefully unaware of the hornet's nest he stirred in her chest when he said her name. "You're probably right."

"I am absolutely right, Charles. The country would be a far superior place if women were allowed to vote their convictions."

"Women, Hollie?"

The lout! "As though you men were made wiser by virtue of your codlings."

"My codlings, madam?" His sultry eyebrow arched, thoroughly, charmingly scandalized.

She hadn't meant to shock the man, but the word was out and there was nothing dangerous in it—despite his catching her up in the unhurried curve of his smile, despite the intimate tugging at the center of her, the coiling thread that tightened between them with every breath.

"I am terribly sorry, Charles. I was raised in a print shop—a man's world. I'm afraid I know them all."

"All?" Less scandal, more amusement.

"Indelicate euphemisms." Gad, this was a dangerous direction to take. "But you know what I meant."

"My testicles, I assume."

Oh, dear. Oh, God. She shouldn't have glanced down at the front of his well-fitting breeches, at the strong, straight shadows of him, the erotic maleness of him. She flushed to the roots of her hair.

"No, that's not what I—"

"I'm afraid my codlings don't make me wise, Hollie." He became awfully tall again, encompassing, drawing the air out of the diminishing distance between them. "Quite the opposite, in fact."

"They make you unwise?"

"Extremely."

Oh, my. There was far too much of him to fight off, and far, far too little left of her sensible self to want to try. Because it seemed like he was about to kiss her. "We've gotten well off track, Charles."

"The subject was yours, Hollie. I was merely following."

"The female vote."

"Ah, yes." His smile slanted off center, a slight easing of the delicious tension. "Just don't look for your right of suffrage to happen soon."

"Of course not." Dizzy from the nearness of him, Hollie ducked away and collected the chalk into its box and set it on the mantel. "But how can that ever happen when my fellow sisters can't even bring themselves to demand authority over their own lives? Or maybe they've just been seduced by their men. I've pledged myself never to be."

His gaze smoldered and strayed to her mouth, making her wonder when he'd come so near, realizing that she'd gone to him.

"Never to be what, Hollie? Seduced by a man?"

"That's right."

He dipped his head as though he didn't quite understand and asked the oddest question. "But doesn't he object, Hollie?"

The fluttering in her chest spread deeper, making her breathless and yearning for something more than a kiss could bring. "Doesn't who object, Charles?"

"Your husband," he whispered, his breath as palpable as a kiss.

"My . . . ? Oh." She suddenly wasn't following the strain of the conversation very well. It had turned somewhere, this new path wildly different and intoxicating, because Charles was standing very close, looking very intently at her mouth.

"Doesn't he object to what, Charles?"

"I'd think your husband would insist upon seducing you regularly." The blaze in the hearth limned his features in shimmering orange; the shadows sharpened and deepened them, scattering her thoughts and making her dizzy with wonder. "I know I would."

A flush rose out of her bodice to make little spots of heat at her cheeks. And it all had to do with the half-lidded look in Charles's eyes, the low murmur of his voice. His broad shoulders, the lean trim of his waist.

His codlings. And the hard shape of him. The breadth of her imagination.

"You'd what, Charles?" She couldn't recall the subject.

"Seduce you regularly, Hollie."

Regularly. Oh, my!

Chapter 19

No, he'd said something about her husband.
And seduction.

"Well, Charles, he . . . uhm . . . no, he doesn't."
All this soft and close conversing had drained
her will and tipped her off balance. The only
remedy was to brace the flat of her palm against
Charles's chest.

Oh, he was warm beneath her hand and
thrummingly alive, the sense of him speeding up
through her fingers.

"You mean that Adam MacGillnock doesn't
seduce you regularly?"

"I mean that he—"

"Not much of a marriage, Hollie, if he's that
neglectful."

"What? Oh." She could hardly find a breath to

answer. "You misunderstand completely, Charles. What I mean is that I won't allow my husband to . . . to seduce me from my thoughts and my opinions."

Oh, this was a fine and dangerous how-to, watching his mouth as he spoke, wondering how it would feel to be kissed by him.

"Ah, your thoughts." He trailed the pad of his thumb lightly across her mouth, a traveling kind of kiss. "And what about the rest of you, Hollie?"

Oh, the rare way the man's lips caressed his words—though she really ought to be listening better to him, answering him. Yet her chest ached with the need for air.

"The rest of me, sir?"

His eyes were tracking hers, as soft as his lashes, as intensely as the thudding of his heart beneath her hand; he followed the course of her jaw, drew his fingers to her chin, and tilted it up to him.

"Your mouth, Hollie?" His gaze was steady and warm, his breathing as unsteady as her own, breaking across her mouth like a kiss. "Does he take time with you here? To seduce your mouth as it deserves?"

"My mouth?" This wasn't real, of course, none of it. She wasn't standing in a cozy gatehouse with Charles Stirling, 7th Earl of Everingham, towering over her in his untamable splendor. And he wasn't exploring her lips with his fingers, shooting stars out the ends of her hair, warming her from the tips of her fingers where she was clinging to his vest, to her toes and to that growing fever so low in her belly.

"And your eyes, Hollie. Does he see you as I do, I wonder? Does he know the color there? This remarkable green."

"Of course he . . ." Oh, this millstone of a husband she'd created. She'd lost track of the conversation entirely. He was leaning against the arm of the sofa, and she was standing in the crook of his long legs.

"I shouldn't be thinking this way about you, Hollie." He caught her face between his exquisite hands; threaded his fingers through her hair with blissful care.

"Which way is that?"

"Thinking that I want to kiss you."

He'd looked at her this way many times before, following his gaze with his feather-light touch, his smile crooked and his breathing ragged and wild. But it had always been followed by one of his furious frowns.

He wasn't frowning now. He was . . .

Oh, my, he was nuzzling her temple, lighting fires along her hairline, whispering at the ridges of her ear, breathing softly there.

"You're thinking that about me?"

"Constantly," he said keenly against her ear. "And I haven't the right. Bloody hell, woman, you've turned my life upside down."

"I'm sorry."

He touched her lips with his trembling fingers. "Don't ever say that, Hollie. You shame me with your apologies."

"What do you mean?"

"Oh, Christ." He left her, growling as he scrubbed his fingers through his hair. "You have me at a disadvantage, madam."

"I do?" Her printing press forfeited, living in his gatehouse, completely at his mercy while he plotted with the government to have her hanged at the next quarter sessions? "In what possible way have I disadvantaged you?"

He paced to the entry and braced his hands against the doorframe, looking thoroughly disgusted with himself. "Do you know that I'm holding you here in the gatehouse in the hope of luring your husband onto my estate so that I can capture him?"

And do you know, my dear, unwary earl, that I plan to steal your correspondence with Lord Sidmouth and share it with my fellow radicals?

"I'm not a fool, Charles." *And I'm not married.* "And you're the magistrate." *And we're even.* "I assumed that was your plan from the first."

But her deeper confessions were too dangerous for any sanctuary but her heart, so she let him struggle with his moral dilemma, admiring him all the more for it.

"So why hasn't he come to claim you, Hollie?"

Oh, what a roundabout, exhausting discussion. "Because he doesn't want to be caught."

"Have you sent him messages?"

It was so awkward and hateful, speaking in riddles and evasions. "You know that I haven't."

"But he bloody well knows that you're here, doesn't he?—the way the rumors fly in his circle."

"I'm sure he knows where I am."

"You know how his rabble-rousing annoys me. The fact that he calls me and my commission corrupt irritates the blazing hell out of me. But nothing matches my disgust for his leaving you to defend his actions on your own."

It had been so easy to dislike him for his aristocratic arrogance, for a hundred other offenses she'd once charged him with. These startling moments of gentleness drained her, made her heart ache with the loneliness that would come when she turned her back on him.

"It's all right, Charles. I don't mind and I really don't expect him to—"

"To what, Hollie?" He blocked her from tidying the remains of her tea tray, slipped his fingers between hers, and tucked their clasped hands into the draping folds of her apron and the warm wool of his trousers. "To come rescue you from the wicked earl? You should expect nothing less from the man who loves you."

Dear God, he was actually worried about her,

this prowling lion of hers. She wanted to soothe him, or to tell him that she was safe here with him. That she couldn't possibly be safer. That his hands were amazing.

"Hellfire, Hollie! If you were my wife, I'd have torn through solid rock to get to you."

"You would?" It felt so good to believe, in this little moment, that he cared so much, that he truly would tear though solid rock to save her from harm.

"With my bare hands I would."

His bare hands! He was trembling in his anger, his fingers quaking as he smoothed his free hand along her neck and down to the base of her throat, his flesh on hers, his pulse matching the beat of her heart—a caress so profoundly gentle that tears filled her eyes. "Does he know how magnificent you are?"

"Am I?"

He caught the tear that spilled down her cheek. "Has he ever told you that, Hollie?"

"No one has."

"Has your dear Adam ever risked his life for you?"

She shook her head, hating this obnoxious strawman she'd created so blithely. She wanted him and all her falsehoods gone from her life. Wanted to stand up for herself and let Charles believe the worst of her instead of believing the best.

Because it wasn't right. They should be honest enemies.

"Does he tell you that he loves you? Does he show it at all?"

"He's not—We're not—Oh, Charles!" Tired to her soul, Hollie slipped away from him, went to the mantel, and doused the lamp.

But he came up behind her, lifted her hair off her shoulder, and whispered, "Do you really want to have children with a man like that, Hollie?"

"I do want children."

"With *him*, Hollie? What kind of father would he be if he doesn't even have the courage to protect his wife? He's a threat to you. He'll drag you down with him. There are courts for this sort of thing—extenuating circumstances can dissolve a marriage."

"I can't, Charles. It's a dangerous relationship." *Heartbreaking, in fact.* "He wouldn't like to be thwarted."

"What the hell do you mean?" He turned her, studied her clinically, carefully felt the bones in her arms, her ribs. "Does that bastard strike you? Is that the sort of coward you're married to?"

"No. He'd never hit me." She had to get away from all his questions, to turn him from the subject. "He's rarely home to talk to me, let alone to strike me. Gone for weeks at a time."

"Weeks?"

"Oh, weeks and weeks. But that's the life of a radical, my lord."

He narrowed his eyes.

"Gone for weeks in only two months of marriage? What sort of wedded bliss can that be?"

"Well, more like a soldier's marriage, I suppose. Though my dear Adam stays away only weeks at a time instead of years."

"I'll wager that your dear husband Adam has a wife in every camp."

She should have resented the idea, but it was so utterly silly, and she was so weary, she wanted to cry. "Oh, I doubt that very much."

"He's a very selfish man, isn't he, Hollie? Out for his own pleasures and glory. I know the type."

He's me, you lout. "Just because you would cheat on your wife if you had one, Charles—"

He went utterly still, grew taller, more intense. "Why do you assume that?"

"Because you and your lordly class marry for power and wealth, not for love. You find your love matches outside of marriage." She'd never seen him quite so calmly outraged. "Don't you?"

"Mark me, Hollie," he said, in a deep and dark voice, "when I marry, it will be to a woman that I love well enough to blind me to any other."

She wanted to believe this of her earl, that his

heart was loyal and true. "You cultivated quite a reputation in your youth."

"I'm no longer that man, Hollie. The marriage bed is far more attractive to me now than any brief dalliance could ever be. And I'd make it so for my wife."

"You would?"

"Her pleasure before mine. An adoring husband's duty, one that I would take very, very seriously."

Sweet aching heaven. That's just what she needed to hear from him. She didn't want to be dreaming of him when she was gone and he'd found a lucky wife to cherish and adore. "So you're discounting my marriage to Adam because he travels?"

"Hollie, I mean that two months ago you married a man you'd only known a week."

"Yes, I fell desparately in love with him." What a flat-sounding litany that had become. Yet the great man flinched when she said it.

He gathered back his determination. "MacGillnock's gone most of the time, isn't he?"

"Alas, he is." She wanted her bed, wanted his arms around her there and his bristly cheek next to hers, the scent of him in her bedclothes, his breathing matched to hers.

"You last saw him a week ago, and then for barely twelve hours."

"That's right." She hadn't the slightest idea

where Charles was going with his heartrending inquest or how long it would last. She pinched out the candles on the side table and the room went nearly dark.

"He's been seen all over the North and the Midlands in the last two months, spends days and days on the road."

"So?"

"So, by my calculations, Hollie, you couldn't possibly have been with your dear Adam for more than two weeks in the entire time you've known him."

She opened her mouth and then closed it. "A sacrifice I'm willing to make."

She picked up the remaining candlestick and started up the stairs to her room, not caring if he followed or not, hoping that he would.

"So how could you possibly know him?"

Indeed. "It seems like a lifetime, Charles."

"It seems like a farce of a marriage to me. And what if he's left you with child, this nearly invisible man who makes you support him with your printing?"

"He hasn't left me with a child." She heard his Hessians on the step behind her, heard the slightest hesitation in his stride.

"But he will, Hollie. One day he will."

"He won't, my lord. I can assure you of that."

"Damnation, woman!" Charles could no longer abide her dismissive lack of interest in the magnitude of the mistake she had made in her

choice of husband. She looked like a sprite leading the way up into the forest canopy, among the
crucked rafters and the bracing that laced the
low ceiling just above her head.

"Where are you going, woman?"

Her shoulders sagged, and the candlestick.
"I'm tired to the bone, Charles."

"Well, I'm not finished."

"I'm going to bed." She disappeared in a whisper of skirts and a flare of slippers.

"Dammit, Hollie!" He had a point to make—
though he wasn't altogether sure what that was.
So he followed her the rest of the way up the
stairs.

"I know that you understand how children are
conceived, Hollie. You made that very clear to
me days ago."

Her bed was tucked under the low-slung eaves,
piled with pillows and a thick counterpane, the
window opened slightly to the night air. There
was a washstand at the wall and a small room beyond that, a closet perhaps, which glowed inside
with the candle she'd taken with her.

"Of course I know how children are conceived, Charles," she called, the barest lilt in her
voice. "What exactly are you getting at?"

You, Hollie. Yet he could only stand by the window and burn for her, grateful for the cool
evening breeze, enjoying the sounds of her undressing, stealing a look at the deliciously dancing shadows she cast across the wall.

She was willowy arms and a waist he could span with his hands. Breasts that swayed, or that he imagined swaying, buoyant in the cup of his hand and uplifted, bare and sweet to his mouth.

Good Christ, spare me.

He cleared his throat and took a gulp of cool air from the window while he tried to recall the train of his thoughts. Something about MacGillnock getting Hollie with child—God curse the man with empty codlings and an unwilling prick.

"And so, Hollie, on those rare occasions when your dear Adam is at home . . ."

She came out of the dressing room in her nightgown, as familiar as though she belonged in his bed and he saw its flannel every night, just before he lifted it over her head and covered every part of her with kisses . . .

"You were saying, Charles?"

He was roused to bursting, hoping to hell she couldn't see the front of his trousers. He cleared his throat again.

"I was saying, Hollie, that on those rare occasions when your dear Adam is at home, I assume that you and he have . . . that you have marital relations together. . . ."

Charles shut away the images of Hollie in another man's bed, watching her face for memories of the man she said she loved. But the woman only blinked at him, catching her lower lip in that way she did when she was upset.

"You do have relations with him, Hollie?" he asked, his heart beginning to pound with an absurdity, a flicker of hope that the bastard had never touched her.

"No, Charles, I don't."

"You—don't?" He wasn't sure she had clearly understood his question, the full weight of it, or the exact meaning. "Do you mean to say, Hollie, that your husband has never taken you to bed?"

She shook her head, and all that golden hair, glanced up at the ceiling, then to her folded hands, and then at him. "Never once, Charles."

Holy hell.

She gave a long, almost growling sigh, snatched up the hairbrush from the washstand, and began brushing forcefully through her curls.

Never once.

He didn't know what to make of this startling news, what it meant to both of them in the long run, let alone in the short. Only that he wanted to shout and celebrate with her in some entirely pagan way. With water from the nearest spring and thick cream and Hollie's naked, moonlit body.

"Good Christ, Hollie, is Adam MacGillnock completely mad?"

"I don't think so." She seemed wistful and worried, as though she were mulling something over.

"Is he incapable?"

But that suggestion only wrinkled her brow. "He's just a very busy man."

"Busy?" He hadn't meant to shout, but he must have because her eyes widened. "Too busy to take his wife to bed? To pleasure her? What the devil kind of marriage do you have, Hollie?"

She shook her head.

"Certainly not a very convenient one, Charles, as I'm discovering the hard way. More of a business relationship, I suppose."

"You suppose? Didn't you talk about it while you were falling madly in love with each other?"

"At times like these I think I even regret the marriage altogether."

"Times like what?"

"Like this particular time, Charles." She spread her hands to him, and he realized she was wearing a different nightgown from before. Not flannel. Transparent in the moonlight, with small buttons that reached to the hem.

Or else his imagination had gotten sharper with his rioting desire for her, because he was sure that he saw a shadowy triangle through the light folds of the fabric there at the joining of her legs, knew it would be dark blond, scented for him, for his mouth and his exploration.

"The confusing times, Charles. When I think I must have married in haste."

"To a man too busy to make love with you."

"That and so much more, Charles."

"He's a fool—and I'll tell him so one day."

"What would you tell him? That he is a neglectful husband?"

"That he ought to have done right by you when he had the chance."

"As you would have done?"

"As I want to do."

She lifted her eyes. "Regularly, Charles?"

"I'd have a hell of a time keeping my hands to myself."

"You'd take my nightgown from me?"

"In good time."

"Not right away?"

"Not until you were aching for me."

Hollie *was* aching for him, deeply. Nearly fainting. "How would you know?"

"I'd see it in your eyes." He lifted her chin with the end of his finger. "And here on your neck— the blush of passion. It would lie like a fever across your bosom." He lifted aside the collar.

"And here, Hollie, on your breasts." She closed her eyes, her dangerous imagination coursing where he wasn't yet touching, where he wanted his hands, his mouth. "But I'd have started at your toes, Hollie."

"Oh, Charles." She opened her eyes.

"And I'd have taken my time."

"And I would be aching long before you got to my buttons."

"Christ, Hollie!" Like a raging storm, he swept her up into his fury, enfolded her in his strong arms, and took her into himself, spreading her knees slightly with his until she was almost straddling his thigh and indelicately pressing against him where her ache was the keenest. She formed herself against him until his rigid erection was cradled wonderfully against her belly, the only place she could ever have him.

He breathed roughly and trembled as he held her, hip to hip, his erection standing stiffly and so fine. It had a pulse like the beating of her heart, and a deep connection to the answering part of her.

But he finally controlled this marvelous passion of his once again, controlled his breathing.

"This is deeply wrong of me, Hollie," he whispered next to her ear.

"No regrets, Charles," she said quietly. "Only that I envy the woman who will someday be your wife."

He closed his eyes for a moment, then smiled wanly. "As I envy your captain, my dear, to the end of my days."

And then he left her, aching for him, wishing she didn't care, certain that she always would.

Chapter 20

⁓◯◯⁓

Hollie soon became dreadfully adept at rifling Charles's mail and stealing a look at Sidmouth's letters. It was a simple thing to slip out of the conservatory before supper and have a quick spy in the library or in his office. Charles spent far more time in the fields than he did at his accounts. And when he was there, Bavidge was too, taking dictation and writing letters, running in circles for the earl. It seemed an old and efficient routine.

Sometimes the letters were lying exposed on the blotter, right beneath Charles's fingers. So since reading upside down and sideways was like breathing to her, she often did her spying in the open, while Charles was looking up at her, setting her pulse on fire with his dark gaze and his rumbling questions, making her want to weep.

But still there was nothing but Liverpool's political posturing, rarely anything at all about Peterloo, as though the matter was nothing to the Prime Minister but an inconsequentially bothersome episode that would soon die away.

The Handbook of Song Birds was coming along nicely, not that it mattered in the least. There was no customer called the Dunsmere Avian Society, no deadline. The etchings had been left in the shop years ago by a customer who had never come back to pick up the project, so they served as a simple cover to keep her press operating.

Now another page of birds was ready to be printed, and Charles was nowhere to be found. The conservatory had become a center of activity; the Stanhope seemed to draw everyone. Even Mrs. Riley wanted to know if Hollie would print the Stirling family recipes for her.

Charles had started out merely watching her, standing around as she used the devil's tail and removing it when she was finished. But the man was as curious about the press as was his son, and from the first page of the *Song Birds* he began to involve himself in the mechanics of the press. From inking the plates and loading the paper to running the bed and the platen.

And she couldn't think of a single reason to dissuade him from offering his considerable strength in the process.

Charles Stirling was an unrhymed poem. He was huge and handsome, had shoulders built for labor, was broadly muscled, thickly sinewed, and wildly passionate. He was a joy to watch, his sleeves rolled to his elbows, the brawny muscles of his forearms straining.

But this afternoon she was alone in the conservatory, and her favorite pressman had locked away the blasted handle somewhere, leaving her unable to continue without him.

She hurried off to Charles's library, but the room was empty and echoing, and she remembered that he was off on his estate rounds today. She was about to turn and leave when she noticed a tempting stack of letters lying open on his desk.

This spying business roiled her stomach, spun it sideways. But her cause was just, she kept telling herself. And the vision of her father lying mortally wounded with all the other victims on St. Peter's Fields steadied her considerably.

With her eyes always on the door, she leafed through the stack of envelopes, looking for the Privy Council marks. But the bulk of them were from Charles's lawyers and land agents, a mining lease holder, and a horse breeder in Yorkshire.

There were two from Sidmouth at the bottom— probably more of his babbling. She watched the door and opened the first: a meeting announcement.

The second letter froze her feet to the floor.

"The Blasphemous and Seditious Libels Act." Dear God. Exactly what she'd been expecting, what she'd been praying would never come. Her breathing caught on her ribs as the words scrambled and blinked into view. "Stronger punishments, including banishment, for publications judged to be blasphemous or seditious." Judged by whom?

And what could possibly be stronger punishment than spending long years in prison or transportation across the world or the gallows?

A chill crept up her spine as she quickly scanned the rest of the pages. Five other acts of suppression were to be proposed to Parliament in November.

"A prohibition against public meetings of more than fifty people without the consent of a sheriff or magistrate." When did they ever consent to anything more than a market fair? And that only because it lined their greedy pockets.

She had to let the others know so that they could be on their guard. Or march on Westminster. Or hide out in their cellars.

She needed to get a note to William Prentice that Captain Spindleshanks would be making an appearance at his next meeting of reformers.

A door slammed somewhere in the house, a startling reminder that she had been living in the belly of the beast, snuggling up to him, dreaming of his kiss, yearning for the touch of his hand.

And now footfalls in the corridor, moving inexorably closer to the library. A stride as dear and familiar as her father's had been.

Charles was too close for her to return the letter to its envelope, let alone to its place at the bottom of the stack. She popped them both into the huge pocket of her apron, raking her mind for a legitimate reason for being in his library.

Reading, of course!

She grabbed a book from the nearest shelf, then threw herself into a lounging position on the settee, wrapped one arm across the book on her chest, and nestled her head in the crook of the other, then pretended to snooze, wondering which title she'd chosen.

She hoped that Charles wouldn't ask what she thought of it so far; prayed most of all that Sidmouth's letter wasn't sticking out of her pocket like a beacon.

The door opened, and Charles's long strides stopped abruptly. She steadied her breathing—a difficult task, given the thudding of her heart and the way her pulse was shooshing around in her veins.

His stride lengthened, and then he stopped just above her. And though he didn't put a hand on her, she felt caressed and kissed. The best of her daydreams come to life.

All that sensual heat left her for a brief instant, like the sun slipping behind a cloud, only to return even hotter, closer, a moment later.

So close that she could feel his minty breath

•

against her cheek and then at her ear when he whispered so softly that she could barely hear, "Fancy my great luck at finding a beautiful nymph sleeping in my library."

Beautiful! Hollie's heart went wild, spreading a crimson blush like a wildfire above the top of her gown, leaving her no choice but to yawn and stretch and flutter her eyes open, feigning surprise.

"Charles! What are you doing here? What time is it?"

He was sitting on the ottoman, elbows braced on his knees, his grin at a wry angle.

"Ah, my nymph is awake."

She adored his smile and tried not to dwell on the heady pleasure of his touch.

"Your nymph, Charles?" Hollie harrumphed and sat up, swinging her legs to the edge of the settee while she clutched the book against her lap, not daring to look at the title. "Your nymph came in to find the devil's tail."

"And did you find it?"

"You weren't here, were you?"

"Inspecting my new inn out on the post road. And so you stayed on to read?"

"I thought I'd wait. But I guess I fell asleep."

"The book was that exciting, was it?"

Hollie read the title for the first time and cringed.

Hints to Gentlemen of Landed Property, by N. Kent.

How would she explain that one? Head on, perhaps. She perched it in front of him, resting it on her palm. "Have you read Mr. Kent's manual?"

His mood darkened abruptly. He stood and went to a cabinet. "I haven't."

The change in him unsettled her. Something about the book? Or her questioning his estate management? She fanned quickly through it and frowned.

"The pages haven't been cut yet, Charles. I guess no one could have read it."

"I guess not." He shut the cabinet door, then laid the press handle for the Stanhope against the desk. His manner was sternly foreign to her and frightening for its inward turning. A sadness shading his eyes made her heart ache for him.

"*Hints to Gentlemen of Landed Property*," she said with a shrug, trying to fix whatever it was she'd broken. "From what I've seen of Everingham, Charles, you could write your own book on the subject of gentlemen and landed property."

His shoulders relaxed as though he'd been holding his breath, waiting for a powerful judgment that would fell him. His frown became the sardonically confident smile that made her pulse rise and surge.

"I think I prefer your book of song birds, madam." Her handsome earl hefted the handle of the Stanhope onto his shoulder, caught her around the waist, and drew her out the door of the library, unaware of the stolen letter tucked away in her apron pocket.

Unaware that she'd be leaving him in the next few days.

And that her heart would be breaking.

Chapter 21

Deception had been so very uncomplicated back when Hollie was committing it against the corrupt vipers who ran the Home Office from Whitehall. Now the guilty weight of it settled like a shroud against her days and stole into her dreams.

It whispered to her in Charles's dark baritone and danced through her heart in Chip's laughter.

The false wife, played to Charles's careful husbanding. The false mother, stealing the innocent love of a child.

As father and son grew closer, they drew her into their circle, tempted her to dreams of a better life. Home and hearth and all the precious things denied a radical reformer with a price on her head.

And still she practiced her treachery against Charles, who was a better man than she could ever have imagined. And she practiced wilfully, because there was far more at stake than simple happiness. Her father to avenge and a truth to expose.

If the Home Office's answer to the tragedy on St. Peter's Fields was not only to blame the victims, but to crush the life out of any future chance of even discussing the problems that led to the debacle, then her choices were few.

Her chance of being caught increased with her daring, but time was flying past. The Home Office would be proposing its heinous acts of suppression as soon as Parliament reconvened in November. She had time enough to print a warning blast revealing its secret strategies. And the best place to warn her fellow radicals was at Prentice's meeting coming up in a few days.

Captain Spindleshanks was going to have to come out of hiding and take a stand for liberty.

And then what?

She shoved the question from her mind, because the answer would make her weep. She went back to inking the seditious plate that she'd composed in secret in the shadows of her gabled home, hoping that Charles would stay busy with his estate manager and that Chip would find Mrs. Riley's cakes too delicious to miss a chance to lick the spoon.

The process of printing was as much an intricate dance as ever.

The paper.

The tympan.

The easy slide of the bed.

The perfect fit of her fingers around the Stanhope's handle, the precise pressure.

Paper meeting ink, her indelible self, the words of her heart, the risk, the need, the end of the journey and the beginning.

Then the precious dance in reverse.

Until she pulled the paper from the plate and spoke her sedition to the world.

"Hollie! Guess what, Hollie! Hollie!" Chip's voice sailed in from the garden and then his skidding footfalls across the flags as he hit the conservatory door and threw himself in from the afternoon sun.

"Hollie!" His face was lit with his brilliant smile until he caught his foot on the sill and tumbled toe over tail across the floor.

"Chip!" Hollie dropped everything and met him as he landed, then pulled him into her arms, expecting to find scrapes and whimpering.

But he bounced up out of her lap and stood grinning, his dark hair wild and littered with bits of straw.

"I rode Briscoe all by myself, Hollie!"

Great heaven, the stables! Those tiny stalls and

the huge beasts and her fearless little Chip. "You've been in the stables again, Chip?"

"And the paddock."

Doubtless alone. "You could have been hurt."

"I held on to the saddle and kept my seat really good."

"Does Carlson know you were there? Did anyone help you?"

He nodded vigorously.

"Oh, yes, Hollie."

"I did."

Charles! He was standing in the doorway, the stern magistrate, and now a fiercely protective father. At least she'd have that happiness to keep her warm—that Charles had found his son.

"And guess what, Hollie! Papa said he'd let me help take care of Briscoe's baby horse."

Hollie's heart melted at Charles's smile. "That's a very important job, Chip."

"And guess what else, Hollie! Papa says the baby horse will be mine when he grows up."

"If you learn to take care of him, son."

Son. Tears clogged her throat.

"I'll learn really good, Papa. I promise. Isn't it great, Hollie!"

"Your papa is a remarkable man, Chip." And she would miss him as she would miss her heart.

Because she had just printed off the last of her sedition on her Stanhope.

Dear God, the broadside! It had fallen when

she ran to help Chip, and now it was . . . somewhere.

She turned to see that it was stuck under the
leg of a chair—just as Charles stooped to pick up
the page.

God, no!

He righted it in silence and studied the page.
Top to bottom, taking it all in so that he could
rage at her.

SIX ACTS OF SUPPRESSION!

She wanted to run, to close her eyes so that she
wouldn't see him realize how blatantly she'd betrayed him. But not looking at him was like trying not to watch some horror unfolding in front
of her eyes.

He took an eternity, and she held her breath,
prayed that he would send Chip away before he
shackled her again and sent her to prison.

He turned slowly, frowning slightly. And then,
as though he didn't care at all that she'd stolen
Sidmouth's letter from his desk and replaced it
right under his nose, that she'd created a
scathing broadside from it, that she would
broadcast the information to the populace before
Parliament could enact a single measure, Charles
set the page on the bed of the press and looked
directly at her.

"Do you ride, Hollie?"

She couldn't hear, couldn't understand a word for the roaring in her ears, for the intimate familiarity in his smile.

You've betrayed me, Hollie. Is that what he said? *You're under arrest, Hollie.*

I loved you, Hollie.

"What's that, Charles?" she asked finally, only to have Chip grab her hand and pull her a few steps toward the garden door.

"We came here to see if you wanted to come with us, Hollie. I want to show you how good I can ride."

Charles was wearing a most peculiar smile, relaxed and sensual and entirely unthreatening. He tilted his head. "Do you ride, madam?"

"I—well, I have ridden some, Charles, but—"

"Oh, then come, Hollie!" Chip was pulling harder on her hand, hopping in his delight. "You must! Mrs. Riley even made us a dinner basket."

And Charles was the picture of Sunday afternoon charm.

"Please come," he said, offering his hand with the tenderest smile she'd ever seen, nodding to the press and her broadside. "There's time for this later."

This! Her heart shuddered. He knew what she'd done, and he was going to mete out his terrible punishment after sharing a country ride and a dinner basket.

She had no choice but to agree.

The fields and forests of the late October afternoon whispered of golds and scattered greens. The sky was a cloudless blue, and the breezes that caught in her hair and her skirt were unseasonably warm.

She waited for Charles's hinted accusations as they tracked the margins of his estate, Hollie riding sidesaddle, Chip on a stubby little pony, and Charles mounted like a crusading warrior on Briscoe.

But no threats came, or condemnation, or any hint at all of seething anger or shock or anything but genuine contentment. No sign of the wrath she expected, though Charles Stirling was a man of action and wore his moods and his nature openly.

And today his mood was newly tender, almost courting, if her heart was any judge.

Nor did his accusations come when they had dinner together in the dining room or when Chip fell fast asleep in her arms in the library under his father's watchful gaze or even when the boy was in bed and he was looking down at his son.

She could barely catch her breath when Charles slipped his hand around hers and said in a whisper, "Thank you, Hollie."

Not "You're a thief and a liar, Hollie Finch."

Not "How could you betray me like that?"

Or even "Why?"

Only "Thank you for my son."

"Oh, Charles." Such a simple confession. Tears welled up in her eyes, spilled over. Her heart hammered at the stunning contact with his hand, at the magnitude of her deception, and the softness in his eyes.

"He was yours all along."

"But you made me stop and see him." His hand was a trembling caress, and his voice a little shaky. "And I think that I've seen all too much of you."

"Me?" Her spying had finally come to swamp her. *Oh, but not just now, Charles, not here in Chip's room, where he will hear me weeping.*

"Christ, Hollie, how I—Bloody hell!" But he didn't char the air with his wrath as she feared.

He merely blew out a huge breath, took hold of her hand, and led her out into the hall. He stopped twice in midstride, both times about to speak, only to continue on his journey.

This was it. He was taking her to his dungeon. He had every right: she'd stolen Sidmouth's letter, then had reproduced it nearly word for word. And he'd waited all day to bring down the full force of his rage upon her until they were out of Chip's hearing and the boy was filled up with a joyful afternoon and her own heart was filled with yearning for what might have been.

She trailed along behind him like a calf to slaughter. The guilt was overwhelming, because no excuse in the world would serve.

His terrifying mood seemed to break wide open at the bottom of the back stairs, when he fi-

nally caught both of her hands and then her arms
and then forced her up against the wall.

"Do you know why I've brought you down
those stairs, Hollie?" There wasn't a spot on her
face where his gaze didn't alight, leaving her to
imagine the scope of his anger.

"I do know, Charles, and I'm so sorry for it."
Sorry for so many things.

"You're sorry, Hollie?" That only seemed to
make him more thunderous. "Good lord,
madam, I don't need that kind of temptation
from you."

"Temptation?"

Charles was near to exploding with madness
for the woman and her disarming magic, had
just saved her from a sound ravishing at his own
hands, and here she was telling him that she was
sorry for his chivalry.

Though just now she looked thoroughly terrified at the prospect, her back stiff against the
wall, her eyes wide and blinking. It was long
past time for honesty. For telling her that he
burned for her, for her mouth and the sleekness
of her skin, that every moment he spent with her
was a trial of restraint that he was rapidly losing.

And all this heady sweetness so very few
inches from him, quickening his heart as well as
his flesh.

"Hollie, I can't have you saying things like
that."

"But I need to, Charles." She looked woeful

and ready to weep, touched his mouth with her peach-fragrant fingers. "Because I do care, whatever you think of me."

He caught her hand and kept it, laced his fingers through hers. "Hollie, I think you're the most remarkable woman I've ever met."

She bit at her rosy lip again and tilted her head as though he was speaking in a foreign tongue. "You do?"

"In case you didn't realize, Hollie, I brought you downstairs just now to keep you safely away from my bedchamber and my bed." Though he hardly needed a bed; these stairs would do.

"You did what?" Her lovely cheeks went pale; he'd never seen her eyes so wide, so green.

"Bloody hell, woman—every thought I have in my head right now involves making love to you until dawn."

"You want to make love to me?" Fat tears gathered in her eyes, a great puddle of them. "Oh, my. Oh, Charles, why are you doing this?"

He'd halfway hoped she would be shocked enough to run to the gatehouse and lock the door behind her. And the other half of him wanted just this. The softness of her blush, the unsteady rise and fall of her breasts, so close he could cup them.

Her eyes were wide and wonderful, and he wanted to speak the rest of his mind, but he couldn't. Shouldn't.

He caught a handful of her hair, soft wisps of curling sunshine, reminding him of wheatfields and buttercups. "Do you know what your smile does to me, Hollie?"

"No." It was a little sound. She shook her head, loosening the tears so they streamed down her cheeks.

"It makes me think of honeybees."

Her mouth glistened as she opened it in a breathy little O, a lush, compelling sound. "Bees?"

"And honey fresh from a hive." He was hotly roused and desperately wanting what he couldn't have. "And the soft petals of a foxglove. Warm places, Hollie, and tight places, subtleties and sunlight. You. The taste of your mouth."

He wanted *all* of her. Damn the husband and his trial!

"My smile does this to you, Charles?" She was breathing in sharp little gasps, her brows still winged in worry. "Just my smile?"

He wanted to carry her up the stairs and make love with her until the dawn came through the windows.

But he had to end it now, before it was too late. "Hollie, I'm sorry."

"Please, Charles, no. Don't be." Her eyes were watery as she pulled slightly away from him, stunning him when she put her fingers to his mouth, as if to stop him from speaking the words that would separate them. "It's me. I'm to blame."

He knew he was doomed to the hottest part of hell for taking advantage of the moment, for questing where he shouldn't. For tasting her when she wasn't his.

For this kiss would leave him suffering for her when it ended and only wanting more, wishing for miracles that didn't belong to him. That never would.

Hollie had been expecting prison and worse— but she'd found only his bewildering confession and his warm fingers slipping through her hair. Hardly the actions of the man who had caught her stealing from him.

He so carefully cradled the back of her head with one hand, was so intently looking at her mouth as he tilted her chin with the other.

Then she was tugging at his lapels, shamelessly balancing herself on her toes because his breath was close and sweet and so disorienting. And he was taking the better part of forever bending down to her mouth. This was the last and the only chance she would have before she left; a moment of magic that would have to last a lifetime.

It wasn't wise to steal from a man like Charles Stirling, not a kiss or a letter, and fatal to give away his secrets, especially when she would some day have to face him and his dark disappointment across a courtroom.

"Stop me, Hollie."

"I don't think I will, Charles."

There was a moment when his exquisitely shaped mouth was poised above hers, his intensely dark eyes blue-black in the shadows; when she wondered if he'd just been tormenting her all along, if this was his punishment—all this wanting and yearning for him.

Then in the next breath there was nothing else in the world but the deeply shattering bliss of his wonderful mouth on hers, soft and hot and hard.

Oh, my! The savory taste of his plundering was exotic spice and passion and danger; the faint stubble of his beard was a delight beneath her hands.

She never could have imagined that her blustering, wicked-hearted earl would have such splendid lips, let alone that she would be standing in the circle of his arms with him kissing her and whispering her name against her mouth or that she would be climbing deeper into his embrace.

Yet of all the unimaginable things that had happened in the last few weeks, the very last thing she could have imagined was that she would come to love him.

But she had fallen hard, deeply and forever.

She loved her greatest enemy. The man who threatened her life and her livelihood and everything that was true and dear to her. Somewhere in the midst of all their wrangling, he had ceased to be her enemy, this remarkable man she'd once believed was wicked and unjust and sought only the truth that he wished to find.

But that wasn't her Charles at all. He was a man of honor, and she loved him. Loved that he was making growling noises in his throat and holding her face steady with both hands, cradling her head, strewing his lingering kisses everywhere.

His kiss was deep and thrilling, reached to her core, and left her breathless with wanting more. He was forceful in his embrace, caressing and completely marvelous. She welcomed the touch of his hand at her neck, his fingers slipping just under the edge of her bodice, leaving a searing trail of longing.

And then he stopped as suddenly as he'd begun. His dark eyes flared when he raised his head, and his brow deeply furrowed.

"Enough, Hollie," he whispered against her ear, where his words were a flame that left her aching and wanting more of him, because she was wicked and she would lose her soul for it.

"Yes—enough, Charles."

Enough of paradise.

And yet she found it again when he caught her inside his cloak and protected her with his heat all the way to the gatehouse. And when he lifted her hand and touched an astounding kiss to her palm.

"I'm more grateful than you could ever know,

Hollie. Wanting so much more than I am entitled to."

He left her at the gatehouse door, her knees weak, her heart soaring and swooping, still having said nothing at all about her most recent crime.

Almost as though he approved.

But that couldn't be the case.

There was a far deeper reason for his silence. Something that had niggled at her all day long, yet nothing she could put her finger on.

Something profoundly important.

And, she suspected, utterly devastating.

Chapter 22

Hollie waited until Charles was long gone from the gatehouse and his heady kiss was just a lingering ache before she crept back up the drive and into the conservatory, where she'd left her broadside so long ago.

Throughout the staggering magnificence of the day, when his hair shone obsidian in the autumn light, when Chip was turning his pony in trotting circles, and later while he was intoxicating her with his lovemaking, it had been so easy to forget the terror of a few hours before.

He'd picked up the broadside and read it through, of that she was certain. And yet he'd set it aside as though it meant nothing that she'd obviously rifled his desk and stolen secret papers.

And not only stolen his private correspondence, but was preparing to broadcast the information it contained.

She lit a candle against the moonlaced darkness and studied the broadside that he'd so purposely ignored.

It seemed clear enough to her.

PUBLIC WARNING AGAINST
SIX ACTS OF SUPPRESSION

Lord Sidmouth's threats enumerated, simplified, emboldened. The terror of random search and seizure, the prohibition against political gatherings, an impossible increase in the newspaper and stamp duties, banishment for those writing papers found to be blasphemous and seditious. And the other cruel acts.

Was her broadside missing the point entirely, had she lost her touch?

Didn't he recognize his own ministry's text? Or had he yet to read Sidmouth's letter? No, it was there on his desk, opened with the others. With notes in his script, or Bavidge's.

He must have read her broadside. The words were bold and crisp-edged and clear enough for anyone to read at a dozen paces.

Unless they were blind or utterly stupid or—
Dear God!

Read it, Bavidge. The hair stood up on her nape.

How many times had she heard Charles say that when she'd first arrived at Everingham?

How many times had he gruffly tossed a document in his clerk's direction and then turned away to listen?

Read it, Miss Finch. The note from the village farrier. And she had done so, because he'd ordered her to.

Read it, Hollie. All that lounging grace and arrogance, his long legs stretched out as she read *The Times* to him, offering her arguments, debating his opinons. In the shadow of all those books.

But he'd read all those broadsides and handbills that first night, hadn't he? No, he'd barely looked at them. Had memorized them.

And the word "forever," the last word in the Magna Carta. He hadn't been looking at that either; he'd been looking at her. He'd only known the last phrase because he had committed it to memory at some time before.

And his anger at her note about their indiscretion and the rags—Bavidge must have started reading it. That's why Charles had been so angry, so misdirected.

And though she'd thought it odd at the time, there had been two lines of writing below his name on the sheet she'd printed for him. His son's primitive C-H-I-P, and above that, an entirely different hand: C-H— uncertain, but bolder, larger than the boy's.

Oh, my dear God. Charles can't read.

But that was impossible. Completely absurd. He was a politically powerful earl, educated at

Oxford. He was wise and disciplined. She'd seen him transfix the members of parliament with his speeches, laying out his arguments point by point.

Without a single note. Holding nothing in his fine hands. Not a single reference.

Because he couldn't read it anyway.

And nobody knew.

Nobody but her.

Her heart dropped into her stomach. Charles was illiterate—and was so ashamed of it that he had been hiding it from everyone for a very long time.

But how? His life revolved around paper.

And what about the Peterloo file? Dear God, he'd never read a word of the evidence for himself! If he had, he would have come to better conclusions, because he was a good and intelligent man. He would have known that his commission was corrupted—if not deliberately, then simply because Charles couldn't oversee the truth.

Impossible.

Improbable. But Charles Stirling was improbable in so many ways.

She needed to be sure that he wasn't leading her on, that he wasn't using her to further his plans to capture her "husband."

He would discover her deception as soon as her broadsides began appearing in the countryside. In three days Captain Spindleshanks would put in an appearance at the reform meeting at Wolverhampton.

She'd have to leave the Stanhope behind—and all her memories. She'd need to leave Everingham tomorrow night after she'd read Chip a good-night story one last time.

After Charles had left the gatehouse.

But how to test him and yet not break him? Anyone could pretend that he couldn't read—though she couldn't imagine why he'd want her to believe that of him.

Whatever the test, it had to be something remarkable, something startling, something that he couldn't hide his reaction to.

Not an open threat or a curse. Something that would strike him in the heart. Something she could see in his eyes.

I love you, Charles Stirling.

Yes, that. Because it was true and startling and would break her heart in two.

Forgive me, Charles.

Chapter 23

Charles found Hollie busy as usual in the conservatory the next morning, fast at work on the book of songbirds. Chip was at his lessons, making long lists of his name.

"Papa!" Charles caught the boy's embrace around his knees and planted a kiss against his cheek, then helped him back into the chair and turned to Hollie.

"Good morning, Hollie."

She looked up at him from across the hulking Stanhope. Her eyes sparkled with the intense green of springtime, edged with an intense brightness that might be the remains of tears, or a night of sleeplessness to match the interminable night he'd had spent himself.

It had been filled with restless, yearning

dreams of Hollie, of impossible miracles. With what ifs, and an enlightening, thorny study of his honor.

And then this morning's news: an unequivocal reminder of the insubstantial claim he had upon her.

I have news of your husband.

"Good morning, Charles." She offered a tremulous smile, overly brave. "I trust you slept well."

"Well enough, madam."

He'd learned through the Home Office spies that Spindleshanks was to make an appearance in Wolverhampton the day after tomorrow, at a meeting of Peterloo petitioners.

This time he'd make the damned arrest himself and be done with it. Done with MacGillnock.

Telling Hollie in advance was a risk he couldn't take—the fiercely loyal wife who had never loved her husband but who championed the man as though he were her matchless hero.

A darkly jealous voice inside him didn't want her to know of the man's whereabouts. Because he didn't want to have to imagine her charging off into the night to warn him; couldn't have borne finding her in the man's arms, whatever their marital custom.

And though he wanted to relieve Hollie of her misbegotten marriage, it wasn't his place to act for her. He'd done enough to tarnish her honor. Stepping away from the situation as soon as the man was caught was the only way to keep his balance, the only moral action.

Above all, he wanted the matter to be finished: to finally catch the man in the act and hand him over to the courts to be tried and sentenced. The fate of Hollie's husband would be decided elsewhere.

Mumberton bustled in, wiping his hands on a dishcloth, his clothes smelling of sweets from the kitchen. "Mrs. Riley says she has cakes to be tested. Is there a cake tester anywhere around, my lord?"

"Me!" Chip took hold of his father's hand and jumped like a jack-in-the-box. "Me, please, sir."

Charles touseled his son's hair, unable to resist casting a grateful glance at Hollie, the woman who had turned his life upside down, who'd gifted him with this miraculous bundle of happiness. "Are you a cake expert, Chip?"

"I am, Papa."

"Well, then, you'd best go give Mrs. Riley and Mumberton a helping hand."

He was off in a streak of laughter, Mumberton hurrying after him, leaving Charles alone with Hollie, the cool air in the conservatory heavy with the scent of ink and orchards.

He wanted to thread his fingers through her hair, to nuzzle through its curling wildness to her ear. But last night's stolen moment of joy would have to be the end of it.

For now, at least. Forever, if it had to be.

"I'm to see my lawyer today, Hollie. To make it official that Chip is my son. My heir."

Her eyes pooled with starry tears. "I'm so happy, Charles. You're making it right for him. I knew you would. I knew you loved him."

It was a roaring, aching thing, this kind of love. Invasive and unrelenting. It squeezed his heart and gouged at his gut. It made his hands cold and his belly hot.

"Christ, Hollie, I wish I could make it right for you just as simply." He wished it wouldn't mean damnation and shattering repercussions.

"We make our choices, Charles, and live with the consequences."

And the fathomless ache. And the yearning for something better.

She turned away from him, tears sliding down her cheeks as she went back to inking the plate in her printer's dance, the one he'd grown to love as much as he feared the product of the Stanhope's clanking and straining, secrets she could so easily keep from him if he wasn't vigilant.

But it wouldn't matter soon. "I must go to Westminster tonight, Hollie."

"Tonight?" Hollie's heart leaped, dropped again in misery, then sputtered in great relief: Charles would be gone when she left for the meeting. She wouldn't have to make excuses or skulk off under his nose with her ill-gotten words in her bags. "Is Parliament in session early this season?"

"Business with your good friend Lord Pudding." Sharing a smile with him had become so unconsciously natural. When had it started to ache like a cold fire?

"Please give him my best regards." She took the page of threatening ravens from the print bed and hung it on the drying line, feeling his gaze on her nape like a caress. "How long will you be gone?"

"Why? Will you miss me?"

Like I will miss breathing and laughing and all of my better dreams, my love. She couldn't answer for the sob that was caught in her throat.

Banter would have to serve, words that pinched, that might cause him to pace the conservatory as was his wont. Something that would make him find the faithless test she'd laid out for him to happen upon in his stalking.

"What if my dear Adam comes to rescue me while you're visiting the Pudding?"

He snorted in his arrogant way, arching an eyebrow at her. "I'll be thoroughly stunned, madam."

He sounded utterly certain that Adam wouldn't come, sending her pulse into her ears with absolute terror. Maybe he had been misleading her after all. Maybe she was wrong. Of course she was! He'd read her broadside after all and was plotting to trap her.

She was already damned for her crimes; now

her ridiculous test would lay bare the threat to her heart.

"Then have I lost my charms, Charles? If I'm no longer a provocative enough lure for my husband, why do you keep me around?"

His gaze was steady and heated, and it broke her heart into a million pieces when he shrugged his broad shoulders as though he didn't care. "You're free to go, Hollie."

I'm not free at all! Not with everything she loved tangled up here at Everingham. "But not with my Stanhope."

He turned back to her and said with dark amusement, "Not on your life."

"You still don't trust me alone with it?"

"I'm taking this damned devil's tail with me all the way to Westminster, madam. Just in case."

Too little, my love, and far too late. She wasn't ever coming back.

Hollie watched him out of the corner of her eye as she inked the panel of ravens, watched in guilty horror as he picked up the handwritten page that she'd planted where he couldn't possibly miss it.

A traitorous trap fashioned just for him; the deepest confession of her heart.

She watched his dark eyes move across the page, the midnight of his lashes lowered. Then he turned to her, an unreadable frown set into his brow, a gruffness in his voice.

"What's this, Hollie?"

I love you, Charles Stirling.

She waited for his thunder, her pulse pounding in her ears. Waited for a sign of his astonishment, his anger; waited breathlessly for any reaction at all beyond his elegantly ordered curiosity.

And the waiting told her more than any stumbling attempt to mask his response would have.

He was so careful, her beloved earl. So guarded with his strategies, so expert at turning the charge back on someone else. Making them read to him what he could not.

Her heart ached for him, for the obstreperous boy he must have been in the schoolroom, and the clever student who must have fought his way through university with every ounce of his courage, terrified of failing, shredding everyone in his way for fear of being caught and having more shame heaped upon him.

Who'd grown into the unrelenting earl who enraptured Parliament and the heart of a young woman in the press gallery with his off-the-cuff speeches.

Because he couldn't read.

Because he had never learned how, and plainly it shamed him to his soul. Though it didn't lessen him in her eyes in the least.

"Oh, it's of no moment, Charles." *Only my heart and all my love for you. For my sweet Chip and all the might-have-beens.* "A reminder to myself that I have a short time left to finish the *Handbook of Song Birds*."

A short time left to look at you, my love, to wish on the last star in a very inky night.

His smile was as trusting as it was relieved. He had succeeded one more time in sheltering his secret from those who might betray him.

"Very well, Hollie. But you'll have to wait the three days until I return from Westminster."

"Yes, Charles. I'll wait three days."

A lifetime. Longer, my love.

Hollie caught the sob in her throat and turned away as he began inking the plates for her. He made his jests and broke her heart to bits when he lifted the returned Chip onto his shoulders and planted a smacking kiss on her forehead.

She could hardly feel more wretched: she had stolen secrets from a blind man who believed that she was as honorable as he.

He was so trusting of her, so honest in his dealings, that she would easily be able to walk out of his life tonight with damning evidence tucked away in her satchel—evidence against him and his commission and the whole bloody Privy Council.

Her wicked earl had become her heart.

"Good-bye, Papa!" Hollie held Chip in her arms and watched from the gatehouse as Charles cantered off down the drive and into the late afternoon sunset. They both waved until long after he had disappeared beyond the coppiced wood.

"How long is three days, Hollie?" The little boy's tears ran freely down his cheeks.

"Three nights, sweetheart. Three breakfasts."

"Three stories."

"Just that, Chip." What a dreadfully easy liar she'd become. "And then you'll have your papa back."

As though nothing else would ever change, Hollie taught her reading lesson that night in the gatehouse, then carried Chip back to the main house and tucked him in this one last time.

"You'll grow up to be a good man like your papa."

"And a printer like you, Hollie."

"He loves you, Chip."

"He loves *us*, Hollie."

Dear God. Allowing him to love her was the worst sin of all.

She held the boy until he fell asleep and then left him to his dreams.

Hollie packed a small bundle of her belongings along with Captain Spindleshanks's costume and a few dozen fresh broadsides to distribute among the members of the meeting, tucked her love note to Charles into her bodice, and then started off across his tidy fields.

She boarded a post chaise in the village at

midnight and was standing in the bustling lobby of the Fleece Inn at Wolverhampton by the following afternoon, exhausted and dusty and wanting nothing more than to weep.

"Hollie Finch!" Mrs. Conners took her hands, met her cheek to cheek. "What a lovely thing to see you again, sweet girl. I have your favorite room for you. Do tell me you're staying the night and not just passing through on your way to chase one of your stories."

Hollie embraced the woman and her chattering, a dear friend from her other life, back when she was as familiar with the country's roads as most people were with their own village high streets.

"I'm here for a day or two, Mrs. Conners. Maybe longer." Until Charles realized that she'd betrayed him, that she'd duped him. In the meantime, she was back in her element. A little wiser and so much sadder than she ever could have imagined.

"A hot bath will do you a world of good, lovey, after your long trip. And a tray of dinner. Let's give your bags to Tommy here, and I'll go see to your comfort myself. Sit, sit, sit. I'll come down for you when it's ready."

Relieved and heartsick, Hollie was about to drop into a chair in the lobby when she heard her name called out from the low-timbered dining room.

"Hollie Finch! As I live and breathe, girl!"

"Major Cartwright!" Hollie hurried past the other diners and threw herself into the old radical's spare embrace, inhaling the familiar pipesmoke that clung to his coat. "It's so good to see you."

"And you, my dear girl. I don't know where you've been hiding, Hollie, but I've missed you sorely. In a cave somewhere? You look pale as a ghost." The old man peered at her through his spectacles and brushed the rough pad of his thumb across her cheek. "What's this? A bit weepy too. What's happened?"

She could never hide a thing from him; he'd known her since she was a babe. A dear friend of her father's, he'd often been in her parlor, involved in noisy discussions with other radicals.

She'd learned at the knees of the greatest reformers of the age. And now she was back again, from her holiday in the country.

Where she'd lost her heart and most of her soul to a man who shouldn't have been so easy to love.

"It's been a difficult year, Major."

"Ah, your father—I know, my girl. I miss him too. Damn them all." He leaned forward in twinkling conspiracy. "But you're here for the petition meeting, I hope."

"Yes, I need to see Mr. Prentice—"

"Hollie Finch, as I live and breathe!" Joseph Howe plunked himself down on the chair beside her, another old friend, florid and always merry, a lawyer who practiced on the side of right and liberty. If only Charles could stop in his thick-headed crusade long enough to understand. "You disappeared after Peterloo. I didn't know what to think, girl."

"I had some thinking to do."

"Parliament's in session in just a few weeks. We'll need you in the gallery, taking down their blasphemies and seeing them published."

Sidmouth planned to put a stop to that soon enough—blasphemy being judged in the eye of the beholder, and Parliament determined to make the sinners pay.

"I hope to, Joseph." She would no longer be free to sit undisguised in the gallery—not with Charles scanning there from the benches, on the lookout for her to return to the scene of her crimes.

The woman who had betrayed his trust. Who had loved him for all his goodness but couldn't stay.

"What about the Tuppenny, Hollie?" The Major wrapped his bony fingers around her wrist. "I heard your father's old printing press was taken by the Home Office."

"It was. I barely escaped, myself."

Joseph took on his lawyer's air, whipped a notebook and pencil from his coat pocket. "You weren't arrested, were you?"

Oh, if the earl had merely arrested her and

thrown her into his darkest prison, as he should have done!

"I was able to talk the magistrate out of it, Joseph. Pleaded innocence." And a false marriage to a cowardly radical, whom she'd grown to dislike with her whole heart. "Since then, I've been investigating the massacre on my own. Because it wasn't going to happen any other way, and I was given an unparalleled opportunity."

The major scooted in closer, intent. "What have you got, Hollie?"

"Information from Captain Spindleshanks."

"Coals to Newcastle, Hollie," Joseph said, leaning back in his chair. "He's coming to the meeting himself."

"Yes, I know. He's sent me in advance." She'd kept the secret from everyone: her colleagues, her father's closest friends—men she looked up to. She'd always hated secrets, and this one had gotten far out of hand, leaving her to wonder who she really was, and where she would go after this, after Charles learned what she'd done and who she was and set his bailiffs against her this one last time.

"What's he been up to, lass?" The major patted her hand.

"Spying on the Home Office."

"The bloody fool," Joseph hissed through his teeth, then looked around the crowded dining room as though they were being watched.

And they might well be, though not by Charles or his bailiffs. Not yet, at least; he was in Westminster.

But that knowledge suddenly didn't feel nearly as solid and certain as it had an hour ago. A coincidental trip that took him away from Everingham Hall, just when she needed to make her escape to Wolverhampton?

Yet nothing at all had changed here. The Fleece was a busy coaching inn, with hundreds of people bound for hundreds of places, at all hours of the day and night.

The noise was clamorous, and yet a sudden chill made her whisper, "Captain Spindleshanks wanted me to let Prentice know that he's gained certain highly secret information."

Joseph leaned into her whispering with his penchant for drama. "Highly secret, Hollie?"

State secrets. High treason, without a doubt.

"I have on me a copy of the parliamentary bill that the Home Office plans to enact against the press and the public come November."

"What lunacy is this, Hollie?" The major took hold of her hand and squeezed it. "Have you been party to stealing from the Privy Council?"

"Not from them."

"I don't care from whom. You must hold fast by the laws, Hollie. Don't give them any reason to arrest you."

Lying to a magistrate, then impersonating a

married woman, falling madly for a peer of the realm, and finally stealing him blind.

"I'm well past that point now, Major. They think I've been printing material for Captain Spindleshanks."

"Have you been?"

She nodded to the major, and the two men groaned in unison.

She'd never told a soul about her secret life. Too great an opportunity to be accidentally betrayed, to hurt the people she loved. The less they knew, the better for all concerned.

"And I would again, if I still had my press. I applaud the captain's measures."

"As I do, girl, but not his tactics, the fool."

"I don't think you understand him, Major."

"I do, girl. And I can't think of a better way of putting the noose around your neck than associating yourself with a felon. You're playing a dangerous game here. Your life is in the balance."

"But life is always dear," she whispered, "no matter how we live it. And like it or not, Captain Spindleshanks will be in attendance at the meeting tomorrow morning. Please let Prentice know if you see him."

"Your room is ready, Hollie." Mrs. Conners bustled over to the table, her guileless smile as wide as the sleeves of her stylish gown.

Hollie was suddenly tired to her soul and aching for a bath. She smiled bravely at the concern in the major's eye and met Joseph's stalwart approval with the feeling that she was about to set her world spinning out of control.

"Thank you, gentlemen," she said, "I'll see you in the morning."

She left the dining room and followed Mrs. Conners up the stairs, ready to sleep the night away.

She dismissed the odd sensation that she was being watched, because it felt so much like the steamy heat of Charles's gaze.

But Charles couldn't possibly be here.

He was in Westminster.

Chapter 24

⎯⎯◦◯◦⎯⎯

Hollie stepped into the tub of steaming water, gasping at the shock of the heat. She shut everything from her thoughts, breathing in the calming scent of the lavender oil, savoring the slip of the soap along her legs and arms. She stood up in the cool night air, scrubbed at her skin, washed and rinsed her hair, and then settled back into the tub, hoping she wouldn't fall so deeply asleep that she missed the meeting entirely.

There were too many important things to do there. Life-changing things.

The chamber was perfect for her mood, tucked way up into a corner of the Fleece, the ceiling so raftered and gabled that it hadn't a single right angle to it. The bed was tucked into one shadowy dormer, and a small table and its pair of chairs in another. A single candle burned on a table beside the tub in the center of the room.

She'd discovered the room years ago and stayed there whenever she found herself at the Fleece Inn, though it was the sort of room that most guests refused for its eccentric simplicity. Her home for the moment. Perhaps for the week.

Or maybe just tonight. It might be Coldbath Prison, after the morning's meeting. There would be spies and informers on the benches and magistrates waiting outside to arrest her.

She was tired of the itch and the sweat of travel, no longer looking forward to the meeting as she used to, dreading the hour when she'd have to don the captain's coat and hat and make an appearance.

Most of all, she was exhausted by her deception. The constant checking and rechecking of every thought before she spoke a word. Always running, yet never staying ahead of her heart. It lagged behind and preached at her to stop, to stay and face Charles with the truth.

But it had gone beyond that now.

A spectacle was called for, if a full accounting of the massacre was ever to be made public and the responsible parties brought to justice. Flash powder and swirling capes—Captain Spindle-shanks making a grand entrance into the court-room itself.

If she was brave enough and lucky enough tomorrow to escape the magistrates.

Charles would surely attend her inquest and trial. He would be there watching when she made her grand entrance as Captain Spindleshanks, when she threw off her costume and confessed that she was the crusading captain, when she pointed her finger and accused the Privy Council to their faces of encouraging barbarism against unarmed citizens.

Charles would stand up and courageously agree with her, would defend the innocents who had died at Peterloo, then take her into his arms and . . .

Hollie started and came awake a moment later, the bathwater still warm and sloshing, the candle the same height as a moment ago. But something had changed in the blinking instant that she'd dozed off; the room felt darker, more familiar somehow.

Charles. The memories of him, clinging to her like the dear scent of him.

She stood up in the tub and let the water sluice off, wrung out her hair, and was stepping out of the bath when she felt a shift in the cool air— eddies of warmth and the voluptuous sensation that she was being watched, tasted, longed for. Which was utterly impossible up here in the garret; it was too small and out of the way.

Dismissing the unsettling feeling as her foolish

imagination, she dried off and donned the white shirt of her Spindleshanks costume she'd set out on the bed and started fastening the buttons.

Charles's shirt. It had gotten mixed with her own laundry weeks ago, and she'd really meant to return it, but she'd loved the texture of the linen, the faint smell of lime. And now it was a reminder of him that she would wear against her skin.

His warmth, his scent—

"I hope your husband appreciates your tender preparations for him, madam."

Charles!

Hollie gasped and whirled toward the dark voice.

He was a part of the curving cruck of the rafters, a midnight shadow leaning against a lighter one. Her heart battered at her chest as she clutched her thin shirt around her.

"You're supposed to be in Westminster," she said, with barely enough air for a breath. She couldn't allow him to intimidate her, no matter what he knew or why he'd come after her.

Because she could imagine that too well.

"And you, madam, are supposed to be at Everingham."

Charles grabbed for the blazing anger that had sustained him through the last hour, for the fury that had brought him up the stairs and into her ill-guarded chamber, that had allowed him to stand by and watch her at her bath.

Christ, she was beautiful, candle-shadowed and lush-limbed, gold dripping off the ends of her hair.

He hadn't believed his eyes at first. His Hollie in the dining room of the Fleece, hours from Everingham. An illusion of the shifting crowd perhaps or a flickering memory of her, of her matchless cascade of golden hair, her green eyes.

He'd blinked and she was gone. Then she had reappeared in the lobby and followed the proprietress up the stairs.

Hollie! Here in Wolverhampton. There could be only one reason.

To meet her bastard of a husband.

The one she loved madly enough to risk her life for.

He'd carefully steeled himself against her excuses, had let himself into her room with no thought but to continue using her in the way he'd been using her these last weeks: to bait a trap for MacGillnock, to see the man's reign of arrogance finished. And now, to shut her out of his heart as easily as she'd betrayed him.

All those falsehoods about her loveless marriage. He'd been fool enough to pray they were true, that she was a casualty of her own goodness. But she'd run to her dear Adam at her first opportunity. She'd used Charles well in her game.

And now she was standing insolently in front of him, surpassingly beautiful in the simplicity of a man's shirt. Doubtless her husband's. And just as doubtless, she had been waiting in her lavender-scented garret for MacGillnock to return from a triumphant meeting with the radicals.

He didn't want to see the sorrowful brightness of her eyes as he came out of the shadows, didn't want to hear the harrowing thunder in his heart that said how much he dearly wanted all her devotion for himself.

"How did you get in here, Charles?" Her voice was etched with a sad impatience, a trembling roughness that made him want to believe better things.

"It doesn't matter how, madam—only that you clearly left Everingham as soon as my back was turned."

She raised her stubborn chin. "I'm not your prisoner," she said, clutching her fists against the linen folds, her sudden breath causing the dark peaks of her breasts to lift against the loose shirt, beckoning his hand, his mouth. "You said so yourself, Charles. You also said you were going to Westminster."

He tossed his cloak easily on the back of the chair, as though his arms weren't quaking to drag her into his embrace.

"I'm here for the same reason you are, madam. Waiting on your husband's return."

She huffed and turned away to the gable window and the darkness beyond, her head bent and her elbows winged as she worked privately at the front of the shirt. She was all slim legs and a shapely, linen-clad bottom. "How did you know he was coming, Charles?"

"Spies, madam. The best that money can buy."

She turned back to him, the shirt's pearly buttons fastened now, its hem hanging to just below her knees. "I take it you didn't catch him."

"And if I had?" he asked evenly, his breathing remarkably steady for a man waiting on her verdict, though his heart had become a dead weight.

"Then I would plead mercy, of course." Her gaze was a steady challenge, her lower lip caught between her teeth as though she'd meant to say more.

"The dutiful wife after all, supportive to the bitter end. You led me to believe differently." But that was the woman's way—blind loyalty, however mad and impossible the cause.

"I think I said that loyalty was a delicate thing, Charles. Easily injured."

"What I want to know, madam, is how he got word to you of this meeting."

"He— It's been scheduled for a very long time. An important meeting of men who only wish to be heard, to have their opinions considered." She shook her head impatiently and clutched her arms around her waist, her hair wilder than his memories. "I wasn't sure, but I was hoping he could keep the appointment."

"And so you thought you'd come here and

find him, arrange a marital tryst while you're here in town?"

"I needed to be here, Charles."

"After your confession to me that he never touched you. Never took you to his bed."

Her shoulders sagged, and she tilted her chin to the ceiling for a moment, then sighed at him. "You're completely wrong about all this, Charles. Wrong about so many things."

"Isn't that why your bath is scented? For him—your *dear* Adam?" He dipped his fingers into the warm water, brought them to his nose. "Is this his favorite scent?"

"It's mine, Charles," she said, her words clipped with anger.

"Lavender, Hollie. But you are peaches and apples and the barley harvest. You smell like that, madam. All day long. I smell you on my hands and in my hair."

Her face crumpled. "Please, Charles. Don't."

"Is he in town?" he asked through the cramping of his throat.

"I don't know."

"So he hasn't come to you yet. Your brave, radical husband who dashes from one heroic event to the next, leaving you behind. The man who supposedly loves you. The one you'd risk your life for. Where is he?"

"Captain Spindleshanks is not a fool, Charles. He knows he's being watched and knows better than to show himself."

"Because you told him."

"No, Charles. He just knows." A shuddering sob escaped her. She raked her fingers through her hair, the finest tendrils curling at the edge of her face in a gilded halo. And she was weeping, tears sliding down her cheeks and landing on the shirt, making wet oriels of the linen. "It isn't safe for him, my lord."

"Ah, and it is safe for you, Hollie?" He was unable to understand her tears, let alone the excuses he was creating for her treachery. He caught her shoulders and risked looking into all that weeping sadness. "Running his errands for him, printing his handbills. You're doing that still, aren't you? Against my orders. Against your own best interests."

Her cheeks were pink, her brows winged in her unnameable fury. "An old pledge, as I said."

"So you pledged yourself to follow him to the ends of the earth. For what? Is he grateful, do you wonder? Has he ever once said?"

"He doesn't have to say a thing. I know the captain's heart." She yanked herself away from him and went to the table strewn with her papers and inks, then fingered the yellowing pages of a small book. "I do it because I must."

"He forces you? Is that what you're saying?" He wanted to believe that the man gave her no choice in her loyalties. That fitted so much better against his aching pride.

"Nobody forces me to do anything against my

beliefs, Charles. You should know that of me by now. The only thing I can assure you of is that I'm not expecting my husband tonight. He's not coming here."

"Because he's a coward, Hollie."

"No, dammit. I mean . . . well . . . yes. He probably *is* a coward." The sob in her throat made his heart catch, made him want to hold her in his arms. "You're absolutely right, Charles. Captain Spindleshanks is the most cowardly creature in the entire world."

Her agreement ought to have delighted him, but it only made him angry.

"He's a rake and a bounder, Hollie. Take it from me, I've been one. I know the worthless life he leads. From one lightskirt to another, unconnected to anyone or anything. He doesn't care."

"And you do, Charles?"

He'd never imagined caring as much about anything. "I do, Hollie."

Yet he was acting the rakehell again, calling her husband vile, wanting her outside her marriage vows, wanting to make promises of his own, to make the man vanish from the earth as though he'd never been. He ached to hold her, to take her to bed and make love to her every night of their lives.

But she was better than that, deserved far more than a stolen life. So he kept his distance.

"You married the wrong man, Hollie."

She shook her head, emphatic, sniffling back her sorrow. "No, I didn't, Charles."

The slice to his gut nearly bent him in half. She should be *his*, damn it. He should have found her first. There on St. Peter's Fields. If the magistrates had kept the swords and tempers in check.

"I should have known better, Hollie. You wear his damn shirt like that, like you've just come out of his bed."

It threatened to fall off her shoulder, for the collar buttons were undone. A trail of glistening tears ran down between her breasts.

Her clear eyes caught his gaze, lit up with a sudden determination. "It's not his shirt, Charles. It's yours."

His stomach flipped, dragging a sharp breath out of him. "Mine?"

She raised her hand and the sleeve slipped down over her fingers. "See, Charles. It's yours."

Calling himself a fool for getting this close, for wanting to believe, he lifted the cuff, found his monogram and then her steady, tear-starred gaze.

Not MacGillnock's shirt.

"*My* shirt."

He didn't need to hear this. Didn't need to be standing on the brink of paradise, a breath away from the angel who was holding out her hand to him.

"I love you, Charles."

"Christ, Hollie." He *really* didn't need to hear that either, so beguiled by the scent of her, unable to move.

He wanted to unfasten the buttons, to lift aside the linen and take her lushness into his mouth. If only she were free and his wife and the mother of their children. "Why? Why not your husband's shirt?"

"Because . . . Oh, Charles." She grabbed a breath and another heart-stabbing sob. "Because he . . ."

"What, Hollie? *Tell* me, damn it."

"Because he . . . isn't my husband."

"Not your—" He flinched, feeling gut-punched. And then confused, because she wasn't that sort. "Adam MacGillnock is *what* to you, then, Hollie?"

"Oh!" She covered her mouth, and her eyes shot wide in scandalized shock. "Oh, God, it's not that, Charles. Not at all. I wouldn't. He's nothing, Charles."

"What the hell does *nothing* mean?"

"I mean, Charles, that he's *nothing*." She slipped past him, brushing her arm against his chest. "Just a man. Just . . . a name to me. That's all."

"A name?" His head was spinning with her unimaginable landscapes, with possibilities. "What the hell does *that* mean, Hollie?"

She lifted her arms to the side, her sleeves drooping, a supplicant. Her hair hung loose at her shoulders. The shirt molded around her thighs, taunting him with shadows and glorious ecstasies.

"It means that I'm not married to anyone, Charles."

Not married. Holy Christ!

The whole world tipped and teetered. Joy was filling him so fast with bits of sunlight that he couldn't contain it, felt it shooting out of his fingertips.

And yet Hollie was staring numbly at him, terrifying him.

"What the bloody hell are trying to say, Hollie? You're not married?"

"Not to Captain Spindleshanks or to Adam MacGillnock or to anyone." Now she was weeping into her sleeves. *His* sleeves.

Because she loved him.

And he loved her. Madly, irrevocably. Because she had become the air he breathed and the morning dew on the fields. And because she would be his wife and the mother of all his children.

"I'm sorry, Charles."

Christ, he wanted to see happiness in her eyes. But she looked utterly defeated.

"Hollie, why?"

She turned sorrowful eyes on him, pleading for something he couldn't imagine. "I . . . I thought I could help. I . . . admired his work. His crusade."

His beautiful, grand-hearted reformer. No wonder he loved her. "Admired him so much that you did his printing for him."

"Yes."

"And lied to protect him."

She only sobbed into her cuff.

"To preserve all the good that you believe he stands for."

"Yes, of course."

"A damned foolish thing to do, Hollie."

She nodded carefully, obviously terrified when she needn't be.

For she'd just made him the happiest man in the world.

And he was about to show her just how madly a husband could fall for his wife.

"Do you know that I love you for it, Hollie Finch."

Charles Stirling loves me.

It was all Hollie could do just to breathe, for happiness, for the terrible half-truth that she'd just told him. Her inescapable little lie made nothing better, except that Charles was looking at her in a delicious way. Like he was going to devour her and make her love every bite, every kiss.

"You've no reason to love me, Charles. You shouldn't. I lied to you in the most unforgivable way: I told you I was married when I wasn't." She couldn't move for the sudden change that came over the man—a bewitching power that should have sent her out the door and down the stairs, except she could swear he was smiling.

"But you *will* be married." A crooked, slanted smile, with a whole lot of devil in it.

"Maybe someday."

He shook his head with a savage sort of arrogance and shrugged slowly out of his fine wool coat, the hungry look of the hunter in his eyes. "A month from now would do very nicely."

"A month, Charles?" Hollie laughed at his absurdity and then ducked out of the way of all that broad-shouldered brawn. "I doubt very much that I could be married in a month." Or ever.

"And I have no doubt that you *will* be."

The impossible man was unbuttoning his waistcoat slowly, inexorably. Moving closer to her, leaving her no escape, and no reason to escape; because he'd backed her against the thick face of the cruck and he was simply wonderful to look at, to smell, to feel.

"Easy to say, Charles, but first I need a groom."

That made him smile all the more, so charmingly cocky she thought her heart would burst with hopeless love for him. He was looming over her, looking thoroughly at home in her bedchamber, thoroughly handsome.

And terrifically intentional as he braced his elbow against the slanting arch, then dipped his head and caught his mouth against her neck with a kiss that buckled her knees.

"Will *I* do, madam?"

Oh, yes. "Will you do . . . oh, my . . . what, Charles?" Ah, and now he was nuzzling her with his fine mouth, nibbling along the ridge of her shoulder. *Yes, yes, yes.*

"*Will* I do, my love?" He caught both his hands around her waist and fitted her hips against his, her belly and the glorious ridge of his erection.

"Will you do for what, Charles?"

"A groom." He touched his searing kiss along the underside of her jaw, then followed with the drift of his fingers.

So lightly! Oh, yes, down her neck and across the base of her throat, before he caught the collar of the shirt with his fingers and slid it part way off her shoulder.

"Groom, Charles? What do you mean?" *And what are you doing?*

He murmured her name and pulled gently at the fabric, tugging ever downward in his bewitching assault, following the swell of her breast, making her squirm and wait for him and hurry him, until she was holding his hips against hers, braced against him, writhing shamelessly.

"Charles?"

He hissed out a thrilling groan.

"Christ, Hollie," he growled as he took a deeply ragged breath. "You're a miracle to me."

No, the miracle was the intimacy of him, the fever blooming in her stomach and at the joining of her legs.

"You've made the sun shine, Hollie." He cupped her face in his hands, threaded his fingers through her hair, and cradled the back of her head. "Do you know that, my love? You've shown me the sky and the moon."

My love. He kissed her lashes and the side of her nose and the hollow of her throat, leaving her clinging to the lapels of his vest.

A sideways smile appeared; his eyes were soft as smoke. "But you see, Hollie, the thing that I couldn't reconcile with the rest of my life, no matter how hard I tried, was not having you beside me."

"Beside you how, Charles?" He was making it so very difficult to think. "Do you need a printer?"

"I need a wife, Hollie."

Of course he did. He was a massively eligible peer. But she didn't want to hear about his plans for the future Lady Everingham, not now. She wanted to weep. "I wish you well in your quest, Charles. In your marriage."

He frowned, tilted her chin with the tip of his finger, and gazed down at her. "Hollie, I need *you.*"

And I need you, Charles.

He went down on his knee and took her hands inside his, his eyes alight with passion and promise and miracles. "Marry me, Hollie."

Marry me, Hollie?

What an impossibly lovely song that was, right out of her imagination. The wicked earl and the reformer.

"Will you, Hollie?"

"Will I . . . ?" Dear God, he meant it! No, but he couldn't possibly. "Are you asking me to marry you?"

"The woman I love, whose life I cherish. I'd be a fool to let you go, my love."

Marry him! She slipped to her knees because they'd stopped working and carried his hands to her cheek, wishing with all her heart that she could say yes.

"I can't, Charles." *I'm a liar and a thief, and there is a wrong that I must put right.*

He narrowed his eyes. "You can do anything, Hollie. You've proved that to me."

"No, no, Charles. I can't do this." They were two different people who lived in two wildly different worlds. She was a radical reformer with a price on her head. And he was the man who had put it there.

This splendid moment was merely a dream that she could pull out of her memories when she was in Coldbath Prison and he was orating against her and her kind in Parliament.

She slipped away from him and took refuge beside the little hearth and its dying fire.

He didn't look at all convinced, only more determined when he stood. "I'm gainfully employed, Hollie."

"And you are a good man, Charles. The very best."

"You love me. You just said so."

"I do. Madly. I didn't know it was possible to love as I do. But I can't. I shouldn't."

"Why the bloody hell not?"

"Because you're a lord. And I'm a—"

"You're a snob, Hollie."

"I'm not, Charles. I'm being practical." He was the law and she was a lawbreaker. And she loved him with every bit of her soul. Loved his goodness and his greatness. And his little son, who had captured his heart because it was a good and gentle heart.

And she'd only break it.

"I've never heard of anything so impractical in my life, Hollie." He walked toward her, rakishly loosening his neckcloth and tossing it onto her bed while he kept on coming, finally trapping her against the side table.

"I'm a businesswoman, Charles. A printer." Not a wife. Never that.

"And I love you for it."

"You're a Tory and I'm a Whig. Our opinions differ."

"You'll be the wife of an earl, my love. You can think and say whatever the bloody hell you wish."

"Can I vote?"

"In our house you can. Marry me, Hollie."

"Please don't ask me to do this, Charles."

"*This*, Hollie? This bountiful thing that would be our marriage? The fine children we would have together?"

"The unforgivable trouble I would bring to your life, Charles. You can't talk me into marrying you. No matter what you say or do." Not even if he kept kissing her like this for the rest of her days, catching her ear with his teeth, breathing his words of love.

"Yes, I can, Hollie."

Wouldn't that be lovely—if he could convince her that dreams were possible? If he could promise that she could preach reform all day and come to her magistrate husband's bed at night?

"My love, I only ask for the chance to change your mind."

An extraordinary chance—to be loved by Charles Stirling. Her pulse had become thready and hot, as if it knew what he planned and was joining his conspiracy, leaving her heart without an ounce of resistance.

"I won't budge, Charles."

He laughed low in his chest. "Oh, my love, you'll do more than budge by the time I'm through with you. You'll be squirming and calling my name."

"Oh, Charles!" Her limbs lost all their will, the words of his enchanting threats stealing across her breasts though he hadn't yet touched her with his marvelous hands. "How do you plan to do this . . . convincing?"

"I have my ways." His sultry grin thrilled her. He braced his hands on either side of her.

"Does this involve kissing?"

He didn't say. He merely kissed her deeply, thoroughly. But only that, plundering her mouth until she was kissing him back, winding her fingers into his hair, pulling at him, at his hips, grinding indelicately against him.

"Yes, lots of kissing, Hollie. Everywhere." She couldn't imagine that, only the skiff of his fingertips along her collarbone. "And I have other strategies in mind too."

"Like . . . ?"

Without a word of warning, he scooped the pitcher and washbowl off the side table, then lifted her onto it, her backside meeting with the lace cloth, her shirttails bunched to her thighs, and her knees spread on either side of his waist, a wantonly unimpeded position.

"Husbandly strategies, Hollie."

Which brought startling thoughts of his exploring wherever he wished to explore.

Especially with his broad hands spread across her naked bottom, pulling her closer, riding her hips until his thumbs fitted in the indentation where her thighs joined her body, just near enough to her curls to send her senses reeling.

"I've dreamed of this, Hollie," he breathed against her mouth. "My hands here where you're soft, and my mouth."

He couldn't mean there, where his fingers

were kneading softly, were pulling her closer against him.

"I like your strategy dreadfully well, Charles." Feeling thoroughly brazen, she slipped her arms around his neck and lifted herself closer to all that delicious straining at the front of his trousers, knowing she couldn't let him win.

But dear God, she could encourage him to try!

"Christ, Hollie. This is my war, isn't it?"

And who'd have imagined that merely slipping her fingers between the buttons of his shirt to the soft fur on his flat belly would cause such a nostril-flaring fury of passion in the man?

"Then do your worst, Charles. I will not bend."

That made him smile all the more. "I'll do my *best*, Hollie, my *very* best."

His eyes gleamed and then his wonderfully damp mouth encircled her nipple right through the linen, a stunning riot of sensation that shook her to her bones.

"Oh, Charles!" She clutched at his shoulders and thrust her breast into his kiss, begging him to come closer, to be sooner, while a swirling madness made her rub against him.

Her nakedness and the wool of his trousers.

"You're bending, my sweet."

Bending? Dear God, she was arching backwards, supported by his arm around her waist, begging him. She laughed and sighed, because he'd known all along how to play her.

He cushioned her breast with his warm hand and nipped at her through the linen, stealing her breath and filling her with the wonder of him. He teased his way down the placket with his fingers toward the joining of her legs.

"But I'm not convinced, Charles." Not yet! Just a little farther—though she couldn't allow it. She would only ache for him when the night was finished and the morning had come.

"And now, my love?" She gasped when he touched her through the linen, tantalizing the curls that concealed her sex.

"I'll kiss you here too, Hollie."

She couldn't imagine it. Not the possessive way he kissed her mouth. Not when the merest brush of his fingers struck the breath from her and made her dizzy. "Not fair at all."

"You'll think differently, my love." She watched in delicious anticipation as he unbuttoned her shirt just far enough to slide it off one shoulder, exposing the bare and yearning cleaving between her breasts.

He slid his hand beneath the linen and watched her face, smiling down on her in his seduction as he cupped his hand around her breast.

"Oh, my, Charles. That's . . . oh, dear, love!"

She arched backward again, farther this time, moaning, when he closed his mouth over her nipple, and shamelessly sliding her hips closer to his as he nibbled and played there, until she had nestled herself against that throbbing rod of heat that had grown against his trousers.

She wondered if he planned to use that too. *Please, Charles, just this once. Just you, the one man in all my life.*

"You taste of lavender, Hollie." The brush of his sweet words and the tugging of his teeth stole her breath.

"My bath."

He met her mouth again and breached her lips with his dashing tongue. He groaned out a melody with her name wrapped in it, lifting her and holding her against him, making a cradle of his hands across her bare bottom.

"Are you convinced, Hollie?"

Yes, oh, yes! Convinced that she would love him forever. That she would miss him like the sun.

Her blood was pulsing madly, her skin aching for him. He was filling her heart with his yearning, filling her thoughts with his glorious intentions.

"Not nearly, Charles. Not nearly."

Chapter 25

❦

Stubborn woman! Magnificent wife. He'd been diligently maintaining his control for weeks, but now Hollie was his. By her own admission, unmarried and in love with him.

"Very well, Hollie, my love—I've warned you well."

His proposal of marriage, her ridiculous refusal, and this delightfully stunning challenge for him to convince her to marry him took even more restraint, and at the moment he was lucky to have an ounce of it left.

Yet he knew that she meant every word of her refusal, that he had some sound convincing to do.

But here she was in his own shirt, her lithe legs spread around his waist, this relentless reformer who had turned his life upside down.

"God, Hollie, you're beautiful." She was so much more than that to him.

But she smiled and shook her head. "It isn't going to work, Charles. No matter what you try next."

He planned to try everything in his considerable experience. A bride had the right to know her groom's skills. "Next, Hollie, is that damned shirt."

She clutched her fingers around the placket. "This?"

"It comes off." He was ready to peel her of every stitch, to kneel before her, to find her most sensitive parts, a secret pathway to her misgivings.

But now he simply caught her up in his arms and carried her to the center of the room, where he stood her on her feet.

"These will have to go, Hollie." She pouted from under her exquisite lashes, her breathing unsteady, her breath falling across his fingers as he unfastened the buttons that ran down the front of her shirt to the shadowed joining of her thighs.

"Strip me, sir, if you wish."

Three buttons gone. "Oh, I plan to, Hollie."

"Kiss me till I faint. I still can't marry you."

But he knew she would, because the buttons were free and the shirt hanging off one shoulder, tormenting him. She moaned a ragged sigh as he trailed a line of slow kisses across her neck and tilted her head away as he caught his finger in the collar and then let the shirt fall behind her.

"You're magnificent, Hollie." Every inch of her, creamy gold, her breasts rose-tipped and a ready, rousing handful.

Far, far too much temptation for a man in love and with a deep craving. He dropped to his knees and trailed a steaming kiss down the lavender-scented valley between her breasts.

"Oh, Charles, this isn't fair." But she urged him closer, gasped as he kissed the very peak of her, and sung out a sigh as he played there.

"I don't mean to be fair, sweet." He pulled her nipple into his mouth and nearly burst when she growled out a lusty groan and threw her head back, when she reached for handfuls of his shirt and gathered him still closer.

"Oh, Charles, you're doing too much." But she was calling him closer with her arching, her bending, her unbridled and sublime curiosity, and she would soon have him dragging her to the bed and filling her with his seed if he didn't stop this.

Yet he wanted to stay and stray lower, to the curling shadows between her legs.

"Marry me, Hollie. Be my wife."

That brought her out of her reverie. She backed up suddenly against the tub as though he'd pinched her.

"I told you, Charles. You're not being fair."

"But you're bending, Hollie. And I like that."

She set her frown and pointed to him. "Take your clothes off, Charles."

"My what?" He hadn't expected these tactics. They would gain her nothing but the full measure of his boundless need for her.

She threw out her arms, her limbs cast in candlelight, her curves sleekly rounded, her face dazzle-eyed, pointing impatiently at his clothes.

"I don't mind all this kissing, Charles. But I'm not going to do it while I'm naked to my skin and you're all trussed up."

This had possibilities. For tonight's "convincing" and for all of their tomorrows. He held back his smile.

"Be my guest, Miss Finch." He opened his own arms, doubting that she would set to undressing him. "If that's what you want."

But wouldn't that be a fine thing if she did? He'd been living in a nearly ceaseless state of arousal since the moment she arrived in his life, but now she was free and he was rock-hard and throbbing for her. And she was tilting her head to the side, tapping her lips with her finger, inspecting the length of him as though preparing her tactics.

She had him shucked of his waistcoat, his shirttails out of his trousers, and his shirt buttons undone in the next breath.

"Well," was all she said, reaching into the draping panels of his shirt, spreading her fingers out across his chest and then around his waist to his hips, dragging the breath from him. She purred and snuggled her cheek against his chest. "Mmm . . . you're very comfortable here, Charles. Hard and resilient. Just like I knew you'd be."

Bloody excellent news.

"You've been thinking such things, Hollie?" His pulse rose and quickened, that she'd thought of him in that way.

"Your chest?" A kiss where her fingers had just been. "Oh, yes, Charles." Another kiss, hotter, wilder, wetter. Her foot hooked marvelously around his heel. She made wonderful little noises in her throat as she tasted her way across the breadth of his chest, following a sinuous trail that might lead her to places that would undo him completely. "Too often since that first night—when I caught you in your room."

He remembered the moment only too well. "Another quarter-minute, if I recall rightly, and you'd have caught more than my bare chest."

Her eyes sparkled with delicious mischief. "I know."

She wrapped her arms around his neck and pulled him down toward her mouth, to the flick of her tongue that wetted her lips, that invited his imagination. Light kisses and hot, deep ones sampling his collarbone, the hollow of his throat, leaving him breathless, his arms quaking to be filled with her. To fill her with himself.

"You're remarkably good at this, Hollie," he managed as she tucked a kiss just below his chin. "Peeling a man out of his clothes."

She took hold of his collar band, bringing her nose to his and a lush and languid kiss to his mouth. "I'm not finished yet."

He couldn't help but smile through his breathlessness, wondering if he was convincing her that marrying him was the right thing to do. Not that it mattered. She would marry him eventually, because she loved him. And he was wildly in love with her, finally able to admit the miracle to himself and to anyone else who asked.

And after all, she was thoroughly naked, making love to his mouth, the heated points of her breasts tracing magic against his chest.

And now she was sliding his shirt off his shoulders. He tried to help by shrugging out of a sleeve, but she made him wait while she yanked at the linen, while her breasts bobbed and shifted sweetly and she murmured something about not ever being convinced of anything.

"Because I love you, Charles."

"Yes, I know." And he loved her stubbornness and this having to convince her.

"Now your trousers."

Well, then. He smiled but caught his breath in a hiss as she found the top of his trousers.

"You're always very hard-looking here, Charles." She spread her fingers wide against the bulging front panel, held them there firmly against his encumbered penis, and sighed against his chest in a little storm. "So sturdy. And long."

She was driving him mad, one thudding heartbeat at a time, hers and his, pulsing together.

"Enough, Hollie!" He caught her hand at the first button, held it flat against his groin so she couldn't move.

"But you unbuttoned me, Charles."

"But you're not dangerously ready to burst as I am."

"What do you mean?"

"I mean, love, that I want to lift you into my arms and fill you with this hardness you've engaged."

He'd hoped to shock her, but her smile was worldly, had been born with her and her womanly curves, and it was meant just for him. "Then I must be ready to burst as well, Charles, because I want you to do just that."

"You do?" Hellfire.

"Your trousers, Charles."

"Go gently, Hollie." He'd meant only for her to follow his hands down the remaining panel of buttons, but she raced ahead, tucking her fingers into the spaces between the buttons until he was panting and she was touching her mouth to his waist. He grabbed her wrist, kissed her palm in warning. She looked up at him, his wild-hearted radical, mischief bright in her eyes.

But he was thinking of her other lips, of slipping past the curls and into her warm dampness, of a kiss that would surely make her bend to his wishes.

"You're still in your trousers, Charles."

Demanding woman. He kept his delight to himself, turned from her curious gaze before it set him afire, and shucked his boots and his trousers.

He was about to shuck his drawers but Hollie had moved to stand before him, and now was staring at the tented linen, the blazing evidence of his desire for her.

"Oh, my, Charles!" Hollie was sure she would die of the pleasure of just looking at him. He was tall and magnificent and dangerously savage, even in his skin-fitting drawers. They were so white against his bronze. She wanted to see what was beyond them, what that dark arrow of hair was pointing to.

She looked up from the marvelously alive part of him and into his eyes, into a ferocious passion that set her head spinning. He tucked his thumbs into the waistband, bent for a moment as he stripped off the white linen, and when he straightened again . . .

Magnificent wasn't a fine enough word.

Erect, certainly. Utterly monolithic!

The long, rigid length of him, the fascinating dark shadows . . .

Mighty? Masterful?

For the first time in her life, Hollie was left without any words.

Oh, my heart! My love.

Charles seemed fully aware of his power over her and wore his smile as he wore his masculine pride. "My need for you in the flesh, my love."

He was building a tight, drawing fever low in her belly, between her legs, just because he was looking there—a tautness that had all to do with Charles, with the dreams and possibilities that he was strewing in her path like rose petals, making her stumble.

"I had no idea you would be so . . . well . . ."

Compelling.

His smile deepened, darkened, as though he'd made yet another inroad into her resistance. "Let me show you the rest, my love. Let me make you bend to me."

"*Budge*, Charles. I said I wouldn't . . . budge. Oh!" He'd closed the distance between them, become a wall of intoxicating muscle and lime-spiced heat as he met her mouth with his.

He kissed her deeply, thoroughly, making her ache for more of him, for the touch of him everywhere. She didn't want to beg—that would seem too much like bending, too near to budging. But she strained desperately toward him, toward his mouth as he plundered her and made her moan with wanting. Until he finally fitted his hands around her waist, spread his long fingers slowly, wondrously across her bottom, and pulled her against the burning heat of him.

"Ohhhhh, Charles!" He was his own blazing fire, his penis a thick rod of new-forged iron against her belly. This wasn't wise. He was winning.

And he was smiling and lifting her into his arms and then carrying her to the bed. She climbed so deeply into his arms that he was forced back onto his heels on the mattress, and now she sat brazenly astride his lap, her tender, swollen flesh snuggled against that simmering male hardness of his, yearning for him to touch her there.

"I don't mind telling you, love, that I've only just begun my assault."

"You're a scoundrel."

"And you will be my wife, Hollie Finch." He left a nibble beneath her ear, trailed others along her throat, and then took her mouth in a raging kiss as he skiffed his fingertips along the curve of her waist and across her hips, ever downward toward her belly and beyond, to all that roiling expectation.

Her blood pulsed for him; her skin ached. He looked into her eyes as he rose on his knees and slid her back, onto the mattress and up against the pillows, her legs parted around his.

He made a slow pilgrimage down her belly with his mouth, murmuring sweet words against

er skin, until he was kneeling between her
nees and she was nearly swooning.

Then he was back again, kissed her mouth and
he aching tips of her breasts, making her arch to-
vard him, bending as she'd promised she
vouldn't and parting her legs further, inviting
is touch, the kiss he had threatened—had
romised.

"Charles, I. . . ."

He looked up from his delicious torture.
Yes?"

"I was just . . . You are . . . Never mind." She
hook her head, hardly believing the request she
ad been about to make, just because he was
preading his fingers across the breadth of her
elly, just because the heel of his hand was
rushing across the curls at the joining of her legs
nd he was hovering above her, grinning at her
s though he'd already won.

"Never mind what, my love? Because I think
ou're about to budge."

"I'm not. It's just that you said . . . oh! That I
vould squirm, Charles, and I'm—Ohhhhhhh . . .
ny!"

Oh, the bliss of it. She was fully cupped in his
alm and fingers, as though she'd been mea-
ured and made for him, for this perfect fit be-
ween her thighs. The feeling of possession
wept her like a storm.

"Are you convinced, Hollie?" he breathed

against her ear. But she couldn't answer, could barely breathe.

He flexed his fingers, a slight, delicious harrowing of her curls.

"Charles!"

"Convinced, Hollie? Because you're calling out my name." He was so devilishly large and so savagely gentle as he leaned down to kiss her mouth.

"I want to be, Charles. More than anything in the world."

Now her remarkable earl was kissing the inside of her knees, her thighs, and then her belly, and then he spread his fingers through her curls and kissed her—there! Lightly, sweetly, and with his tongue, sifting through curls, teasing his way toward the place where she was wet and fully awakened, where she was aching for him.

"Hmmmm . . . You're budging, Hollie." A kiss at the indentation of her thigh. "And squirming and bending, my love." Another. "I can feel it."

And then he was at the core of her, teasing her with his steamy breath, taking her curls between his lips, toying, kissing. Unable to abide another moment, Hollie arched her hips to meet his intimacies, as stunned that such a kiss was possible as she was certain that she would die if he didn't do it quickly.

"Oh!" She wanted him—all of him. Wanted him to hurry with his clever convincing. Though she could never give in.

But he was maddeningly slow in his torment, dazing her with a blinding stroke of his fingers, and then a nibble on her breast, an ardent calling that made her feel ripe and sun-warmed, that drew her pulse in a thousand and one directions and created new cravings for this man who was drawing these ecstasies from her.

"Charles, may I . . . ?" He rose up from his amazing love-making, kissed her temple.

"What?" His eyes were glazed with a smile.

But then she decided not to ask permission. Fair was fair, after all. She braced her arms against the bed and sat up, driving him backward onto his haunches.

And there was the root of her curiosity, blissfully rising up between his thighs, surpassingly rigid, erect because she'd made it so.

Oh, the power of a kiss.

Charles watched in disbelief as Hollie rose up on her knees and kissed his mouth and nearly shot out of his skin when she closed both hands around his penis, the full throbbing length of it, holding firmly. So perfectly, he couldn't breathe, couldn't move for the terror of spilling himself into her hands.

"Oh, I like this, Charles." She sighed into his ear and fondled him, the sensation deep and binding and drawing great, gasping breaths from him.

"Stop! Please, Hollie!" He grabbed her hands and stopped her movement.

"Not fair, Charles." Her eyes glittered as she dropped her hand into the space between them, gathered up his scrotum with her gentle fingers and sighed. "I like this part of you too."

Christ, he couldn't breathe for the sweet ecstacy of her kneading, the delicate grazing, could only drop his forehead onto her shoulder and groan. His tether was as taut as a thread, near to breaking. He couldn't last a moment longer with her hands roaming free.

But two could play at this game.

And he was larger, stronger. With a lifetime of passion and miracles in the balance, he lifted her onto his lap, where he could better tease and toy with her.

"Oh, my! Charles!" Her eyes widened, and her hands grabbed at his hips with a fury and brought the length of his erection against her dampness.

"Much better, my love." Then he carried her back to the pillows, while she whispered that she really couldn't and certainly shouldn't and wouldn't ever, ever marry him, interweaving every other denial with her sweet words of love for him.

He needed her like he needed air and the sunlight, needed to be inside her. With her. His bones ached and his muscles had long ago cramped into thick, useless ropes.

"Just come to me, Charles."

The very miracle he wanted to hear.

"I love you, Hollie."

"I didn't mean you to, Charles!" But she sighed and tugged at his hips and watched his eyes as he slipped his hand between them where she was wet and ripe for him, her thighs lush and welcoming.

"Too late, Hollie." He nibbled at the peak of her breast, tried not to think about her belly wriggling and rolling against his erection. "I'm mad for you."

"No, Charles. Please don't be!"

Impossible woman.

"Dear love ..." Charles suspended himself above her, his mind a fog of peach and lavender and sweat and his beloved gazing up at him with her clear green eyes. She tilted her hips in a heady, pulsing greeting, made little sounds of awe, grew bolder with her squirming and ringed him with her fingers, then slid them upward around his shaft.

He laced his fingers through hers where she held him, then shifted his hips and nearly lost his way in blinding pleasure when their flesh met.

"Oh, Charles, you are very large and warm."

"And this will pain you, I fear."

"I've heard as much, Charles." She slipped her arms around his neck and snuggled while he pinned her hips to the mattress to keep her from moving another inch; his restraint was far too tattered. "I've also heard that I ought to lie still and think of pruning roses. But I'm not thinking that at all. Only that I want you and I don't care. You won't hurt me." She was open to him, taking him slowly inside her until the barrier wouldn't give.

He caught her smile and held it in his heart. "I think you're going to have to budge just a little, my love. For now. For us."

"Oh, yes, Charles!"

Like a man possessed, and with Hollie urging him home with her ankles clasped around his hips, he drove upward through her maidenhead in a single, exquisite thrust, joining himself to her with a ferocity that must have hurt but drew only a singing sigh from her.

She was tight and flexing and fever-hot, and he wanted to thrust and drive and lose himself in the heat of her. But tears were sliding from the corners of her eyes. He lifted his hips to withdraw, but she gasped.

"No! Charles! Don't leave." She tightened her legs around him and tilted her hips, taking him more deeply.

"Hollie!" He propelled himself forward again, filled her selfishly, so stunned by the sense of utter possession, he couldn't move. He was on the knife-edge of his restraint, held there by nothing more substantial than the need to see to her pleasure before his own.

"I have to warn you, Charles." Her eyes widened as she took up a stirring measure with her hips, a rolling, rising rhythm that was fast becoming the surging of his pulse and the thrumming of his heartbeat. "I think I'm about to squirm."

"Too late, sweet." He loved her impatient grin, loved that she was moaning shamelessly and that her lips were rosy and damp from his kiss.

"Please, Charles!" she breathed against his ear, tearing at his control.

"Marry me, Hollie?"

Oh, Charles, if only I could. Hollie loved her wickedly handsome earl, the savage power of him, the tethered straining of muscle in his thickly corded arms, and the deep concentration he focused on her eyes. She loved the rich roughness of his breathing, the flare of his nostrils as he drew himself out of her and then filled her again.

She loved the slow convergence of his hips against hers, as though each tightly coiled stroke might undo him if he broke this delicately controlled rhythm that was driving her to madness, that had her threading her fingers through his hair.

And him—she loved him. Adored him. Ached for all that might have been between them.

"I do love you, Charles." She knew he was doing this for her sake, holding back something of himself as a gift to her, not knowing that this would have to be enough to last a lifetime. This shattering intimacy between them, his nose beside hers, his nuzzling, his sweat mingled with hers, his hair damp against his forehead.

Hollie broke his cadence, dipping her hips into the mattress and then raising them to take him deeper this time. He groaned, sending a hot surge of pleasure licking upward from where they were joined, as though his tongue were there lighting fires.

"Christ, Hollie, I don't know that I can last." His breath was thundering out of him as she arched her back and met him, as she moaned and paced his rhythm and then increased it. She cried out his name when he closed his mouth over her nipple, aching with the sundering pleasure of it.

"Oh, Charles, I—" He spread his fingers down her belly, then slipped his broad hand between them where she was waiting and wet and already filled with the thickness of him.

"You what, my love?" he whispered. His dark eyes glittered as his simple, skiffing touch filled her with an undefinable bliss, a longing for him that only deepened, that broadened and left her breathless and wanting more of him.

All of him.

He was all around her now, in her nostrils and on her lips, feathering his words of love against her ear, making dear promises, and watching her, smiling down on her.

"I love you, Hollie. Marry me."

And then the heavens exploded. The stars and the constellations scattering into bits. Pulsating pleasure upon pleasure. A bedazzling radiance and wave after wave of brightness. Blinding peaks and pulsing valleys that rose and fell and rose again.

And in the midst of this dizzying explosion of unimaginable bliss, Charles called her name, caught up her bottom into his splayed fingers, and then plunged into her far, far deeper than he had been before, hotter still, and again and again and again. Then, with a convulsive groan, he filled her with a rapturous, spilling heat—his seed.

A child? What a blessed joy that would bring to him, to her.

But it wasn't to be. This wasn't the right time in her cycle, and she wasn't the right kind of wife.

She caught her magnificent earl as he fell back to earth, held him as he nuzzled and kissed her, leaning on his elbows like a tent over her.

"Marry me, Hollie."

She kissed his mouth, savoring the raspy closeness of his cheek against her.

They were still connected, steamy and pulsing, making her want him again.

"Can we do this again, Charles?"

"Why? Do you need more convincing?" His dark eyes shimmered under his soft, sooty lashes.

He was already sliding his huge hand between them to find her nipple and dragged a gasp out of her when he rolled it between his fingers.

Another weapon in his arsenal, a stunning pleasure that seemed tied directly to her sex.

"I still can't marry you, Charles."

"You're squirming again, my love. Fully budged."

"I can't seem to help it, Charles." So Hollie rocked her hips and took him deeply again.

And prayed for the miracle that would keep the dawn away.

Chapter 26

Hollie woke to the emptiness of the bed and a desolate darkness in her heart. Panicked that Charles had left her, she reached out for his pillow but found him standing at the foot of the bed, fully dressed but for his jacket, a look of suspicious confusion on his face that made her stomach roll.

"What's this doing here, Hollie?"

The broadside. The breaking point between them. She couldn't keep this truth from him, not for long. The meeting was to take place soon, and she would announce the government's secret new strategies, even though Charles would be standing at the rear of the assembly room. He'd realize then that she was a thieving radical, not a wife.

Besides, she could no longer pretend ignorance of his own secret, even though her heart would break along with his.

"What is it, Charles?"

"This."

She heard him shake the page at her, and knew he was frowning. Next would come the demand that she read to him, like a lion rattling a tree for his food.

"Oh, that," she said, yawning dramatically and sitting up, because he would soon be in a towering rage and she would need to calm him. "It's a broadside."

"Yours?"

So brusque, so well rehearsed. She should have seen through it long ago.

"Yes. The one you saw in the conservatory."

He dropped the page onto the bed as though it burned his fingers. It fluttered sideways and landed on his pillow.

"You printed this on the Stanhope?"

"I did."

"Against my orders."

"You weren't watching." She hated his look of helpless fury, the squaring muscle in his jaw, hated it because it hurt him deeply. So deeply that he didn't even ask why she'd acted so blatantly against him.

"Read it, Hollie."

Dear God, she didn't want to hurt him this way. It took every ounce of courage and compassion and determination to slip her legs out from under the covers on her side of the bed and stand up.

And even more courage to refuse him. "I don't think I will, Charles."

Hollie heard him go still, like a forest of hornbeams coming to rest in the instant before the wind whips a storm across the landscape and uproots them.

"You wrote it, Hollie," he said evenly, though his breathing hinted at raggedness and his hands were shaking slightly. Her arrogant, self-possessed earl. The man she loved with all of her heart. "You'll read it."

She braved his growing thunder as she left the bed for her shirt laying on the floor, his shirt tossed there in his passion to convince her that she should marry him. In his belief that there was a chance for them. What a damnable liar she was.

"But I don't need to read it, Charles." She lifted her shoulder as though she didn't care, as though her heart wasn't breaking to bits. "I already know what it says."

"Yes, but damn it, Hollie, I d—"

"You *don't*?" She finished his sentence flatly and made no other move. It was his turn now. God keep him.

She knows.

Charles couldn't breathe. Couldn't find a single one of his defenses, because she'd dismantled them, scattered them. Because she was standing adorned in his shirt and scented with their lovemaking.

Waiting for him, for his confession.

"Never mind," he said.

"But I do mind, Charles. I mind terribly. And so do you."

Her gaze never flinched, nor her challenge. He wanted to leave her to her damnable supposing, but he was rooted in place by his fear and by his relief that she must have known for a while and hadn't told anyone.

At least, not yet.

"Leave it where it is, Hollie."

"Don't you want to know what that says, Charles? It might be important to you. To me. Maybe even to us."

He snatched the page from the bed, balled it up in his fist, and tossed it to the ground. "I told you not to put yourself in the way of things."

"But I'm already here, Charles. You led me right to it."

"I said leave it be."

"Charles, I had no idea at all that you cannot read until the day before yesterday." She hugged the shirt tighter around her slim shoulders, her limbs quaking in the cold.

"You've known that long, madam, and you haven't run off to London to spread the word? To have my shame printed on one your damnable broadsides and flogged on every street corner?"

"Don't be absurd, Charles. I'd print this broad

side against you and your Privy Council, but I'd never print anything that would shame you. It's none of my business at all, except that I love you and that it hurts you deeply."

It took every bit of courage to ask, "How did you know?"

"By chance, Charles. You're an artist at this masquerade. I only suspected because . . ."

"How?"

She dropped her gaze. "One little clue after another until I finally realized."

"That the great earl is a clod who can't read," he said bitterly.

She shook her head, and tears welled up in her eyes. "That's not what I thought at all. I would never."

"Have to be pretty stupid to have attended Oxford, to have reached the grand old age of thirty-two, and not know how to read."

"That takes unimaginable skill, Charles."

He hated her concern, her pity. "It takes everything, Hollie. And shreds it."

"Is that what your father did?"

Christ, had he confessed his entire life to her? "He was a miserable man and an even more miserable father. But you suspected. Not even a month in my care and I've given myself away to you. How? What made you so certain?"

"It doesn't matter."

He grabbed the back of the chair and jammed it out of his way. "By Christ, it *does* matter."

She caught her breath and stepped back, as though he'd struck her, new tears in her eyes. "You're right, Charles. I owe you that much."

A shadow crossed his vision, a muting guilt and that dark shame that ambushed him when he wasn't on his guard.

Hollie had turned from him to sift through her satchel. "I had to be sure, Charles, and so I . . ."

"You did what?"

"I tested you."

"You . . ." He swallowed back the bellow of shame. "Tested me how, dammit? Did you stick a pin in me to see if I would cry out?"

"Oh, Charles!" She flinched as she unfolded a note that had been tucked in her shirt pocket, against her heart, then offered it to him. "I wrote this and put it in the conservatory where I knew you'd find it."

Her simple gesture hurt him deeply, widened the ache in his chest, the rawness of his shame. But he took the note anyway, because it was scented like a summer orchard and still warm.

And it was hers. He looked down at the scrawling lines, the swells and swirls. He remembered seeing it in the conservatory.

Believing her without question.

"Do you mean to humiliate me completely? I obviously fail your test once again. You know very well that I can't read this."

"I would never do anything to humiliate you Charles. You mean too much to me."

"And so you pity me instead? Me and my convenient shortcoming."

"No, Charles, never." She reached for his hand as if he were a wild animal, and held it at a distance. "You may not believe this, but you're the most remarkable man I've ever met."

"And is that what this says, madam? Or is it, 'I'm running off to meet the husband I never married, you great clod.' "

She dropped his hand. "It says nothing of the sort."

"Then what else could it say? 'I'm deserting you and your son.' 'I've betrayed your trust.' "

"You *are* a clod, Charles Stirling, if you really believe that I could choose to blithely hurt you. Or Chip. You don't know me at all if you think that. My note has nothing to do with reading or writing or books or broadsides. It has all to do with you."

Charles hated this moment most of all—the swimming ink, the scent of the woman he adored and still couldn't have, her words that he couldn't read. "Then what, madam?"

She had her fists stuck against her hips, fury on her brow. "It says, 'I love you, Charles Stirling.' "

He couldn't breathe. He looked down at the page, at the lines and squiggles that had suddenly become the most important thing in the world.

"This does? You wrote that here?"

"Yes."

"Why?"

"Because I wanted it to say the most meaningful thing I could imagine, in case I was wrong. 'I love you, Charles Stirling' seemed quite a perfect sentiment at the time. It still is."

She whirled away from him and stood in the middle of the room, her chest heaving as she jammed her slim legs into a pair of large linsey-woolsey trousers that hung loosely at her hips, until she cinched up the fat belt.

"And this, Charles, is the reason that I can't marry you. Not now or ever." She picked up the balled-up broadside and tossed it at him. "I'm a liar and a thief."

He caught it in his fist and tightened his fingers around it, because her words were sinking slowly into his brain, melting his outrage and the fear in his gut.

"I stole it from you, right off your desk. Outsmarted the earl of Everingham, and through you, the entire Privy Council."

A new, unnamed fear slipped over his shoulders; not for him, but for her. "What have you done, Hollie?"

"For a start, I've read every letter you've received from the Home Office." She sat down on a chair and pulled on a tall boot that went to her knee.

"Not very sporting, madam, but I knew that."

She lifted her brow. "How could you have? I was careful."

"One of the skills I learned long ago. Never lose track of exactly where you put a piece of paper. Bavidge knows better."

"So Bavidge knows—"

He shook his head, his heart beating again, thrumming for her. "Only you, Hollie. And now you wield a great deal of power over me. All the power you've ever wanted."

She pointed to the broadside in his hand. "That, my lord, is all I need. Six acts of law that Parliament plans to enact against me and the people I love. Six vindictive measures to silence the opposition forever."

So that was her deadly game. "That's privileged information, madam." And high treason to steal it.

"It's the truth. And all I've ever asked for, Charles, is the truth about my father's death. I just want someone to care that children died and wives and mothers and sons. I want someone at Whitehall to tell me that the Peterloo Massacre matters. And that it won't ever happen again."

Tears had welled again in her beautiful eyes and spilled over. His blindsiding radical.

"That's not possible, Hollie—"

"Damn you, Charles, how can you say that? The truth is here in Wolverhampton; it's at Everingham in your files. It's in the depositions."

"I've studied those."

"You couldn't have, Charles. You can't read the bloody words, can you?"

Cold fury came instantly. "I've gotten by for thirty-two years."

"And look where getting by has taken you: to a botched investigation into the death of nearly a dozen citizens. And reports that have so many holes in them, you don't know what's true and what's assumption."

"I get by as I always have."

"How?" She stood before him in trousers that didn't fit and a single, too-large boot, her arms spread, the shirt hanging up on her elbows.

"Bavidge reads to me." He didn't want to meet her eyes, but he couldn't stop himself.

"Everything, Charles? Every word?"

He glared hard at her. "He tells me what's important."

"What's important to him. And how do you know what's in all those other reports?"

"I have a staff at Westminster. They cover that."

"But that's their truth, Charles, not yours. It's Liverpool's truth. And Sidmouth's. I know you well enough to stake my life that you wouldn't knowingly allow a falsehood or a misstatement. You're a good man, Charles, the very best. I expect better of you."

She waited a beat for his denial, then screwed up her face into a teary scowl and turned her back on him to pull on the other boot.

You're a good man, Charles, the very best. His heart was slamming around inside his chest again.

He lifted a knobby woollen scarf from the table, then a tattered tricorn hat with a tangled curtain of black, shoulder-length, theatrical curls attached to the inside of the crown band. And draped across a chair, a long black cloak and a huge coat.

Christ Almighty. His blood suddenly ran cold.

Spindleshanks. The rage felt good and just, a righteous blaze of anger that would separate him from her and her falsehoods. And break his heart in two.

"Are you expecting him soon, Hollie?"

She turned to him in her boots and trousers and oversized white shirt.

"Him?" she asked, grabbing the cascade of her hair and beginning to plait it.

"Your captain."

She hung her head for a moment. "No, Charles, I'm not expecting anyone. I do this alone. It's the best way I know." She grabbed the scarf and the hat from him and bundled them into the cloak along with the coat, then stood at the door as though she was leaving him.

"I'm sorry, Charles—for so many things. But

I'll never be sorry that I love you. Give my love to Chip. Tell him that I'll miss him."

And then she was gone. Vanished with his secrets and his shame. And that blasted costume.

Hell-bent on treason.

He was out the door and after her a moment later. He made the lobby, but she was nowhere. She couldn't possibly have gone through there without causing a stir in that shoddy pair of trousers, her shirttails flying.

She took the back stairs, of course, and the back roads to her damned meeting. To give her bloody captain his costume.

Charles dashed behind the inn, to the small alleyway there. His gut twisted with helpless anger and molten jealousy for this nothing of a man whom she would follow to the ends of the earth.

Charles breathed a grunt of relief when he saw her bootheel disappear as the narrow alley turned, and he caught her by the shoulders a few moments later.

She whirled on him. "Stop it, Charles. It's over. Let me go."

"Don't be a bloody fool, madam; there are magistrates posted at the meeting."

"Spies and informers." Her mouth, well loved from their long night together, was fixed in a line. "Yes, I know. It's what they do, Charles. But it's what I do too. This part of me that you don't condone."

"It isn't a matter of condoning, Hollie. This is your very life at stake."

"Then so be it. I have a mission." She yanked out of his grip and started away, trailing the tail of the cloak and then the hat. She saw it fall and stopped, but Charles got to it first and held it for ransom.

"Please, Charles. I have to go. I'm expected."

"I can't allow you to go to him, Hollie."

"There's no him, Charles."

There was something about the hat. It was all wrong. The essence of Captain Spindleshanks, exactly as he'd been described. But Charles had expected the hat to reek of the stale must of sweat and poverty. Just as he had expected the enormous greatcoat, with its broad, cotton-batted shoulders, would. But it was another scent that struck him with a costly shock. Peaches and pears, familiar and lovely and completely out of place here among the tatters of Captain Spindleshanks's disguise.

Pears and peaches and Hollie.

The scent was hers, woven through every strand of hair, every fibre of the wool.

As was the passion.

And the foolhardy recklessness.

Bloody hell! A rattling sense of dread shook him as he looked up at her.

Spindleshanks wasn't some broad-shouldered radical Scotsman or a renegade from the House of Lords or her lover or her husband.

"Hollie!"

He knows! Hollie swallowed, and her heart stumbled, then thudded around inside her chest. It was too soon. Needing to make it to the grange, she yanked the hat out of his hands and started running.

He knew, and now he would truly throw her to the lions if he caught her. And yet she couldn't outrace him. He caught her at the edge of the churchyard when she slipped on the dewy grass and lost her stride.

He lifted her off the ground and pulled her close. "The game is up, madam."

"What game?"

He sat her on a stubby stone wall. "This is your costume, isn't it? Your bloody hat, the cloak, the scarf"—he tossed them onto the ground, one piece at a time—"and it was your bloody sedition, my dear Captain Spindleshanks."

She couldn't let him believe that, couldn't let him be a party to the danger. This was her secret, not his. No one else's.

"Are you completely mad, Charles?" Hollie fought the flush that was rising in her chest. She felt as though she had suddenly been tossed into a raging river, fighting a strong current with the man she loved trying to take them both under. Another few yards, and she'd have safely made the meeting. She could have spoken her piece and taken her punishment if they'd caught her. "You can't be serious, my lord."

Oh, but he looked altogether serious. She wondered how far she could get if she broke from him again and ran into the misty morning. Her last taste of freedom.

"I was a bloody fool, madam, for not noticing immediately. But you were such a distraction."

A distraction. He'd said that before. Now his mouth was so close, she'd have thought it a kiss only an hour ago.

"Your father was killed on St. Peter's Fields. You have no brother to protect, no cowardly uncle, husband, or lover. I find a cartload of seditious material in your printing office—I couldn't have been more blind."

"You really think I'm Captain Spindleshanks."

"There's only been one thing in the world that I've ever been more sure of." Hollie was certain that he was about to close his mouth over hers. But he went on, holding fast to her arms, his accusations as breathtaking as his kiss. "You are my nemesis, Hollie Finch, in so many ways. No wonder I couldn't catch you, Captain: you were too close by. Too busy rousing the weavers—and me—too busy spreading sedition and wild rumors that I'd tainted my commission of inquiry. Too busy teaching me how to love my own son."

Hollie hung her head. "I'm not your captain."

"Rennick believes that you are nearly seven feet tall, that you ride a steed out of hell and can disappear at will."

"Lord Rennick employs young children as

piecers and scavengers in his bloody mill. Have you ever watched them, Charles? The children? They walk twenty miles every day in their endless bending and collecting, picking gobs of loose cotton from under the looms—while the machinery is still working! Can you imagine Chip working there? He might have become one of them if you hadn't rescued him."

Charles stilled; his eyes clouded over as he looked skyward in his silence.

"That's why I do this, Charles. The mill owners purchase their members of parliament with bloodstained money. The children have no voice—"

"None but yours, Captain?" She'd never seen his mouth so pale with fury.

"Yes." Defeated, too weak to fight him any longer, Hollie stuck her hands out, bared her wrists to him. "So go ahead and arrest me, Charles. I'm not guilty of sedition or libel or any other crime you might come up with. You have no proof it's me you want."

"But I do, Hollie."

"What proof?"

She thought at first that he wasn't going to answer, watched a muscle move in the strong line of his jaw, as though the admission would cost him dearly. Then he narrowed his eyes and said the most unbelievable thing she'd ever heard.

"The costume, Hollie—it smells like you."

"It . . . what?"

But she had no chance to ask more. Her splendid beast laced his fingers through her hair and kissed her deeply, sent her heart spinning out of control. Put dreams in her head, and hopes.

"Oh, no, no, Charles! I can't." She had a crucially important job to do. Peterloo and her father. The children. She pulled away from him and tried to run, but he caught her and swung her back into his arms, held her improperly close for a churchyard but splendidly for a man who used to love her.

"Where the devil do you think you're going?"

"To make my appearance at the meeting, Charles. You can't stop me."

"Haven't you heard a word I've said? You'll be arrested and out of my reach. Christ, Hollie, I have sheriffs waiting at the doors for you—for your bloody captain!"

"Then I'll be arrested. Yes."

He seemed terribly cocky all of a sudden. "And then what, madam?"

He released her slightly, as a cat releases a mouse, blocking her way and the coming daylight with his shoulder.

"Then I'll go to prison, rats and all, until my trial. Isn't that how it works?"

He folded his arms and peered down at her as though he had an answer for all this tangle, and was waiting for her to notice. But there were no answers that didn't mean losing too much.

Dear God, if their lives had been otherwise . . .
Oh, the children they would have had together.

"And your defense will be, my dear Captain?"

"I'll tell them exactly what happened on St.
Peter's Fields, and I'll be damned proud to be
telling them. I'll tell them what I've tried to do to
right the wrongs. And then I'll take my punishment."

He shook his head. "No, you won't."

"Charles, you can't talk me out of this." She
tried to scoot around him, but he caught her
around the waist and held her fast.

"How can I make you understand, my love,
that sacrificing yourself won't make a damned
bit of difference to anyone? There's no truth that
will satisfy your sense of justice or the Privy
Council's ability to prosecute or Henry Hunt's
outrage at his arrest."

"It doesn't matter, Charles; I have to warn
them all about what's coming. I'm going to the
meeting."

"Then so am I." He grabbed her hand and
started rushing her along, the remains of Captain
Spindleshanks tucked under his arm and a terrifying light in his eyes.

"Why, Charles?" Hollie stumbled after him,
her nerves spent, still jangling from the night in
his arms and now this monstrous morning.
"What are you going to do there, Charles?"

He bolted through the churchyard gate. "I
plan to stand beside you and defend myself

against your accusations as best I can. To confess my sins."

"What do you mean?" Had he lost his mind? "Do you mean us to debate?"

He pulled her from the brink of the lane and back into the churchyard. "I mean that you've finally made your point, Hollie."

"Which is?" Because the man had a devilish way of twisting up the truth.

"You've censured me in the press, madam. You've questioned my integrity, my readiness to oversee the Peterloo commission, the commission itself, and made me realize that . . . you're right."

"I am?" No—he was toying with her. "Why?"

Because I'm a damned fool for not understanding sooner.

"Because this damned costume smells like you, Hollie." He dropped it at his feet, his hands itching to hold her.

"It's you, Hollie. Every thread of you, woven together into this godforsaken thing. You're Captain Spindleshanks. And you're the editor of the *Tuppenny Press* and the beautiful reporter in the press gallery. You're my conscience and my patience. You're the ink stains here on my fingertips. And the breath in my lungs. Chip's favorite teacher, his friend—his mother, Hollie."

"Charles, don't." She was sobbing freely, her arms crossed against her chest.

"Hollie Finch, you're the woman I love more than my life. I'm thick-headed and illiterate—"

"No, Charles, you're—"

"And happier than I ever knew was possible. And if I want you, Hollie, that means everything of you. The scent of you that's caught in this hat, your inks and your linseed, and the chalk dust. All the inseparable, priceless parts of you."

"But it won't work. It can't." She shook her head, and her hair tumbled out of its loose knot, a sobbing panic in her eyes. "You're not a radical, Charles."

"You're not either, Hollie. You're sensible and just and determined. And I adore you for it. Marry me."

"I can't."

Bull-headed woman—he'd just have to show her how. He took her hand and started away. "Come, then, sweet."

"No." She stayed rooted to the ground, holding onto his hand with both of hers. "Why, Charles?"

"Because I would like to ask your colleagues a few questions."

"Why? So that you can put them in jail? Charles, don't make me do this."

Oh, what a soulless bastard she must believe him to be.

He got down on his knee, cupped her face between his hands. "My solemn pledge to you, Hollie—on the lives of all our children. I may not be a reformer, but, sweet love, you have re-formed me."

Her chest shook with her sobs, her tears streaking her shirt. "But I have to tell them, Charles. About Liverpool's terrible plans—the acts of suppression. And as soon as I tell, then I'm committing treason. And you have to arrest me for it. And I can't put you into that position—"

"Then *I'll* tell them, Hollie. I doubt I'll be sent to the gallows for it."

"The gallows!" Hollie smothered the cry from the deepest part of her heart, the unimaginable loss of him. "No, Charles, I can't let you do that."

"Ah, then, Miss Finch, you *are* a snob." He looked damned pleased with himself as he stood. "Saving martyrdom for yourself, are you?"

"No, Charles, I'm afraid for you."

"And I'm utterly terrified for you, my love." He reached out his hand for her, so gentle, so capable. "Come, let's try to make it better together. That's all we can do."

Make it better.

Patience, Daughter.

Oh, Papa, he's just so wonderfully wise.

She'd always suspected it—but she'd never suspected that his heart was so very grand.

"You're absolutely sure that Liverpool won't hang you, Charles? Because if there's even the slightest chance of that, then I'm not letting you anywhere near that meeting."

His dark eyes glistened beneath his lashes, lifting her pulse and gathering up her dreams. "I assure you, my love, Lord Liverpool is no threat to me at all."

Hollie was about to protest his certainty, but her marvelous hero slipped his arms around her and lifted her off her feet right there in the churchyard.

"And we burn that damned costume, Hollie, as soon as we get home."

Hollie would happily have agreed if she hadn't been so busy collecting his glorious kisses.

And wondering just when her wicked earl had become so extraordinarily fine.

Epilogue

"H-A-N-D."

"Yes, Charles. Oh, yes, husband! That's very good. Verrry."

Charles loved these private lessons, when his ravishing teacher sighed into his ear, when she reached for him. He loved most of all that she was his wife.

And that she encouraged his vocabulary. "Let me try this one, my love. B-R-E-A-S-T." It look a long, sweet while, and some delicious manipulation.

"That's exactly right, Charles. Oh, my!"

Hers were exactly perfect and warm and beautifully bared to him as she lounged back against the settee, her nightgown in a heap on the floor.

"How does one spell 'quim,' wife? This."

She gasped when he touched her and lifted her squirming hips against his hand where he was playing, delving with his finger. "I don't know, Charles. Pleeeeeease, Charles."

"Hmm. Does it begin with a K, do you think, or something else? English is a damned tricky language."

"I'm not thinking very well at all, husband. Not with you . . . oh, Charles, kiss me, please."

God, he wanted to, wanted to bury his face in her fleece and make her moan again and writhe. But she'd promised to teach him these seven words tonight.

"I'm not quite there yet, sweet wife." The minx was tugging at his hair, at his ears.

"Oh, Charles, but I am. I'm very, very near there now."

"Not just yet, love." But he couldn't resist nuzzling her breast, taking her rounded nipple into his mouth and nibbling for a while.

"Oh, Charles, you're a lout."

"L-O-U-T, my love, 'lout.' " He'd learned that last week. "Now 'quim.' "

"Starts with a Q." The U and the I followed in deliciously breathy gasps, but her M ended in a throaty, drawn-out moan that nearly drove him out of his mind with wanting her.

But he had his lessons to learn before they could play. His own printing to do.

"You're beginning to look like a copybook again, Hollie."

"A handy teaching tool, Charles."

"Hold still, my love." He leaned down and kissed the inside of her thigh, making her sigh and coo and call his name.

"You're very wicked, my lord."

"And you're very beautiful." He inked the letter K against the ink ball with one hand and then pressed it against the inside of her knee. "I don't know why a word that sounds like an N must start with a K."

"Now the N, Charles. If you'll hurry, please."

"And two Es, if I'm not mistaken." He hurried along—a husband could only take just so much of his wife's yearning.

"Oh, my, yes, Charles." He followed his fingers with his mouth, easing his kisses up her leg, parting them, until he found the honey he was seeking.

Hollie thought she would surely die of pleasure as her thoroughly naked husband made love to her in that most remarkable way of his.

Soon she was crying out his name, begging to surrender, grateful that they had chosen the gatehouse for their lessons, because she'd be waking the house if they'd begun this in their chamber.

Just when she thought she would explode, he lifted her onto his lap and filled her with himself, filled her heart with his words.

"I love you, Hollie," he whispered and whispered again and again as he filled her with his seed, holding her tightly against his pulsing strength.

She rode his steep waves and made waves of her own that carried her over the edge.

"And I adore you, husband." She took him to the deepest part of her until he was gasping and clinging to her, his dark-lashed, lust-heavy eyelids looking deliciously piratical.

"Do you know what I think about, Hollie, when you're in the press gallery and I'm giving a speech?"

"This, Charles?" As if she didn't know after four months of marriage.

"Endlessly, my love." He wrapped his arms around her and pulled the blanket over her shoulders. "The very reason I've adopted those damned long-tailed frock coats. They're the only way to hide my passion for you." He was teasing, of course, was the master of control in public. In private was another matter altogether.

"All the while I'm thinking, Charles, that I married the bravest man in all the kingdom. A radical to your core, especially when you do battle against Liverpool and Sidmouth."

"The bastards trumped me on the Six Acts, Hollie. Damn their souls. I'm sorry for it." The loss had outraged him for weeks; he'd felt the loss for the ordinary people he'd met in his investigation.

"But you softened their effects, Charles." Her dear champion. "And I will love you forever."

"You've made me so damned lovable, Hollie, we can barely get through these private lessons any more. And the dictionary has thousands and thousands of words. I'll be dead of pleasure before page twelve. But there's still one more word left in this lesson. What is it, my love?"

"A very special one, Charles." Bundles of happiness, marvelous beginnings. She wrapped her husband in her arms, nuzzled his ear, and then leaned back and looked at him. "How about 'baby'?"

"Baby. Baby."

He took a deep breath and made the face she loved: the adventurous, cogitating one, when he was concentrating on the sound of the word inside his head. He closed his eyes and scrunched up his nose. "Baby. I can do that, Hollie. B-A—"

Charles stopped because his heart just had, right before it became a thundering in his pulse. He opened his eyes and found Hollie's, which were wide and soft.

"Baby? Hollie, is that what you're saying?" *Please, Lord,* he prayed. "Are you . . . ?"

Her eyes were lit with love and wonder, her lashes starred with tears as she smiled and touched her mouth against his. "I'm as certain as I can be."

"A child. Oh, God." He scooted upright and covered her belly with his hand, just where their child was growing, wondering if the babe knew how very lucky she was to have Hollie to mother her. "When?"

"Christmastide, Charles."

"A girl, Hollie."

"We'll see."

They dressed and slipped back into the house, then woke Chip to tell him. But he seemed to already know as he snuggled an arm around each neck.

"How could you possibly know this, Chip?" Charles shared a bemused look with Hollie.

"I made a wish, Papa." Chip yawned and rubbed his nose against his father's cheek.

"Wishes sometimes come true, Chip," Hollie said, drawing her fingers through his soft hair, sharing another glance with her husband, whose eyes were pooled with tears.

"We wished for you, Hollie—didn't we, Chip?"

But the boy was already asleep.

And they had a whole night of celebrating to do.

Dear Reader,

Now that you've come to the end of your book I'm sure you're like me—eager to discover something new to read and longing for a fresh, exciting, sensuous romance to entertain you.

Remember, each month there are four delicious Avon romances to choose from, so even if you've just finished one, there are three more awaiting you where romances are sold. And *next* month you'll be able to choose from these four unforgettable titles.

A Notorious Love by **Sabrina Jeffries:** She's a proper young lady, compelled to join forces with a dashing rogue to rescue her runaway sister. He's a man no proper young lady should be seen with—but he's devastatingly attractive . . . and oh, so irresistible. Sabrina Jeffries is a rising star, whose work sparkles with wit and sizzles with passion—this book is truly unmissable!

Next Stop, Paradise by **Sue Civil-Brown:** If you love contemporary romance that is high-spirited, delightful, and truly unique, then don't miss this one! When a small town lady cop matches wits with a handsome, smooth-talking TV journalist, well, you know something special is going to happen! With a touch of magic and a whole lot of charm *Next Stop, Paradise* should be on your book-buying list.

Secret Vows by **Mary Reed McCall:** It's always exciting to bring you a book by a brand-new author . . . one who has a spectacular career ahead of her. In *Secret Vows* you'll find a soul-stirring love story between Catherine of Somerset and Baron Grayson de Camville. And though severe punishment faces Catherine if she fails in her mission, she can't help but fall in love with this man she's been forced to marry—and ordered to destroy.

An Innocent Mistress by **Rebecca Wade:** He's a rugged bachelor sworn to avenge his imprisoned brother; she's the fiery woman known as the mistress of a fabled bounty hunter—but is she concealing a secret identity? Passion flares . . . and no one is quite who they seem to be in this surefire blockbuster of romance.

There you have it—four brand-new romances from the premiere publisher of romance . . . Avon Books.

Enjoy,

Lucia Macro
Lucia Macro
Executive Editor

REL 0801

Avon Romantic Treasures

*Unforgettable, enthralling love stories,
sparkling with passion and adventure
from Romance's bestselling authors*